Undying Love

Secrets of Roseville • Book 1

Betty Bolté

Copyright © 2017 by Betty Bolté
www.bettybolte.com
ISBN-13: 978-0-9981625-1-5
ISBN-10: 0-9981625-1-5

Digitally published as *Traces* April 2014 by Liquid Silver Books, an imprint of Atlantic Bridge Publishing, 10509 Sedgegrass Dr., Indianapolis, Indiana 46235.

First print edition of *Traces* published 2014 by CreateSpace.

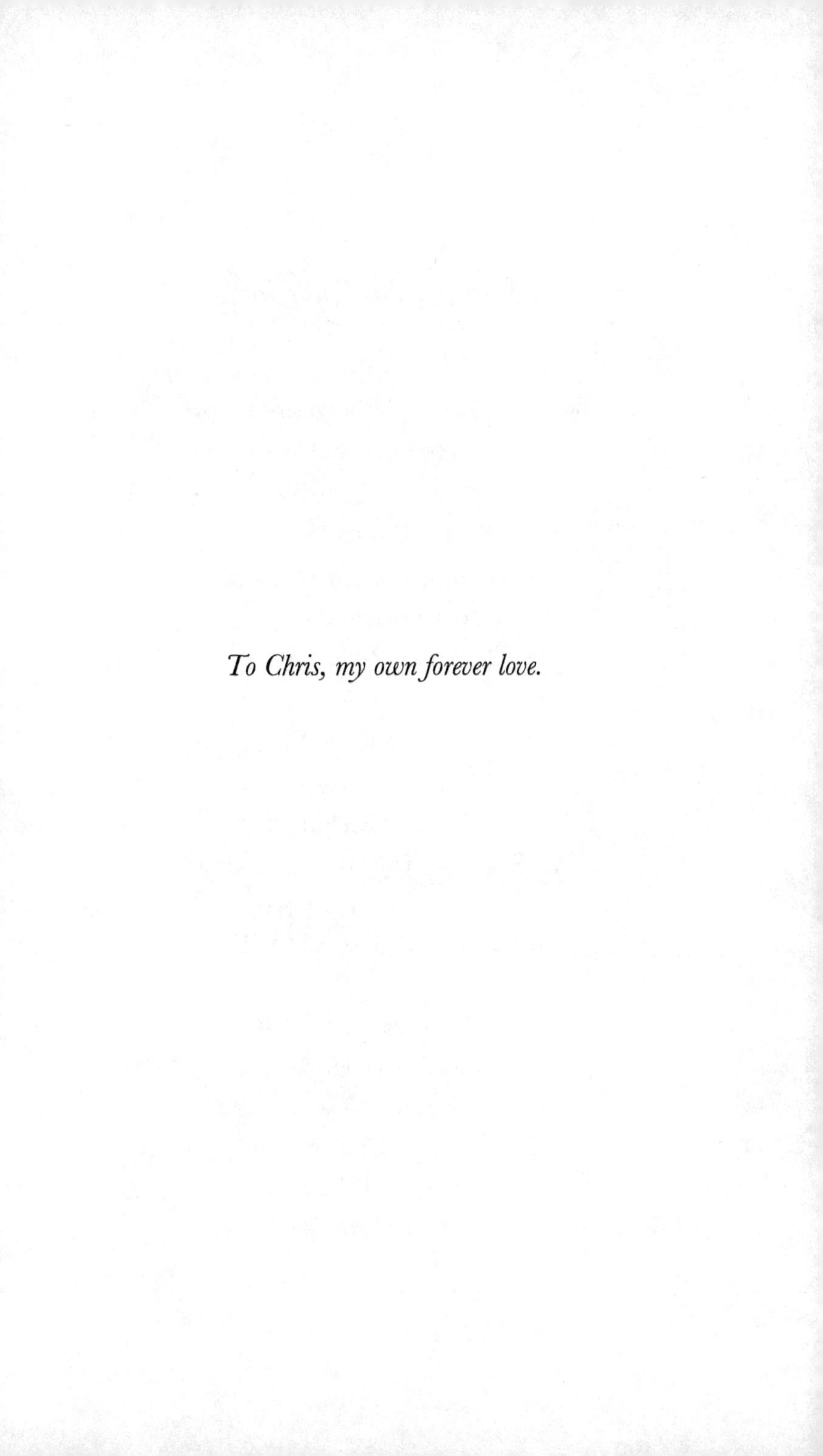

To Chris, my own forever love.

Also by Betty Bolté

Becoming Lady Washington: A Novel
Notes of Love and War

FURY FALLS INN
The Haunting of Fury Falls Inn
Under Lock and Key
Desperate Reflections

SECRETS OF ROSEVILLE
Undying Love
Haunted Melody
The Touchstone of Raven Hollow
Veiled Visions of Love
Charmed Against All Odds

A MORE PERFECT UNION
Elizabeth's Hope
Emily's Vow
Amy's Choice
Samantha's Secret
Evelyn's Promise

Acknowledgments

Not only does it take a village to raise a child, I've learned that it takes one to write a book, as well. My dear friend, Deborah Neel, shared her architect's eye and reaction to architecture to inform Meredith's view of the plantation house. Rhonda Pepper, Facilities Development Engineer at NASA Marshall Space Flight Center, and Thad Stripling, Civil Engineer at NASA Marshall Space Flight Center, provided insights into the world of demolition and restoration of historic buildings. The owners of the Rattle and Snap Plantation, Dr. Michael and Bobbi Kaslow, graciously answered many questions about the history of their property. Jillian Rael, director of the Fayetteville-Lincoln County (Tennessee) Public Library, educated me on the National Register for Historic Places and how Tennessee historic properties are managed. Michael C. Moore, State Archaeologist and Director of the Tennessee Division of Archaeology, answered my questions about regulations and procedures surrounding private cemeteries and burial sites in Tennessee. Patrick McIntyre, Jr., Executive Director and State Historic Preservation Officer of the Tennessee Historical Commission, answered my questions related to procedures to be followed after finding remains on personal property. Last, but by no means least, my nephew, Ben Hay, trumpeter and musician extraordinaire, provided guidance on the appropriate music choices for the high school concert and solo. Thank you all for your willingness to share your expertise with me.

Chapter One

eredith Reed stared at the plantation home she'd inherited from a grandmother she hadn't seen in years. A pair of ancient oaks, the inspiration for the Twin Oaks name, guarded either side of the sprawling two-story brick dwelling, providing shade and funneling cool air through the house. Sunlight filtered through the massive limbs. Meredith raised one hand to shield the glare as she scanned the façade. The architect in her appreciated the symmetry of the Greek Revival style as well as the quality workmanship of the brickwork as she walked around the site.

"It really hasn't changed. Not much."

She studied the once-elegant antebellum house, pausing at the base of its wide front steps missing a brick here and there, its four elaborate Corinthian columns and intricately carved woodwork flanking the double doors. The property description listed ten bedrooms, four bathrooms dating from the early twentieth century, a gourmet kitchen, two parlors, an upstairs ballroom, and several outbuildings.

"It's a real treasure." The estate lawyer, Max Chandler, had driven her out to the four-hundred-acre property. He had barely spoken during the entire trip except to relay

1

pertinent details of the surprise inheritance, including the fact she had also inherited her grandmother's sizable and diversified investment account. A very handy part of the surprise.

She'd have preferred to drive her own car, especially since he drove one of those redneck pickup trucks. Sitting in a vehicle with an attractive man set her teeth on edge. Worrying about what might happen tensed every muscle in her body. He also didn't need to know how edgy being with him made her, as if her skin burned the closer he drew. But he'd insisted until she ungraciously relented. She picked her fights, and that one wasn't worth the effort. The rolling Tennessee countryside had flowed past the window, immense fields dotted with horses and cows. Green shoots poked through the tilled earth in rows, reaching for the early spring sunshine. She'd noticed her surroundings automatically, but none of the hauntingly familiar sights held her interest. Once she no longer sat in the unfamiliar truck, her tense muscles eased, and she drew a deep breath as she studied the building.

Why on earth had her grandmother, whom she hadn't seen in nearly ten years, chosen her to receive the grandiose house that stood for everything she would never have? The family she *could* never have? Pain combined with a deep-seated longing blossomed in her chest. Three front steps led up to a brick porch with its immense white columns announcing to passersby that the building was more than a house. Unlike the small, boxy ranchers and nondescript houses they'd passed on the drive to the plantation, this structure cried out for a large family. Her parents had often carried her and her sister Paulette from Memphis to visit Grandma when she was a child. Back when love and laughter echoed through the many rooms. A great blue heron fished in the two-acre lake in front of the house, where they had once splashed and played. The huge yard, graced with several shade trees—the site of barbecues and softball games, with the extended family arguing over who potentially cheated or whooping with glee when a good shot was made—now stood silent, accusing her of neglect and indifference.

So be it. She stiffened her spine. She would not wallow in self-pity nor give in to the temptation to wrap her arms around her waist and cry. She squinted at the glare from the windows nestled into the brick walls, noting the ivy climbing up one front corner. Willy would want her to move on, build a new life, but she couldn't. Not yet. Even after a year, the grief and anger stewed in her brain, sizzled in her veins, and throbbed in her heart. She led the way around the other side of the house and back to where Max had parked.

"Shall we go inside?" Max leaned his tall frame against the hood of the green pickup, arms folded, his curiosity evident in his expression.

The color of his eyes as he waited for her response reminded her of the crystal blue of glacier ice, and that thought evoked the bittersweet memory of her and Willy on their honeymoon trip to Alaska. The glorious clear sky that day had created a perfect backdrop to the pod of whales they watched blowing. She heard again the cry of eagles as they soared majestically above the surrounding mountains. The trip of her life with the love of her life. Back when they had their entire lives stretching before them, full of promise and hope. The weight of her wedding band drew her attention for a moment. The last connection she had with her husband. She raised her eyes to meet the steady regard of her grandmother's lawyer.

Her phone buzzed in her pocket, breaking the spell of Max's intent gaze. She fished the contraption out and glanced at the screen before answering. "Hey Buddy, what's up?"

"Just letting you know the Murphy job is put to bed."

Her boss's brusque, businesslike voice helped her focus, steady her breathing.

"That's good news. I left it ready to close out."

Buddy coughed and cleared his throat. "I only had to smooth out the final walk-through."

A chill spread through her at his words and the tone of his voice. "What do you mean? It was all set up and ready to rock and roll."

"Don't worry about it. I took care of it."

She bet. Like he always did. With the end result a mess she had to sort back out again.

A flash of blue in an upstairs window drew her attention, and she peered at the pane. Blinked away the lingering image. An illusion. A pair of turkey buzzards spiraling high above reflected off the window, wings outstretched so that the tips of their feathers stood out against the sky. Bringing home memories of how she used to pretend to be dead to lure them in, and then jump up and scatter them on the breeze. Memories she couldn't afford to resurrect. Her stay in Tennessee would last no more than a month, maybe two, tops. She could survive that long.

"Fine. I'll follow up with her when I get back to Maryland."

Meredith ended the call and slipped her phone back into her pocket as Max pushed off from his spot near the front of the truck.

"What is it you do again?" Max strode over to stand beside her.

"I'm an architect." She snatched the manila folder off the hood of the vehicle, a file Max had handed to her at his office. Inside were copies of the legal papers he'd reviewed with her across his massive mahogany desk. "Why?"

"Your grandmother said you were the perfect heir for this property." He let his gaze drift away from her to scan the hundreds of acres of fields and trees, across the lake, and on to the various outbuildings surrounding the plantation house.

A circle of trees nearly hid the old gazebo from view, but they couldn't stop the surge of memories of afternoons spent with her sister playing under its roof. Glimpses of white painted boards and black wrought-iron trim appeared through the dense branches and limbs sprouting with new growth.

Meredith dropped her attention to the folder, severing the thread of the past, and turned a page without reading it. Why did Max care what she did? She slanted a questioning glance his way. "I enjoy designing beautiful yet useful buildings."

"Right. Utilitarian structures rule," Max said, his words clipped. "Let me show you around." He indicated for her to follow him through the kitchen door.

Bristling at his tone, Meredith pinned him with a stare. "Look, you don't need to. It's been a while, true, but I have been here before. I know the layout. We can go." Then she wouldn't have to go inside and relive the happy, carefree days of her childhood through the weary eyes of an adult while Max watched.

He shook his head, his dark chocolate hair touched with gray sweeping his collar, watching her. "Things have changed. You may be surprised by what you find inside." He tapped a hand against one thigh and cocked his head to gaze at her for a long moment. "Either way, you should take stock of what you've inherited."

He didn't appear much like a lawyer, truth be told. Didn't lawyers wear prescription glasses and look nerdy? Not that she believed in stereotypes, but all that studying must make their eyes weak. Max was the other end of the spectrum. Perhaps her grandmother had a need for eye candy when she chose him as her estate planner.

He was delicious to contemplate, that's for sure.

Probably a couple inches taller than a cornstalk with a soccer player's physique, Max could double for a cover model. She appreciated his classic good looks, straight nose, and strong jaw. Dressed in khakis and a deep red polo shirt, he seemed more ready for a round of golf than a client meeting. He represented the unattainable type of man for her. The kind embodying something too smart, too handsome, too *much* for her taste. Even if she were in the market for a man, which she was not. None of that mattered since she would be staying in the area for only a short while. Despite her hard shell of indifference to the opposite sex, she couldn't help a moment of succumbing to the temptation of drinking her fill of his appearance. But only for an instant.

"I don't want to keep you, is all." Meredith waved a hand at the vehicle. "I'm a big girl. Take me to my car. I'll come back on my own."

"Actually, your grandmother made it clear she wanted me to show you around when you claimed the place. She wanted to be sure you appreciate the extent of the inheritance and had an opportunity to see how much work is needed to put it to rights. So, if you'll follow me?" He walked to the screened door, obviously expecting her to concede the point.

"And Grandma always gets her way." With a sigh, Meredith shadowed him through the door. She stopped inside the doorway to look around. The sickly smell of mildew hit her senses like a wrecking ball, bringing tears that smarted the corners of her eyes. Crossing the threshold was like stepping back in time to another era. "It's exactly like I remember. Well, except for the smell."

Max nodded as he ushered her across the familiar sunny room and through the swinging door into the front hall and foyer. "Mrs. O'Connell prided herself on ensuring any necessary repairs matched the original decor and architecture.

But as time went on, she wasn't able to keep up with the issues of an old, historic home. A few repairs will be necessary. Your talents, skills, and expertise are why she left Twin Oaks to you instead of your father. You know, so you can ensure the repairs are appropriate to its original grandeur."

Dark wood floors reached throughout the plantation house. The stairs rose slowly from the left, boasting dark wood treads with white painted fronts, up to a wraparound loft. A cherry table sheltered against the wall beneath the stairs, showcasing a dainty crystal lamp centered on a lace doily. She smiled, spying the small door standing invitingly ajar, leading to the games closet tucked under the stairs. A colorful rug invited guests to cross the space toward the parlor on the right or the double parlor on the left. In days gone by, the gentlemen would have adjourned to the larger retreat after dinner to smoke and drink. Farther down the hall leading from the foyer, light spilled onto the wood floors from the windows in the back rooms. A chill settled on her shoulders. The back room on the right had been her grandmother's sewing room—her favorite spot in the entire house—and the room in which she'd died, according to Max. Meredith shook off the thought and focused instead on the condition of the house.

She moseyed into the parlor, noting the dusty, cobwebby, overstuffed chairs and dark wood furniture. Faded and peeling, the rose-patterned wallpaper competed with the brocade drapes for attention. Above the rose marble fireplace, she spotted the relief carving of the Irish Claddagh: two hands reaching toward the center where a heart wore a royal crown. Her grandmother loved to tell stories about the Claddagh, representing bonds of love, friendship, and loyalty. She inhaled, smelling dust and cold ashes from the fireplace mingled briefly with a faint yet familiar scent she couldn't place. She mentally shook her head. No matter.

Scanning the room, Meredith let her gaze touch each piece of antique furniture, each grimy objet d'art, each vase of tired silk flowers. The dismal scene before her contrasted sharply with how everything once shone with loving attention. She had started debating selling the property before she even packed her suitcase, tucked Grizabella into her cat carrier, and started her car to make the two-day drive to Roseville. Back to her past. She couldn't stay. Tennessee would never be home again. She could call an auction company to handle selling off everything, from furniture to furnishings and the property itself. That would be the easiest route. A shiver of horror set her teeth chattering. What difference did it make if the floors were dusty or the furniture saggy? If cobwebs draped over everything like cotton candy? After all, she couldn't see keeping it.

Meredith wandered through the rest of the house, Max following silently. Her tour of the upper floors was cursory at best. She avoided the attic entirely, not prepared to open that particular door to the past. Max's silence suited her. She didn't want to talk about her thoughts with anyone. Others may not agree with them, for one thing. They didn't understand the hurt and anger deep inside. Hell, she didn't totally understand it. She surveyed the interior, pondering what she'd need to do to put this past firmly behind her once and for all. Her quick survey revealed an endless list of repairs needed to make it livable let alone to restore it to its prime. Best to make it sellable and move on. She glanced at Max when he stopped beside her in the kitchen, his spicy aftershave helping to obscure the odors of the old house.

"I'll stay here until I can make the necessary arrangements." Meredith refrained from touching the white ceramic counter dotted with green mold.

Outside the window, the backyard extended for about an

acre before opening up to a large—perhaps ten acre?—meadow with trees and field beyond. A separate two-car garage was tucked at the end of the driveway near the small caretaker's cottage, out of sight from the front of the property, to ensure its curbside appearance remained faithful to that of the nineteenth-century expectations. Primordial oaks and maples, ones she and Paulette used to monkey in, provided shady oases across the expanse. Two giant magnolia trees stood sentinel at the back, where she knew they marked the entrance to the O'Connell family cemetery nearly hidden at the edge of the open area. She leaned slightly to the left. *There.* The grave stones, some drunken with age, were clearly visible and surrounded by a black wrought-iron fence and gateway. The arch above the gate announced the family name in wide, rounded letters. From here she could discern the weary steps leading up to the ancient gazebo, the gingerbread trim drooping over the entrance to the shadowy inner space.

"Good. You'll have chance to decide what you'll do with such a lovely property." He regarded her and appeared to wrestle with what to say next. "I envy you, Mrs. Reed. I realize it needs work, but this is a wonderful place. Both peaceful and historic. I wish I could afford such a home as you've been given."

Meredith turned and gaped at him, wondering if he was joking. He wasn't. "Peaceful? Have you heard crickets in the summer? Or roosters? God, the roosters crowing all day drive me insane." She wouldn't listen to him go all sentimental on her. Restoring the property was not her agenda. "Shall we go? I have to take care of a few matters, and I'd like to put the wheels in motion." Meredith shook off the glower Max gave her at the abrupt change in conversation. She headed for the door.

"As you wish. Let me know what you need and I'll make sure you have it."

Once outside, she sauntered toward the truck, hearing Max close the door and lock it. She didn't look back as she reached the truck and stepped up and inside. Only then did she permit herself to scrutinize the home—no, the *house*—she'd inherited.

Max joined her in the vehicle and drove for a time in silence, the only sound the symphonic muzak oozing from the stereo. She felt the weight of his assessment. Even after he returned his attention to the winding road before them, she sensed his appraisal, weighing her words and actions and the silences between them.

"I assume you'll go through with the application your grandmother had me submit." Max shot her a glance and then focused on navigating the streets of Roseville. "Right?"

Outside the car's window, the quaint town square slipped past. Roseville had been established early in the nineteenth century and served as the county seat of government. The stately brick courthouse with its white clock tower stood in the center of the square surrounded by a hodgepodge of antiques stores, diners, boutiques, and a two-screen movie theater. A woman holding the hand of a child skipping along the sidewalk hurried toward the Hideaway. The popular restaurant once housed the old jail. Eating in the former jail cell with her parents had been a highlight once upon a time. Shoving away the sharp stab of nostalgia, she refused to allow the past to influence her future.

"What application?" Did the man have to speak in riddles? Keeping her eyes averted, the young family held her attention as she waited for his answer.

"To have the plantation added to the National Register of Historic Places." Max turned on his indicator and waited for the light to change.

"No."

"No?"

"That's what I said." Was he hard of hearing too?

"It's already in the system." He cut her a glance and focused on the traffic. "Why don't you want it to be listed?"

"I have other plans for the property." She looked at him, observed the frown pull down between his brows. "It is mine to do with as I choose. No strings attached?"

He steered the car onto Market Street. "I'd assumed you'd want to honor your grandmother's intent and keep the house in the family. Or at least, appreciate the need to preserve the area's history for future generations."

"You know what they say about assuming things." Meredith held on to the vinyl seatbelt strap to relieve the discomfort of its biting into her shoulder. "And, to be clear, I never said what I intend to do with it."

"But you don't want to have official protection for the structures, to keep them as testimony to the history of this area?" Max eased the car into a parking spot in front of the old house that served as his office.

A white sign hung on a matching post beneath a spreading maple tree growing next to the sidewalk. The building was home to Estate Planning Attorneys, specializing in historic preservation law, with five attorneys listed. She spotted Max's name—James M. Chandler— second from the bottom. Not a ranking member of the firm. Good to know.

"I haven't decided exactly what I'll do, but I will over the next week or so." Electing to keep her own counsel, she opened her door and stepped out into the warm afternoon air. Max followed suit, studying her over the roof of the pickup. The sound of tires on asphalt joined with the thump of music blaring from radios in passing cars. She should say something. "I'll collect Grizabella from your secretary and head back out to settle in for the duration."

"You make it sound like you're preparing for a siege." Max chuckled and closed his door, and then met her in front of the vehicle. "I put my card in the folder I gave you earlier. Call me if you need anything."

"I doubt that will be necessary." She extended her hand and met his curious gaze, steeling herself from any memories attempting to assert themselves. "I appreciate all you've done for my grandmother and for me."

"My pleasure." He engulfed her hand with his larger one.

Never had the touch of a hand ignited such a warm buzz against her skin. Did he feel the same jolt of electricity that zinged through her? He peered at her, probing her expression. When his gaze landed on her mouth, she inhaled sharply, lips parting involuntarily. *Damn.* That did not happen. She would not permit anything to distract her. She pressed her lips together and ended the contact between them. She had no time for complications in her life. No interest in another man.

"Um…is the grocery still off the square on College?" She took a step backward, putting distance between them, away from whatever vibes he radiated.

Max smiled, a slow, sensual movement that implied they shared a secret. "Edna's? Yep, it's still there."

She nodded and strode up the sidewalk toward the office door, careful to step over the eruption of concrete under pressure from a tree root threatening to trip her. "I'll get Grizabella, stop at the store for essentials, and then head back to the house."

Max strode in front of her and opened the door, waiting. She slipped past him, avoiding both touching him and looking at him. She smelled cinnamon and apples as she scanned the homey reception area. More of that instrumental music similar to the compositions she'd heard in Max's truck made her think of happier days with her husband. The antique furniture, flowered wallpaper, and apple pie combined to make the law office feel surreal. If it weren't for the laptops and printers scattered among the vases of flowers and stacks of files, she'd feel like she were visiting someone's home. The secretary, Sue Grimwood, approached her with a smile on her maroon-painted lips and two cups of coffee in hand. The woman had welcomed her warmly when she first arrived to meet with Max, sharing that she loved old homes and had three children and a grandson all in the space of minutes. If Meredith was planning to stay, which she wasn't, Sue could become a good friend.

"No cream with two sugars, and black." Sue handed Meredith one cup and Max the other, and then tucked her hair behind both ears, making her appear like an eager teenager. "So, ready to move in?"

Meredith shrugged lightly. "For a while anyway. Thanks for remembering." She lifted the cup in salute and took a sip. Hot and sweet. Perfect.

"Has Griz been any trouble?" Meredith cradled the steaming cup between her hands. The cat carrier sat where she'd left it, but the top door stood open. She looked around, searching for the feline. "Where is she?"

"She's fine." Sue gestured with a manicured hand to the elegant settee situated in the bay window, sunlight streaming in to highlight the calico snuggled there. "I took pity on her and let her out."

"Thanks for keeping her for me." Meredith took a long gulp of coffee and set the mug on the desk. "I should be going."

"First," Max said, "let me give you a copy of that application so you'll at least know what's been put into motion. You'll want one for your records, I'm sure."

Sue nodded her head rapidly, silky hair escaping from behind her ears to bob frantically about her chin. "You know what Max always says. That beautiful old plantation really ought to be preserved for future generations to enjoy and learn from. You're fortunate to own such a splendid property."

"Yes, it is beautiful." Meredith didn't have the heart to burst the woman's bubble of excitement. She had a vague but emerging idea of her path forward. Once she decided for sure, then she'd stick to it. She never backed down on her plan. That was how she'd built a solid reputation and she intended to maintain it. Max folded his arms, waiting, his expression guarded. She should at least pretend to care. She shrugged. "Fine, but make it quick."

Max motioned for her to follow him and then strode to his office. "I expect we'll hear one way or the other in a few weeks."

She stopped beside him. His desk, an expanse of highly polished wood, reflected not only the late morning sunshine but the apparent extreme orderliness of Max's mind. Or perhaps Sue's. The inbox matched the desk and contained a pile of folders, stacked with military precision. Not the haphazard mishmash of Meredith's desk at home, but with the corners aligned and the tabs all pointing in the same direction. Pens and pencils stood at attention in separate wood cups, likely, Meredith thought with a grin, to prevent them from mingling after hours and multiplying like rabbits. Mixing the two just wasn't done in polite society.

"Working with the National Register is never easy." She fingered a gold-tipped pen, angling it against the flow of the others in the cup to see if Max would notice. She stifled a conspiratorial chortle at her little rebellious act. "I've managed to avoid working with them any more than absolutely necessary."

"We have plenty of time, though. Right?" Max glanced at her and then back to the folder on the desk. One manicured finger, the nail clean and blunt-tipped, toyed with the edge of the manila stock, capturing Meredith's gaze.

Willy's hands sprang into her mind, his long fingers and wide palms calloused and capable. How many times had those fingers clasped her own, squeezing gently to share a joke or convey his feelings? She'd watched Willy work magic with those hands, creating a work of art from bushes and flowers and rocks. They'd joined forces once they married, she designing the homes, the developments, and other buildings, and he designing the artistic landscapes to enhance the overall appearance. Walking through his gardens was like exploring a fairy world, complete with blossoms and lighting and winding paths. Water features, such as reflecting ponds and waterfalls, attracted a variety of birds to add life to the scene. Willy's designs had won multiple awards over the past decade, and she'd been proud to be his wife.

They'd built a good life together, filled with love and promise. Their love had brought a deep abiding happiness into her world. Until the attack stole everything from her.

Paulette O'Connell drew up to the curb and killed the engine. The pale spring sky provided a backdrop to the house she'd shared with Johnny for the last four years. Across the street, the bungalow sat dark and empty, a for-sale sign swinging in the early morning Indiana breeze. She clutched the steering wheel, wishing she felt something akin to the sadness or grief she ought to feel at the end of this once oh-so-promising relationship.

She'd fallen in love with the tall, sandy-haired man with the quick smile. He liked to joke and chat about anything and nothing. He seemed to be the perfect man for her. Only somehow she hadn't noticed Johnny's lack of willingness to share his feelings with her. His inability to actually care about most everything. Or, at least on the surface, he showed no signs of possessing a flicker of emotion, good or bad, about anything. Including her. Even when she finally had had enough and told him she held no ill will toward him but she couldn't live with him any longer. He'd blinked and nodded, as though she'd told him the mail had arrived. Then he'd gone on about his plans to move, alone, to his dream job in Alaska.

Her car held the entire sum of her possessions, crammed into two good-sized boxes and a pillowcase. When she'd thrown her things together two days ago, she didn't think through her actions. She'd crashed on a former coworker's couch while she contemplated her situation. She no longer had a home, a man, or even a job after the house she'd been assigned to decorate had been completed. The firm she'd worked for told her they had to cut back on staff, and she'd been the last one hired. Time to face the awful truth. She had one last place she could go, one person she could descend upon who couldn't refuse her. And after all the sacrifices she'd made, surely her sister, Meredith, owed her. Even though Paulette had tapped her before to get her out of a scrape here and there, they were still siblings. Sisters looked out for each other, right? It was no matter that they hadn't actually seen each other in years or talked on the phone in many months.

Paulette laid a hand on her abdomen for a moment, her resolve slipping as she envisioned the murky path ahead. She'd been astonished when her parents had informed her of not only Grandma's death but also the contents of her will. No surprise that all Paulette got was a small trust she couldn't even touch for five years. Her Grandma made no bones about her belief that Paulette didn't know how to handle money. Which may well be true, but it still hurt. Given that Meredith now owned the plantation, she definitely had the room as well as the means to provide a home for Paulette. There was enough space in the old place that they could go for weeks without ever seeing one another should push come to shove. If only Paulette could manage to stop the impulse to argue with her, perhaps they could coexist in relative peace. Maybe.

She turned the key and slipped the car into gear. Pulling away from the curb, she glanced at the once-welcoming house for the last time. The flowers and bushes she and Johnny had carefully planted when they first moved in were beginning to bud in anticipation of spring. White lacy sheers hung at the windows bordered by green shutters. Her dream home, or so she'd thought. She choked back a sob. Such a forlorn hope, after all.

Johnny had already left for his new job in Ketchikan, one of the tipping points that told her he didn't truly care about her and what she wanted in life or, for that matter, in their relationship. She'd argued against his taking the job, hating the idea of living where it snowed and stayed cold the majority of the year. She'd tried to convince him to look for a different position in the South, where the climate was warmer than the north. Hell, Indiana had been difficult enough for her, with the gray skies and cold, windy winters. She longed for the sun like a cactus longs for rain. He'd ignored her, told her she was being selfish, and continued making the arrangements necessary for his move.

Now it was her turn. Driving faster, she merged onto I-65 southbound and headed for her new home. With luck, she'd be in Roseville in time for dinner.

Chapter Two

*E*dna's Supermarket hummed with customers. On Saturdays, the town of Roseville enjoyed the onslaught of people hurrying to complete the many errands their workday left no time for during the week. Meredith lowered her car windows enough to allow ample airflow on this spring afternoon. She'd parked in a shady spot at the back of the small lot, hoping to avoid dings and scrapes as well as to keep the car as cool as possible. The cat's repeated plaintive yowls reverberated from within the bold yellow car. "I understand, Griz. I'll be back as quick as I can."

Meredith strode across the lot and into the closely packed aisles of the town market. Edna's had existed as long as she could remember and served as the town nexus. Everybody shopped there, if for no other reason than to try to keep up with the comings and goings. The automatic doors ground open, a cold blast of air greeting her when she strolled inside. She hadn't been to this town in years, and yet everything seemed the same. She moved along the aisles, making her choices quickly. The sooner she finished her shopping, the less likely she'd run into anyone she knew.

She paused in the fresh produce section to debate on a spring mix of lettuce or a head of romaine. Suddenly she noticed an older couple—she in blue jeans and flowered top, he in khaki overalls with an open-collared work shirt—standing by the bin of tomatoes, peering at her as though debating whether to speak. Uneasy with their open appraisal when she didn't immediately recognize them, she cleared her throat. "Can I help you?"

"I'm sorry to stare. But can it be our little Meredith? Is it really you?"

The lady's salt-and-pepper hair framed her heart-shaped face. Despite her advanced age, few wrinkles graced her smooth skin. Piercing cobalt eyes smiled at her. Peering closer, Meredith finally recalled the older woman.

"Meg? My goodness, it's great to see you." Meredith embraced her grandmother's housekeeper. "I'm surprised you recognized me after all this time."

"I'd never forget you. You remember my husband, Sean." Meg patted her husband's arm twice and smiled at him, her love for him evident in her adoring expression.

"Of course." Meredith shook his proffered hand. "How have you both been?"

"We were better before that lawyer gave us a pink slip." Sean shifted his weight to lean against the buggy.

"After Grandma died?" She bristled on their behalf. The two longtime employees of her grandmother deserved better treatment than that. Meg occupied a special place in Meredith's heart after all the wonderful times they'd shared during the annual summer visits. "What are you doing now?"

"Looking for work, but at our age it's difficult to find a new situation." Meg's smile became strained. She looped one arm through Sean's, and he stood straight once more.

"I'm sorry. I wish I could help." Meredith gripped the buggy handle, her mind racing through possible solutions but coming up empty.

"I hesitate to ask, but…well—" Meg drew in a quick

breath and smiled. "If you're willing, of course, we could work for you, seeing as how you've inherited the place." Meg shifted closer to Sean, her eyes hopeful. "It's a lot to manage. You are planning to stay, right? That's what Max told us, anyhow."

Max. Stirring up trouble for her yet again. Meredith did not need anyone else interfering. This couple, as helpful as they may be, could only cause complications. Yet the hope shining in their eyes gave her pause. They'd devoted most of their lives to working for her grandmother, and now they were on the street because of Max. Through no fault of their own, they found themselves out of a job and a livelihood. And a place to live in addition to the rest.

"I suppose I could use your help to put things in order," Meredith said slowly. "But I can't promise for how long."

"Thank you, Meredith. I hoped you'd say that." Meg beamed at her. "We appreciate your confidence in us. We won't let you down."

"We'll move our things back into the caretaker's cottage this afternoon." Sean shook her hand again, hope in his level gaze.

"Perfect." Meredith mentally shrugged. They already knew their jobs, so how much trouble could they be? At a minimum, Meg could remove cobwebs and rid the joint of mildew. "I'll see you later, and we'll talk specifics."

They waved as they hurried away down the aisle, chatting to each other with happy animation. She watched them until they turned the corner, wondering how they'd talked her into hiring them back so easily. Shaking off the encounter, she pushed the buggy quickly after them. Finally tossing in several cans of cat food to complement the bag of dry, she wheeled the buggy to the checkout.

She'd nearly made her escape when another female voice, one she hadn't heard in a long time, stopped her in her tracks. "My God, I can't believe I'm seeing what I'm seeing. Little Meredith grocery shopping."

Meredith raised her eyes to confirm that the voice she'd heard was indeed that of Paulette. *Crap, crap, crap.* She had no idea she was anywhere near Tennessee. The last she heard, she was holed up with some bloke in Indiana, doing what she did best: bitch and cause trouble. *Show no fear.* She swallowed but held her gaze. "What are you doing here? Wait. How did you know I'd be here?"

"Is that any way to greet me after all this time?" Paulette strutted over to stand next to the buggy, an alligator advancing on its breakfast. "Mr. Chandler told me when I phoned him earlier on my way. I heard about your fortune, or at least your luck. What did you do to coerce Grandma into handing over her wealth to you?"

She'd have to warn Max about not revealing her whereabouts to others to respect her privacy. And to not share any information with Paulette. Meredith forcibly stopped herself from retreating backward, away from the angry flash of Paulette's tawny eyes. "Do? Nothing. Now if you'll excuse me, I have to go."

"I'm coming with you." Paulette laid a hand on Meredith's arm. "That house should have been mine. As the oldest and all, if nothing else."

"Actually, it should have gone to our parents," Meredith said, wanting but refusing to shake off the hand searing her arm. "Then we wouldn't have this to argue about as well as all the other crap we've argued about most of our lives."

"We don't argue. We discuss heatedly." Paulette winked. "I want to catch up with my little sister. Is there anything wrong with that?"

"Yes. And no, you're not staying with me." A bitter lump formed in her throat, and she forced it back down.

Paulette had once been her closest friend, until she'd started shooting down all of Meredith's actions with stinging remarks that reverberated in her head for years afterward. Cutting, hateful comments. Meredith didn't understand what had changed between them, but something had. It was like a secret she wasn't in on.

Paulette's blonde curls bobbed, denying Meredith's words. "Yes, I am. You owe me."

"I owe you nothing." Meredith drew in a long breath, striving for balance and failing. She couldn't be in the same room with Paulette without wanting to throttle her. Or at least, she became defensive in her presence. Wary and watchful and tense. Paulette deserved only one thing from her. "Nothing."

"Whether you like it or not, Meredith, I'm still your older sister."

"So you keep saying. What of it?"

Where was she going with this? What did she want from her now? The last time they'd seen each other was before she hooked up with Johnny What's-his-name. Paulette had struggled to land freelance jobs as an interior decorator, which turned out to amount to merely slapping paint on walls and choosing fabric for ugly stuffed chairs. As a result, Meredith bailed her out of her rent more than once. Even gave her cash for groceries and utilities. Without a word of thanks in return.

The smile melted from Paulette's lips. Her expression hardened but hinted at desperation. "I want what's rightfully mine. Half of Grandma's fortune."

"What makes you think there's a fortune to be had?" Meredith played for time, trying to find a way out of this hellish conversation.

Paulette could not be trusted to do right by anyone other than herself. Meredith had been burned by her opinions and tirades too many times to tally since they'd turned into teenagers. Now she refused to leave an opening for Paulette to target her verbal darts or missiles. No chinks existed in her emotional armor because Meredith refused to give Paulette any additional ammunition to use against her in these spats and catfights.

"If nothing else, that house is big enough for us to share." Paulette's pink lips twisted into something reminiscent of a pout. "If you don't want to sell it?"

"Ah, so that's it." Meredith pushed the buggy closer to the waiting clerk, trying to shorten the length of time she stayed trapped by her sister. Finally the pieces of the puzzle snapped together. "You need the cash or a place to stay? Or both? Did Johnny leave you?"

Paulette wrapped her fingers around the wire buggy and stopped Meredith's progress. Her pout flattened into a frown. "The bastard. He doesn't know when he's got it good."

"You still can't stay with me." Nothing would be worse than having Paulette in the same house for any extent of time. She pushed the buggy up to the counter and quickly unloaded her items onto the conveyor belt. Paulette's hand remained on the buggy as though afraid Meredith would go running out the door. The beep of the scanner punctuated their conversation. "But there's a B&B up the street from here."

Paulette stared at Meredith for the span of three heartbeats before shrugging, a smile sliding onto her mouth. "You're probably right. We'd hurt each other in the same house. I'll have them send you the bill."

Relief twined with anger flushed through Meredith. At least she'd dodged having her in the house, but she still had to pay the price. Literally. "Right." She lifted the twin grocery sacks hanging off her hands, the weight quickly making her arms shake. "I've got to go. My cat's in the car, and the longer I talk with you, the hotter it's becoming out there."

"Hang on." Paulette caught one of Meredith's arms,

snaring her with an intense regard. "Meet me for dinner. I—I need to talk to you. How about the Hideaway for old times' sake?"

Meredith stared at her. The hint of dark circles under her eyes suggested Paulette's life had some difficulties. Again. Meredith forced tight shoulders down and rolled her neck to release the building tension. Shaking her head, a tiny movement, she admitted defeat to herself if not Paulette. She couldn't dodge the woman forever. At some point, they had to put their hostility behind them. But was now the right time or the worst time to try? Reluctantly, Meredith nodded. "As long as we don't sit in the cell."

The kitchen door squealed as Meredith pushed it open, grocery sacks and the yowling cat carrier bumping against her legs. Her purse slipped off her shoulder, yanking so hard she almost dropped the poor cat. She eased both to the floor before slinging the grocery sacks onto the counter. A puff of dust whispered into the air, making her cough.

Her grandmother had loved to cook, and thus the kitchen was the one room in the house allowed to vary in content and design from an antebellum-era kitchen. The renovated room served as an altar to culinary delights. Paneled doors hid the appliances, blending them into the surrounding walls, so finding the dishwasher and refrigerator became a game of hide-and-seek. Ceramic tiles graced the floor, complementing the tiled table set in front of the rear window.

She opened the fridge and sniffed the cold air inside. Passable, but she'd need to ask Meg to clean it soon. She placed her quart of milk, half-dozen eggs, and containers of yogurt in front of several bottles of wine shoved to the back.

"*Meooww.*" The carrier wobbled on the tiled floor as the yowl echoed in the room.

"Okay, okay. Hold on." No dangers lurked in the corners and shadows as far as she could tell, so she'd let her feline loose. "Just don't go getting lost, deal?"

"*Meooww...*"

Laughing at her vocal companion, Meredith slid the latches open and lifted the carrier's lid. Grizabella's white, black, and orange head popped up and swiveled like a periscope surveying the unfamiliar horizon. She leaped out of the confines of the plastic box in one fluid arc. Griz picked her way across the floor, lifting and placing each paw, nose and tail both twitching at the onslaught of new scents.

"Behave yourself." Chuckling, Meredith found a place to hold her remaining groceries. She reached for the handle on the pantry door, only to have the tarnished brass and glass knob come off in her hand. Sighing, she pulled her Swiss army knife from her pocket and flipped up the appropriate tool to turn the inner mechanism. Finally popping open the pantry door, she flinched at the odor accompanying the spiderwebs stretched across the interior. This place needed more than a bit of work.

Wonder if Grandma kept things in the same places all this time? She hurried to the back staircase, the one once used by the servants of the house and connected the kitchen to the bedrooms above. Similar to the front stairs, a small door led to a closet made from the space underneath the risers. Unlike the front hall closet, this one's door sat firmly shut. Meredith gingerly tested the doorknob before giving it a firm twist to pull it open. A small cloud of dust swirled around her feet, lightly coating her shoes.

Taking a deep breath, she ventured inside. The old straw broom Grandma had always preferred over the "newfangled" ones with plastic bristles rested against the back wall. A dust mop, rag mop, bucket, and round-headed wall brush Meg needed to use on the cobwebs everywhere flanked the yellow-bristled tool. Grabbing the broom handle, Meredith strode back to the pantry and swiped the webs from the shelves. Satisfied, she replaced the broom in its home. A roll of paper towels sat on a faux marble spindle on the kitchen counter. She wet one to wipe down the shelves. Before long, her groceries sat neatly situated in the pantry.

She glanced at her watch. Putting away her groceries only took an hour. If every task took that long, she'd be here until Independence Day, or worse, Christmas.

The light thump of cat paws sounded in the back hallway. Meredith kept one ear tuned to track where Griz explored, just in case she needed to rescue the cat from her own curiosity. Which had happened when they first moved into the little apartment in Baltimore, overlooking the Inner Harbor. Griz had sniffed out a hole in the wall between the kitchen and the living room. Meredith hadn't known anything was amiss until the cat's plaintive cries came from within the wall. Ultimately, repairing the wall was easier than trying to lure her back to the small opening.

Meredith paced through the house until she stopped at the wide doorway to the sewing room. Max had told her Grandma died in her rocker, head back, eyes closed peacefully as though taking an afternoon snooze. Meredith paused, mentally inventorying the contents of the room. Sunshine filtered through the sheers covering the oversize double-hung windows. A cut-glass bowl of lavender-and-mint potpourri sat on an antique table, a spiderweb glistening between the bowl and the wood surface. Two floral-print gooseneck-handled rocking chairs faced the windows, lace doilies pinned to their headrests. Meredith envisioned her Grandma taking her final nap in the chair farthest from the door. The same chair the woman had occupied every Sunday afternoon of Meredith's childhood to do her mending for the week, or to add stitches to one of hundreds of gifts in celebration of a new baby or birthday or other milestone event.

Grandma didn't know what Meredith had endured. What would she have said if she were here? How would she have handled the loss of two dear loved ones in such a tragic way? The horror followed by anger and grief was beyond her ability to describe to people who had not experienced it, and even more difficult for them to grasp.

Meredith swallowed the emotion threatening to sprout tears. The past was dead, just like Willy. Just like her Grandma. She could not permit herself to relive it. She could only press on with her life as she knew in her heart that Willy would want her to do, and pray for the day she joined all those who'd gone before her.

A panicked hissing sounded from the foyer, startling Meredith into turning with a soft cry of surprise.

"Griz? What have you gotten into?" She hurried down the hall. Grizabella stared at the front double doors leading out onto the wide porch where Paulette and Meredith had often played between the columns with the light glinting off the lake's surface. The cat's back arched, and she growled between hisses. "It's okay, Griz. It's only a door."

A low, menacing cat growl told her Grizabella did not agree. The hairs along the ridge of the cat's back bristled. Meredith inched closer to the door, hand reaching to open it. A cold draft floated across her skin, sending a chill through her. Griz growled a final time and then raced past her into the kitchen, claws scrabbling to find purchase on the old wood floors. She jumped out of the way of the terrified feline.

The aroma of honeysuckle wafted past Meredith before dissipating in the silence. She caught a flash of motion out of the corner of her eye and swiveled her head to the right, but nothing moved. Odd. She glanced the other way, searching for anything out of place. All remained quiet. Must be the house settling, its old foundation shifting.

Really? What kind of foundation would take so very long to settle? In fact, if she remembered correctly, this building sat on a stone foundation. Frowning as she contemplated the underlying structure of the building, she walked back to the kitchen doorway. Grizabella sat in the safe haven of her open carrier, head poked up through the rectangular opening like a prairie dog popped out of its hole, eyes wide.

"Poor baby," Meredith crooned. She walked into the airy, sunlit space, a cool breeze caressing her cheeks. She scooped up the cat and hugged her close, stroking her to calm her trembling. "What scared you, kitten?"

The calico replied with a low purring rumble. Grizabella nudged her hand with a warm nose and then butted her head into Meredith's palm. She scritched the cat in her favorite places behind her right ear and under her chin. Did other cat owners refer to the soft rubbing scratch as *scritching*, or something else? She'd never asked anyone that question. Slowly the tense cat relaxed enough that she could put her back on the floor.

"Perhaps some dinner would help you settle better. You can't be so scared of nothing around this old place, or neither one of us will get any rest."

Grizabella wound about Meredith's ankles until she reached down to scritch her again. When the cat sat down to lick one delicate paw, Meredith retrieved a can of cat food from the pantry. She located a small saucer in the cupboard, dumped the food on the plate, and placed it on the floor by the carrier. Grizabella stared at it for a long moment prior to picking her way across the tiled floor to sniff disdainfully at the flat spherical lump.

"I know it's not your usual, but it's all they had." Meredith turned aside from her companion's silent accusation.

Grizabella raised her head from where she'd been nibbling at her supper, ears cocked toward a sound outside, drawing Meredith's attention from her reverie. She peeked out the window. A small dark-blue car drove into the driveway and went immediately to the little cottage, its white walls contrasted by dark-green roof and shutters, situated at the back of the clearing. Meg and Sean, no doubt, moving back into the house they'd shared for decades. Coming home must be wonderful for them. *Home.* Her throat tightened, and she swallowed the lump of nostalgia. She steeled her heart against any other emotion that might try to resurrect itself and turned away from the window.

Her watch showed she had a couple of hours until time to face her sister. Her questions. Demands. Needs. Grievances. Why had she agreed to dine with her? What was she thinking? No matter. Once Meredith made a commitment, she didn't back down. Ever.

Since she had some time, she may as well begin. She'd start at the top and work her way through the rooms, so she could discard unnecessary furniture while she continued to live in the house. Meredith tramped out of the kitchen, down the front hallway, and without giving herself time to second-guess her decision, marched up the steps to the second floor.

Several doors opened off the upper loft-like area. She envisioned the connecting doors between bedrooms creating a kind of rabbit's warren of the top floor: one room leading to another and then another. The ballroom took the whole front of the house, overlooking the pretty lake and large front yard. She had an image of ladies in hoop skirts and men in Confederate uniforms dancing inside the open French doors, and shook the daydream from her head.

The sleeping porch, her favorite place in the summertime, molded itself to the back of the house. She could almost hear the laughter she and Paulette once shared while supposedly asleep on a hot summer's evening. Owls and whippoorwills had created a lullaby for the two young girls on many starry nights. Those happy times resided so far in the past as to be another lifetime. One in which she and Paulette called each other friend. Not now. Perhaps not evermore, which evoked a sadness in her heart. She stiffened, blocking the urge to probe the sore spot lingering between them. She mustn't indulge in such fantasies as to think she and Paulette could ever be friends again.

The stairs leading to the attic beckoned her, the solid wood door at the top closing off the large, musty space where she and Paulette had played on cool days during storms. She relived in her mind the house-shuddering booms of thunder overhead while rain pounded the shingles above. They were only allowed to play among the wire-bodied mannequins and trunks of old clothes and jewelry, books and papers, strange statues, and knickknacks when the weather forced them inside. They had enjoyed playing dress-up with the dresses and necklaces and bracelets on those rare occasions. Indeed, most of her childhood she'd spent out of doors. As a result, the attic contained equal parts memories and mysteries.

Including the memory of the severe storm that had threatened the very existence of Twin Oaks. The severe weather had come in waves throughout that day. She and Paulette were finally permitted to venture into the attic once the air temperature had eased from the cool rain accompanying the storm. The sudden tornado siren blasted moments before a tremendous crash of thunder overhead. The boom preceded a series of lightning strikes around the house, splitting an old oak down the middle. The entire event had terrified Meredith, leaving her shaken and trembling during every subsequent thunderstorm.

She rested a hand on the newel, the one her father

carefully helped her fashion into a carved acorn. She place one foot on the first step. Starting at the top meant the attic. That meant returning to the birthplace of her terror of tornadic weather. Something she hadn't considered carefully before committing to her plan. Traversing the stairs and then passing through the door would mean facing not only that fear but also the many mysterious boxes and trunks housed within. Maybe the old gray and red trunk with its forbidden contents still hid among the others. She'd finally see inside of it. But did she want to? She put her foot back on the floor even as she gripped the wooden cap of the nut tighter beneath her palm, careful to not dislodge it as it was wont to do. Sooner or later she'd have to venture up to the attic and sort through whatever she found. She placed a foot on a step and then joined it with her other one. One stair at a time, she neared the wood door. Four more to go.

Banging on the door below preceded Meg's voice drifting up the stairs. "Hey, anyone home?"

Relief sparked through her like lightning hitting the dead oak. Her breath rushed from her. Why did she, a grown, intelligent woman, hesitate to approach the attic after all these years? She pivoted and hurried down the stairs, entering the kitchen as Meg knocked three times in rapid succession on the wood screened door.

"Come on in." Meredith pulled the door open, the entire frame wobbling in her hand. Meg stood in the open doorway, holding out a plate of chocolate chip cookies.

"I thought you might enjoy some warm cookies," Meg said, walking into the kitchen.

"You remembered." Meg's county fair award-winning baking skills flooded into her memory. The aroma of cooling chocolate made her mouth water. She took an appreciative bite of warm, gooey heaven. "Hmmm. Nobody makes cookies like you."

Meg winked at her. "It's my secret ingredient."

"One of these days you'll have to share with me what it is." Now why did she say that? She wouldn't be baking cookies for anyone. Ever. "What brings you by so soon? I thought you'd still be unpacking, settling in."

"It's all done." Meg set the plate on the counter. "I wanted to check on how bad the place had gotten after I was sacked."

Meredith shrugged. "Bad enough. Dusty and cobwebs, a little mold here and there, but livable for a time. How long has it been since you worked here?"

"Your Grandma died six months ago. Max had even turned off all the power, but when he knew you were returning, he contacted the public utilities to have it turned on."

"For that I'm grateful. But it explains why the fridge smells funky."

"Oh dear. I'll take care of it straightaway." Meg crossed her arms and gazed at Meredith. "What else do you want me to do?"

"Clean. That's the most important thing." She needed the antiques in sellable condition, after all. That and she didn't want to live among dirt and mildew if only for a short while. Everyone suffered when mold entered the picture. She wrinkled her nose as the musty smell drifted past her. Grandma was probably turning somersaults in her grave at the filthy condition of the house she loved. "Grandma would have wanted the mold addressed first."

"I'll start on it immediately."

"And Meg, thanks for coming back. I know it would mean a lot to Grandma. As it does to me."

"My dear, I appreciate your kindness. Your grandma knew you would take good care of Twin Oaks. I'll go make sure a room is ready for tonight. You'll stay in the master now?"

"Yes, I think I will, though I hadn't really thought about it."

In fact, it would be preferable to sleep anywhere but her childhood bedroom with all its memories ready to haunt her. The bedroom she and Paulette shared when they visited each summer. The twin beds with their personalized quilts their Grandma had stitched by hand; Paulette's featuring patchwork planets, sun, and moon, and Meredith's decorated with flowers and butterflies. Her breath caught. Why on earth did she think she could return to this house and have any peace of mind?

Grizabella chose that moment to wander back into the room, her tail a slowly twitching flag, reminding Meredith of an inadequate radar sweep. The distraction enabled Meredith to breathe again.

"Who do we have here?" Meg stretched her hand down to pet the cat, but Grizabella walked out of reach. Meg straightened. "I guess she doesn't know me yet."

"That's Grizabella, or Griz for short. She is rather wary of strangers since she was a stray. I've always wondered what happened in her past."

"She's a beauty."

"In looks, though not always in personality. But I love her nonetheless." Meredith crossed the room, scooped Griz up and cuddled her, moving closer to Meg so she could stroke the calico fur.

"She loves to be scritched."

Meg cocked her head to one side, her fingers poised in the air to touch the cat. "Scritched?"

Meredith chuckled. "Yes, it's what we've always called gently scratching on the kitties."

"Like this?" Meg curled her fingers and rubbed the cat gently.

"Exactly."

"I best get started." Meg swiped her finger down Griz's neck one last time. "We'll have this place shining again in a twinkle."

"Oh, Meg, speaking of time, I'm meeting Paulette at the Hideaway for dinner, so please lock up as you leave, okay? I wouldn't want anyone wandering in while I'm gone."

"Your sister? How wonderful for you. I can fix up a room for her as well."

"No, thanks," Meredith said firmly. "She's staying at the Coldwater B&B."

Meg blinked at her, brows drawing down around puzzled eyes. "I suppose she has her reasons, though I'm sure I don't know why she'd pay to stay somewhere else, even that lovely B&B, when this big ol' house is sitting near empty."

Meredith shifted her weight to her left foot, folding her arms across her chest while looking at Meg. "Let's just say she'll be way more comfortable there."

Chapter Three

eredith peered through the Hideaway's front window, built with thick glass blocks in place of the former iron bars. She spotted Paulette at a table for two, perusing the menu. Taking a deep breath, she pushed open the door. Waving off the eager hostess, a teen with black hair pulled into a severe ponytail and a smile on her freckled face, Meredith sauntered to the table.

"Some things never change." Paulette lowered the one-page paper menu to the small square table between them. "The Hideaway is one of them."

"Change isn't always for the better." Meredith picked up her own menu. "Many folks prefer evolution to revolution."

Paulette sniggered and perused the menu once more before laying it down. She steepled her fingers together, elbows resting on the edge of the table. Meredith made her choice and laid her own menu down, watching her sister scan the small diner. She'd changed, her hair less shiny, her eyes more calculating and wary. She'd always been a bit on the sarcastically skeptical side. Paulette had not contacted Meredith in months—no, make that years. Not since Johnny had cheated on her and they'd split and made up again. What had happened to cause such harshness and bitterness with a hint of panic in her expression? Nothing good, surely.

Meredith let her own gaze wander over the homey establishment. She noted the rows of blond wood tables and chairs, the tall potted plants scattered around, striving to create a warm atmosphere, and the watercolor paintings of Roseville's lakeshores and cityscapes. She lingered on each object as if they were unfamiliar. In fact, nothing could be farther from reality. Her parents used to have dinner there, occupying the old cell in the back of the block structure once a week every summer. Their tradition of eating in the confines of the metal doors stemmed from their first visit to the new restaurant. As the story went, her parents, Brock and Dina O'Connell, worked their typical magic and became fast friends with the owner. That perk secured them the privilege of eating in the reserved space each time they dined at the Hideaway. After her mother became pregnant with Meredith, they frequented it more often because of the healthy menu choices. Then as Meredith grew older, Dina started introducing her to friends by saying that Meredith had been in and out of jail all her life. *Ha. Ha.*

After the waitress took their orders, Meredith fiddled with her fork, aligning it precisely with the edge of the yellow paper mat. Once satisfied, she glanced up and caught Paulette grinning at her, a twinkle in her eyes. Many years had slipped by since she'd last seen such amusement on her face. Usually at her expense.

"What?" Meredith folded her arms, resting them on the table as she studied her sister's expression.

"You always did that," Paulette said with a wave of her hand. "Line everything up. Even your Barbie doll shoes sat neatly in their closet in your dumb dollhouse. Do you remember?"

The image of the oversize dollhouse, a replica of Twin Oaks complete with wraparound porch and electric lights, rose in her mind's eye. She and her dad spent most of a summer on the design and creation of the nearly exact miniature version of the family home. The only thing missing was running water. "Whatever happened to that monstrosity?"

Paulette shook her head, blonde tresses swinging along her jawline. "No idea."

"The house was the first real building project I helped Dad with," Meredith said slowly. "Did you know?"

"How could I forget? You spent months doing little else. I was so bored, and you wouldn't play with me." Paulette's expression sobered. "I hated you that summer."

Meredith toyed with her fork, slowly spinning it like a propeller blade after the motor shuts off. She glanced up at Paulette's words, the heat her voice contained. Did the animosity between them stretch so far into the past? "You did? I didn't realize you'd even noticed."

The waitress returned, carrying a grilled chicken salad for Meredith and chicken-fried steak and mashed potatoes for Paulette. The sisters studied each other in silence as the teen placed the meals on the table and departed. Meredith drizzled balsamic vinaigrette on the greens and chicken and tossed the salad lightly with her fork. The temperature of the space between them warmed, simmering with tension. She stirred in the dressing, aware of an impending change but unsure of the direction the shift would take.

"You and Dad spent so much time together he ignored me entirely." Paulette cut into her meat, stabbed a bite with her fork, and plopped it into her mouth. The earlier twinkle of amusement had vanished, leaving her mouth pinched as she chewed.

At the time Meredith had thought only about what would make her little house perfect. She wanted it to be an exact replica of the plantation house, right down to the scroll at the top of the columns on the front porch. The design of the shutters and even the acorn newel matched the house as closely as her ten-year-old hands could create. The one difference she had reluctantly allowed had been not making the columns hollow because her dad had convinced her they would be easier to make using solid dowel rods. In fact, they had to hunt down wider dowels than usual in order to recreate the correct dimensions. She'd agreed at the time because no one would know the difference, but to this day the modification equated to copping out on the design, which still irked.

"I'm sorry," Meredith said abruptly, "but I was able to be creative, really creative, with that project. Maybe I went a bit crazy."

Her words came out more brusquely than she'd actually intended, but so be it. She couldn't undo what had happened when they were children. Taking a bite, she chewed quickly. Perhaps she shouldn't have come. This powwow had started out an uncomfortable idea, and now all this recollection of the past made it more so. She stuffed another bite into her mouth. The sooner she finished, the sooner she could return to the solitude she craved. Even if it meant being holed up in the very place that embodied her disquiet.

"You never really cared about me, admit it." Paulette speared her with a glare. "It's always been about you. You and what you want. Your perfect life. You've convinced yourself that you're better than me. But you're not and never will be."

Shock reverberated in Meredith's chest. The tension between her and Paulette stretched as taut as the horsehair on a violin bow. Blowing her breath through pursed lips while counting to five, Meredith blinked. Poor Paulette. Always insecure and clinging yet at the same time fighting to be independent and respected. Definitely she was a conundrum, to say the least.

"That's not true, and you know it. I've done all I can to help you over the years," Meredith bit out. "You don't help yourself, but wait for me to come to your rescue."

Paulette leaned forward, her hands gripping the edge of the table. "You've always been jealous of me and what I've accomplished despite the hardships in my life. The real world is very different than the one you live in."

"Like you'd know. You never try to understand anyone else's situation; you assume you know everything. But you don't and you never will. God, why did I even bother trying?" Meredith ripped her napkin from her lap and threw it on the table. She pushed back her chair and stood, yanking her purse strap onto her shoulder. "I knew this was a mistake. I'll take care of the tab on my way out. Again."

"Bitch! Don't walk away from me!" Paulette jumped to her feet, knocking her chair against the wall behind her.

"Right." Meredith waved a hand in farewell. "You're like this restaurant. You never change."

She hurried to the reception area to settle up, hoping Paulette would let the argument drop. The confrontation left her shaken. Their simmering hatred apparently went far deeper into the past than she'd realized. Of course, she hadn't contemplated their relationship in eons, preferring to ignore it and hope time would ease the tension. Paying with cash at the register, she slipped her receipt into her purse and turned to flee the animosity and memories the diner held. Only to run into the broad, strong chest of Max Chandler.

"Whoa, Meredith, what's your rush?"

Embarrassment warmed Meredith's cheeks as she blinked at him, her hands still pressed to his chest. "Sorry. Excuse me." She removed her hands from his shirt and stepped past him, but he caught her by the arm before she could escape.

"I saw your car outside and came in here looking for

you." He squeezed her elbow gently, keeping her beside him. "It really stands out in such a small town."

Meredith searched for a way to extricate herself from this uncomfortable situation as Paulette closed in on them. Not only did she feel her sister's eyes stabbing her from behind, but the zinging electricity from Max's touch heightened her desire to flee. She shook her arm free of his grasp, but not before the bitch noticed the physical contact between them.

"Aren't you going to introduce us?" Paulette offered a hand to Max without waiting for Meredith's response. "I'm Paulette O'Connell, Meredith's sister. And you are?"

"Max Chandler, Meredith's estate attorney."

He was? Meredith glanced up at him and frowned. She didn't recall hiring him as her attorney. She flicked a glimpse at her sister, noting her narrowed eyes and raised chin. She obviously suspected more to their relationship than existed. Or could exist, for that matter. Maybe another time, perhaps another lifetime, she'd find Max both intriguing and handsome. Right now, though, she refused to become involved with any man.

"We spoke earlier. I guess that means you're mine as well." Paulette's features morphed into her alligator smile. "As Meredith's sister, it is only fair we share in Grandma O'Connell's inheritance. Don't you agree?"

Max's smile lost its warmth. "That is up to Meredith, as Mrs. O'Connell only included her in the will. Your name wasn't mentioned as an heir to the property."

"We'll see about that." Paulette's smile disappeared as fast as it had arrived. "I'll be in touch, Meredith. Hope you *enjoyed* your dinner."

Four bites of salad didn't constitute a meal. Meredith shook off the sarcastic comment. Paulette strode to the outside door and pushed through it. The tension between them diminished with each click of her heels. Meredith released the breath she'd been holding. She still reeled from the emotional onslaught caused by their conversation, coupled with the unwanted physical reaction created by Max's touch. She didn't need this, all this angst and emotional turmoil. Stealing every tiny shred of balance and peace she'd dragged into her life. The room slowly spun, tiny black and gray splotches dancing before her eyes.

"Are you okay?" Max grasped her upper arms. "I think you're about to faint. Why don't we sit down and talk?"

"I don't faint." She had never done so, and she was not about to start. What was it with him touching her all the time? She tried to free herself from his grip, but he held firm. She attempted to glare at him. "Did you need something? You said you were looking for me."

"I hoped to catch up with you. Please, let me buy you a cold drink. I can't in good conscience let you drive in this condition."

He practically dragged her back to the bar area situated near the old jail cell. Perfect. Another bout of memories to combat. She stood facing away from the cell. The mirror reflected the assortment of bottles filled with a variety of colorful liquors arrayed along the back wall. Wineglasses and martini glasses hung in racks above the bar, within easy reach for the bartender. The traditional jackalope—the humorous stuffed animal made by combining a jack rabbit and an antelope—peered at her from its place on the wall. Tonight's barkeep, a young man with spiky hair tipped with orange highlights, wiped a red cloth over the polished surface of the bar.

"Sam, how's your dad doing?" Max motioned to Meredith to take one bar stool as he settled onto another one.

Sam tossed the rag onto the bar and stepped closer. He seemed to be about twenty-five. What chain of events led him to work in a small town in such a small bar? The counter she leaned her elbows on only measured approximately twelve feet long. Enough space to serve, at most, four customers. Not like her favorite watering hole in Baltimore that could seat thirty. Of course, he fixed drinks for those at the dining tables as well. Who would have thought this small town with its many churches contained even that many people who imbibed?

"He's recovering, thanks to your quick action." Sam laid cocktail napkins in front of each of them. He nodded at Meredith and then indicated Max with his head. "He stopped my dad from drowning last week after he fell asleep at the wheel and landed his car in a drainage ditch."

"Wow," Meredith said, one hand going to her throat. She pictured a car in dark gray water seeping into the cabin, and shivered. "He's mighty lucky indeed."

"Max was in the right place at the right time and pulled him out," Sam said. "He saved my dad."

"Glad to have been there to help him. He's a good man," Max said. "I'll have my usual. Meredith?"

His usual? "Gin and tonic, please." Meredith angled her head to study the man beside her.

He surprised her on many levels, not least of which being the electrical current that seemed to shoot into her when he moved within a certain proximity. *Like now.* Her skin itched from the static and grew warm from his body heat. His perusal of her face, intimately inspecting each feature from her eyes down to her nose and on to her mouth, made her squirm. Had she plucked her brows this morning? Yes, yes, she had. She ran her tongue over her teeth inside her closed mouth, checking for stray bits of lettuce. His gaze zeroed in on her lips. Okay, so maybe that was a bad idea. She stopped her tongue's mission.

"You come here often." Not a question, but a statement of fact. Meredith's pulse skipped a beat when he met her gaze. She really needed to compose herself. This reaction wouldn't serve her purposes at all. At least he no longer stared at her mouth.

Max leaned on the bar, his legs angled toward hers, a slow grin illuminating his face. "Sam's my cousin, so I come here to support his livelihood. Besides, he makes a killer moontini."

Sam placed their drinks in front of them. He set a small bowl of salted peanuts between the crystal glasses. Meredith grabbed a handful and plopped a few nuts into her mouth. If she was going to have a drink, she needed sustenance.

"I'll bite. What's a moontini?" She watched the motion of his chin, then his lips, as he chuckled in response. She forced herself to look away, focusing on his eyes instead.

"A moonshine martini." Max raised his long-stemmed glass, rotating it slowly so the oversized green olive rolled lazily around the inside. He took a sip and she stared, fascinated, as his Adam's apple rose and fell in his throat. "Ah. Very smooth."

She swallowed a mouthful of her cocktail to gather her wayward thoughts and to tamp down on the unwarranted sensation she experienced as a result of his nearness. "You wanted to talk to me, and I'm sure it wasn't about your superhero status or your drinking habits." She chewed on another handful of nuts while she waited for his response.

"Right. You like to cut to the chase." He lifted his drink, filled his mouth, and swallowed slowly before continuing. "I wanted to know what your plans are for the plantation. You left me feeling uneasy when we parted."

"I'm still considering my next move." Meredith tasted a hint of lime in her drink, swallowing to buy time and cool the sizzle in her veins. "Why unease?"

"I get the feeling you're not planning to live there." He shifted, pointing his knees at the bar and resting his elbows on the counter. His long fingers gripped the crystal stem of his glass. He swished the moonshine, light refracting through the glass and clear fluid. "Your grandmother would be disappointed about that, I'm sure."

Meredith glanced at Sam, who obviously could hear every word they said. How much of this conversation would be public knowledge before she reached Twin Oaks tonight? "I don't plan to live here. My home is in Baltimore. Not here. Never here."

He stared at her, assessing her expression. "Never?"

"I enjoyed my summers here, but this isn't home."

"But you're here now. You know this place, and this place knows you."

What a miserable thought. She shivered and gripped her glass hard to still the tremble before it traversed her entire body. Small towns housed a lot of nosy people who had to uncover every action and secret of those who lived near them. "I'm here for a short time by design. Besides, the people of this town have no idea who I am and what I'm capable of."

"Please, Meredith, reconsider living at the plantation." He gazed at her for a long, searching moment and then laid a hand on her wrist. A subtle change in his expression warned her of something she couldn't interpret. Mesmerized, she watched him. Slowly he pulled her hand away from the glass and curled his fingers around hers. "I think you feel the same connection I do. I want to give us a chance to get to know each other. Find out, like you said, who you are and what you're capable of."

She blinked several times, her eyebrows rising so high she could feel her bangs brush across them. This man she barely knew wanted more than she could fathom ever giving to another man. She might be about to move on with her life, but that didn't mean she was ready to link up. Willy had been the only man she would give her entire heart and soul, and no one could replace him and the love they'd shared. No way would she ever accept the offer before her. She yanked her hand free.

"If that's all you wanted to say, *Mr.* Chandler, then thank you for the drink but no thank you on the rest of it. Good night." She grabbed her purse off the bar and pivoted in her seat in preparation to slip off the stool.

"Wait!" Max grasped one arm. He peered at her, his expression cool. "I'm sorry."

He did *not* just touch her again. His flirtations came and went like an ocean wave. She glared at his hand until he slowly released her. Anger simmered through her, canceling out any chance of Max affecting her composure with his chemistry. She'd always excelled in chemistry, but she had no use for his. "You don't seriously want to get to know me, do you? So what is it you really want?"

The Coldwater Bed and Breakfast hunkered among drooping willow trees, as inviting as a mausoleum. Paulette trudged up the concrete sidewalk and then the steep steps to the wraparound porch. She paused, noting the splashy flowered cushions on the brown wicker chairs arranged around matching wicker tables. The sight contrasted with the cold atmosphere she sensed blanketing the house. Almost as though overcompensating with vibrant colors would warm the environment. The owner, one Angel Baker, had welcomed her with no warmth in her shriveled face. Paulette shivered in the cooling night air. Pushing open the door, she strode into the house. Lamps shed pools of light from side tables in the foyer. A chandelier hung from the ceiling, its crystals dangling, unlit. She'd never stayed in such a foreboding place. Another shiver rocked her shoulders.

The sound of sensible shoes smacking the carpeted hardwood floors announced Angel's approach. Paulette clutched her purse, readying an excuse for hurrying up to her room without engaging in idle chit-chat. After her horrible discussion with Meredith, she dreaded talking about nothing with the proprietor of the B&B.

"My dear, did you have a good dinner with your sister?" Angel bustled into the foyer, wiping her hands on her ruffled bibbed apron.

"The food was good." Paulette sidled toward the staircase to her right. "I think I'll call it a night." She yawned for good measure.

"I turned down the bed for you." The woman nodded as though praising herself. "Scoot on up and get some sleep. Breakfast will be at eight."

Paulette paused with her hand on the newel post. "What are you serving for breakfast?"

Angel winked. "My specialty. You have a nice night, and I'll surprise you in the morning."

She made her way up to her room and dropped her purse on the dresser. Her suitcase stood beside the luggage rack. The canopied bed dominated the room. An overstuffed chair nestled into the corner by the window. A round skirted table held a glowing porcelain lamp, providing a spot of warmth in an otherwise cold room. Her hope that Meredith would welcome her to stay at Twin Oaks had disappeared with the start of the old arguments. She'd needed a place to stay the night. A place that ended up shoving back at her, pushing her out the door. The house didn't want her to remain, but tonight she had no other choice. She'd have the bill sent to Meredith like she'd thrown at her sister. Meredith had plenty of money.

She opened her suitcase and pulled out a short nightgown, the kind Johnny preferred she wear. When she told him about the baby, he'd said he didn't want to be tied down by a family. He wasn't ready to be a father. But he'd already fathered a child, whether he felt ready or not. She thought she'd loved him up until that moment. Why did she keep trying to please the man who had walked away from their relationship? She tossed the gown back into the suitcase and yanked out a pair of short shorts and a soft tank top. Much better.

Leaving the lamp on, she drew the quilt up to her chin. Meredith would be settling in to sleep in that huge, lovely house. While she shivered in this awful place. She needed a plan for her and her baby. A home and a future.

Tomorrow she'd take the first step.

Meredith slammed the door behind her, the loud *bang* echoing the fusion of disappointment and anger seething inside. Griz sauntered into the kitchen, tail flagged and twitching in rhythm with the thump of her paws across the floor. Meredith skirted the cat so she could drop her purse and keys onto the ceramic-tiled table nestled in the bay window, which overlooked the back of the property. If the sun were still in the sky, she'd be able to see the family cemetery. The kitchen light reflected back at her from the dark window, a yellow blot on the darkness.

"Damn him." Her words floated through the house, fading into silence. "I didn't need a frigging guilt trip from Grandma after she's been buried."

Definitely not when delivered by the oh-so-suave and handsome Max Chandler. Right after receiving the riot act from Paulette. What a helluva evening. So worthwhile driving into town to be told how to live by two people—make that three, one of whom was dead—who had no clue what she needed. It irked her when people thought they knew better about everything. Even more so when they felt the need to correct her.

She retrieved a wineglass from the cabinet and sniffed it before holding it up to the light. Good enough. Removing a bottle from the fridge, she poured chardonnay into the vessel. She took a long sip, and the coolness calmed her nerves as it flowed down her throat. Grizabella bumped her head into Meredith's leg, demanding attention. Reaching down automatically, Meredith found the cat's favorite itchy spot. A splash of wine on the floor beside the calico reminded Meredith of the glass she held, and she straightened back up.

"Did you miss me, Griz?" Meredith set the glass down on the table and then scooped the cat into her arms. Machine-gun purring answered her question.

She scritched along the cat's stomach and around her neck. When her arms grew tired, she slipped the cat back on the floor before quickly wiping the spill with a paper towel. Then she picked up her glass once more and headed out of the kitchen.

Meredith drifted through the house, listening to the sounds of the old building creak with each step. The dark of night lurked beyond the windows. The scents of cleaning products told her Meg had begun her work. She paced down the hallway and into the foyer, the floorboards beneath her shoes flexing under her.

Most of all she heard Max's voice laying on the guilt from Grandma O'Connell. The love of the land as an Irish heritage. Honoring her family through maintaining her inheritance and keeping the land and home. She took another long swallow of wine and walked into the sewing room.

"This old house must miss Grandma," she said to the empty room. "She loved this place so much. I don't know that I'm truly even worthy to try to be like her."

Immediately she noticed a change in the atmosphere, a subtle shift in the temperature as the air chilled. Something altered, though she could not put her finger on it. Meredith stilled, searching the shadowy room for differences. What was that? She slowly spun in place, a complete circle, as she scouted out the sound's source. Nothing. She shook her head, her ponytail whipping her shoulders. Just her imagination after all of Max's harangue about her responsibilities and family heritage.

She flipped the light switch. Four frosted globes in the center of the ceiling fan cast their combined glow over the furnishings. An old-fashioned wood loom hunkered in one corner, empty but for a few spindles of wool adding burgundy and steel color to the ambience. A freestanding embroidery hoop stood within reach of an overstuffed chair, a modern white light arched above the afghan cloth hanging from the frame, a half-finished cross-stitched cardinal ensnared by the round wooden hoop. Her grandmother's rocking chair sat beneath the light, which emphasized the worn arms of the flower-patterned upholstery. Threadbare patches where elbows had rested bespoke of the amount of time her grandmother occupied the seat. Beside the chair, a rack overflowed with stitchery magazines.

Grandma's now empty chair sat in the middle of an empty room filled with her most treasured memories. This room had served as the focal point of her grandmother's sewing, where Meredith could almost hear her voice, smell her perfume, and feel her presence. Traces of her loving grandmother woven into the very fabric of the old house.

With a sob born of the grief and pain she carried inside, she turned off the light and made her way back through the lit hallway to the kitchen. Nobody understood what the shooter had taken from her. Not only her husband, but also their unborn child. They'd longed for several years to express their love for one another through the creation of a baby. They'd been trying with no success, which made their lovemaking feel a touch desperate at times. Then one day she felt *different*, found herself crying over a peanut butter commercial, and decided to purchase a pregnancy test. The very night she planned to reveal to her husband that the pregnancy test turned up positive, she lost everything. Including her harmony, her sense of hope, and her future dreams. Everything shattered in the blink of an eye. The only thing left from her previous life was Grizabella.

The prospects and expectations this rambling plantation home stood for stabbed her emotions with each step on its aged floorboards. She once longed to have the family this home deserved, but the doctors told her the damage she suffered prevented her from having children. She could always adopt, they'd said. Many orphans needed loving homes. She'd shrugged off the suggestion. Without Willy, she had no desire to build a future family. Without Willy, she coiled into herself, latching onto the wonderful memories of their life together and hating the robber that caused such inner despair.

After checking the lock on the back door, she rinsed her wineglass and turned out the light. Tonight she'd try to get a good night's sleep. Tomorrow she'd begin the sorting process in earnest.

The electronic beat of music reverberated across the bedroom while Meredith stripped out of her clothes. Griz waited on the bed, a miniature multicolored sphinx. Meredith preferred instrumentals to lyrics so she didn't need to decipher the meaning of the song. To not listen to the voices. But the classical music Max insisted on playing grated on her last nerve because Willy had also enjoyed the sound of stringed instruments. She needed something more alive. More like the driving pulse and rhythm she now danced to that worked their magic on her frayed nerves, much like a deep-tissue massage for the soul. Reluctantly, she turned off the music, silence surrounding her.

She fluffed her pillows and slipped between crisp sheets. Meg's efforts had transformed the dusty room into a gleaming sanctuary. The lamplight pooled on the oak nightstand, reminding her of the honey on toast her mother made for her when she'd suffered with a sore throat. The matching triple dresser with its large mirror reflected the bed she and Griz occupied. Several needlework samplers and pictures decorated the walls, works by Grandma, no doubt.

Griz stood, stretched, and resettled beside her. Where Willy should be. The other half of the bed, empty except for the eight-pound cat. Meredith ran a hand over the cool sheet, imagining her husband lying beside her, his weight along with his desire for her pulling her closer. The pressure of his lips on hers. His hands moving over her most sensitive areas. Her name when he came.

Stop. Crossing her arms, she focused on breathing, seeing the furniture, the pictures, the cat. Anything but the images in her mind. She couldn't let herself relive his presence. The pain left from his death seared through her.

With a flick of her wrist, she turned the light off and cast the room into darkness. She snuggled into her pillow, tucking the sheet under her arms. A half-moon floated among the pinpoints of stars outside the window, lending a touch of luminescence to the atmosphere. Perfect sleeping weather.

If her eyes would close. She stared at the ceiling. Knotholes dotted the narrow slats. *One, two, three...* Knotholes instead of sheep? *Why not?* Since sleep evaded her, she had to do something to while away the night. Counting knotholes had helped when she was a child as well. Apparently sleeping through the night wasn't high on her list of priorities. Even when tired. Like tonight. She sighed and started over. If she counted long enough, surely she'd drift off. *One, two, three, four...*

The memory of a childhood dream floated into her mind. The Lady in Blue. Inspired by the belles in that old movie, *Gone with the Wind*, most likely. But the dream had replayed for her frequently as a child. It always started with a beautiful young woman dressed in a royal-blue hoop skirt, dotted with sequins twinkling with every step. Her blonde hair pulled up with sausage curls dangling about her petite face. Funny how she could never see the lady's eyes, though.

An icy breeze blew through the half-open window, fluttering the lacy sheers. Meredith opened her eyes at the first blast. Griz lifted her head from where she'd laid it on her paws, staring at the window. Meredith stroked the cat, but the feline leaped up, the hair along the ridge of her backbone slowly rising.

"What's the matter, girl?" Meredith looked at the cat, then the window. She pushed back the sheet and went to the window to close it. The sheers settled into place. "There's nothing there. It was just the wind."

Griz growled low in her throat, staring at the window.

Meredith slipped into bed, pulling up both the sheet and the lightweight coverlet. All was quiet except for the slowly fading complaints of her cat. "It's okay, Griz. Now where was I?"

One, two, three…

Another icy breeze chilled her despite the covers draped across her body. The window remained tightly closed. Her brow tensed into a frown as she sat up and scanned the room. A flash of light drew her attention to the mirror on the triple dresser set against the far wall. She gasped as Griz jumped from the bed and raced out the door. The Lady in Blue appeared in the mirror, standing between the window and where Meredith sat on the bed, the lady's hands reaching toward her. The lady's silk skirt rustled when she stepped closer to the bed, sequins glinting.

Fear, sharp and intense, shot through Meredith. She spun around to confront the woman, only to discover she sat alone among her tangled bedclothes, sleep a distant thought.

Chapter Four

Thunder jarred Meredith awake, fear shooting into her soul at the terrifying sound. She jerked upright, shoving the covers to one side. Lightning flashed, bringing the room into focus. Glancing at her digital watch, she groaned aloud. Not even the damn roosters would be crowing before five in the morning. Rain laced with hail beat against the panes in its own rhythm. At least the weather radio hadn't sent out an alarm, so it was simply a thunderstorm. Nothing to fear. Sleep didn't factor into her plans during such a ferocious storm, so she may as well accomplish something.

Unplugging her laptop to guard against ground strikes by the frequent lightning, she lifted it off the rolltop desk. She looked at her options, having to choose between sitting on the straight-backed chair by the desk or the cushioned window seat. The storm raged outside the glass pane, but she walked toward it, defying her own fears. She perched on the window seat, the flash of lightning at her back, and settled the computer on her legs. Focusing on creating an actual list of chores to do would help free her mind to think as well as provide a distraction.

With the rain and thunder providing antagonistic

background music, she quickly typed a list of tasks, including conducting a complete tour of the premises. She worried about only one room in the entire house. She longed to but also dreaded going into the attic. To finally discover what hunkered in the shadows of the large space. Fifteen minutes later she reread her list, satisfied she had a good handle on the necessities of the effort. The most pressing task: decide what to do with Twin Oaks.

Closing the lid, she put the device on the rolltop and strode into the bathroom to take a shower. Lightning flashed, followed quickly by a boom so loud she jumped, both hands flying to her throat. Better delay the shower with the storm so close. Once dressed, she pulled her hair into a ponytail and then padded down to the kitchen. Grizabella appeared from a side hallway, her whiskers trailing a cobweb remnant.

"Looks like Meg has more work to do around here." Meredith swiped the offending gossamer string from the quivering whiskers and then scritched the cat's back before sliding a hand from the base of her tail to its tip. Griz circled and rubbed against Meredith's legs, her tail curling around one of Meredith's calves. "No time like the present to begin, eh, Griz?"

After starting a pot of coffee to brew, she ate a cup of yogurt. Pulling her phone from her pocket, she found her earbuds in her purse and plugged them in. She turned on her personal mix of underground electronica and R&B so she wasn't surrounded by silence or, worse, the memory of childhood laughter. The tunes made her feel alive and young, and best of all didn't sound anything like the music she and Willy had enjoyed together. James Curd's "Open Up Your Mind" had her bobbing her head in time with the beat and her hands shaking invisible maracas for a moment. Then, while the pot gurgled and coughed, she grabbed a notebook and pen and pushed through the hallway door, walking in time with the music.

She'd avoided venturing into the attic the day Meg first showed up at her door. But the day arrived nonetheless. Delaying only created larger mental obstacles to accomplishing the necessary tasks. Surmounting the ever-growing hurdles must begin with the first step, literally. Resting her hand gingerly on the newel post, she gazed up the flight of stairs, took a breath and let it out slowly, and then started to climb. Griz sashayed into the hall and sat at the bottom of the flight, gazing after her with curious eyes. Meredith turned at the first landing and began climbing the second flight to the attic door hiding in the dimly lit stairwell. She made a mental note to add a light up there, perhaps a battery-powered stick-on kind.

One step at a time she neared the closed door, her imagination spinning yarns as to what lay behind the barrier. As a child they had looked forward to the infrequent times they could play in the attic, considering it a place of mystery and adventure. Of ghosts and spirits of times past. Now she needed to keep a firm grip on her sensibilities and see whatever was in there through adult eyes. That meant no mysteries, no adventures, and of course no spirits or ghosts.

Now why did she think of ghosts just as she gathered her nerve to venture into the attic? Would she see the lady inside among the shadows and webs? Uncertainty fluttered in her chest, causing her to hesitate. Ever since she'd returned to Twin Oaks, she'd been besieged with self-doubt, a feeling she'd banished upon graduating from university with highest honors. Enough.

Gripping the doorknob, she turned it and pushed the door open before she had time to dwell on her thoughts. Nonetheless her throat tightened in anticipation. With her right hand, she searched for the light switch inside the doorjamb. Before she found it, a blur of fur raced past her, skidding to a halt in the near darkness. Reflexively she jumped and then felt foolish when she realized it was only her cat. After locating the switch, she flipped it, and light bathed the room. Griz peered up at her with wide, mirrored eyes.

"Silly kitten, you startled me." Meredith propped the door open with the fabric-covered brick that had served as a doorstop as far back as she could remember. "Now let's see what we have."

Letting her gaze pan the room, Meredith saw an assortment that recalled her childhood. Grizabella flicked her tail from side to side and stalked into the depths of the room, weaving past the brown plastic rocking horse with its fading painted-on saddle, the schoolroom-sized blackboard and sticks of colored chalk in the tray, and most amazingly the large dollhouse that looked like a miniature of Twin Oaks. Tears threatened and won, seeping down her cheeks at the sight of her first architectural endeavor. Her father's patience played in her memory as he taught her about jigsaws and gluing techniques, about angles and perspectives. She missed her father more than she could put into words. Perhaps she should call him later to invite him and her mother to come for a visit. She brushed her cheeks dry and continued her exploration.

A mannequin stood to one side, its wire shape allowing indecent peeks through its interior. Meredith grimaced, and then smiled, remembering its purpose. Grandma had used the dummy to make dresses; ugly and misshapen ones, but made with a depth of love. One of Paulette's hand-me-downs—a light green nightmare with one sleeve longer than the other, an uneven hem, and neon green frogs boasting bright red eyes—Meredith had flatly refused to wear.

She strode into the room to the marching beat of Crookers's "Bust 'Em Up" and quickly searched the room for the mysterious locked trunk. Her ownership of the plantation finally gave her the right to look inside. That had been the one restriction for the girls when they played up here. They couldn't look into or play with the trunks. The other trunks, all unlocked and secretly explored decades earlier, held old books, clothing, and some jewelry from long-dead ancestors. The time had arrived to solve the mystery of the locked trunk. Feeling a little like Nancy Drew, she peered into the shadows and finally spotted the dark gray trunk with red leather trim. She grabbed the handles on each end and dragged the heavy box into the light.

Squatting, she fingered the padlock hanging from the latch. *Damn.* She looked about, finally spying a rusty tool box nearly hidden beneath an old coffee table piled with yellowed newspapers and magazines. She hurried to the metal box, pulled it from under the table and quickly lifted its lid. Empty. *Double damn.* She slammed the lid and strode back to the trunk.

She needed a key, or a crowbar, or a hammer and screwdriver. But she hadn't brought those kinds of tools with her. Maybe the garage had something she could use. For now, her objective had been defeated by a simple padlock. The scent of fresh coffee teased her nose. After her short night sleepwise, she needed caffeine to kick-start her day. She darted a glance around, jotted a quick list of the amount of stuff to be sorted and disposed of, and finally called to the cat. After several summons, Griz emerged with her head covered in dust and cobwebs, but Meredith could swear she wore a Cheshire cat type of grin.

"What have you been into?" Shaking her head, Meredith shooed Griz out the door and turned off the light. "We'll come back later with the right tools to open that trunk and a broom to sweep off those webs. Right now, I need coffee."

Griz trotted lightly down the steps ahead of her. Meredith pulled the door closed with a *thud.* She yanked out the earbuds and hung them around her neck, the quiet sound of the beat of Subb-an's "Take You Back" playing as though from a distance. The storm outside intensified, the drum of rain on the roof echoing the musical base. Suddenly Griz hissed and growled, arching her back when she stopped on the first landing. The hair on Meredith's neck rose along with those on Griz's spine, sending shivers down her arms and back. Involuntarily gripping the handrail like a lifeline, she stopped, fascinated by the cat's behavior even while afraid the Lady in Blue had returned. Meredith looked in the direction of Grizabella's wary stare but saw nothing alarming. Griz hissed again, retreating three slow steps backward. Still her hackles remained up and her hiss became a low-throated growl reminiscent of last night's occurrence.

"What is it, Griz?" Meredith tried to calm her with her voice, but Grizabella paid her no heed. Taking one tread at a time, Meredith eased down the stairs. "There's nothing there, silly girl. Come on now. I want my coffee."

The floorboard beneath Meredith's foot creaked loudly beside the cat. Griz spun and ran into a bedroom, disappearing from view. Meredith called to her but, as she expected, received no response from the frightened cat. But frightened about what? Meredith looked again in the direction the cat had refused to go. She saw only the usual things: floor, walls, ceiling. Nothing scary or even out of the ordinary. Definitely no spectral Civil War belle.

"Look, Griz, it's okay." She walked on, reaching the top of the stairs leading to the main floor. "Come on, kitty. I'll show you. You have nothing to worry about."

Meredith stepped onto the first stair, and the hair on her neck lifted, cold air sending shivers racing down her arms and back. A door banged closed beneath her, making the risers tremble under her feet. "What the…"

She raced down the remaining steps and whirled around

the newel post to hurry down the hall leading to the kitchen. Everything looked as she'd left it, so how did a door close? Obviously it must be her imagination, overwrought by the visit to the attic. Maybe it hadn't been such a great idea to go up there after the events of the previous night. She forced her shoulders to relax as logic slowly prevailed. Perhaps the wind from the storm worked the kitchen door loose and then closed the door as the wind pressure changed. Sure, that must be it. She drew in a deep breath and exhaled slowly, letting the tension exit her body with the spent air. Nothing to worry about after all. The silly cat had her imagining things. She shook her head at her own foolishness.

Thunder boomed and shook the house, the rain continuing to pummel the building. She loved the smell of rain in the springtime, but the thunder was an entirely different matter. She drew in another breath, trying to calm the familiar terror the storm created, and smelled honeysuckle. Only the windows were all closed, and honeysuckle didn't bloom until later in the year.

Strange. Griz eased her way down the stairs, tail sweeping jerkily left and right. Meredith listened to the rain driving against the house. Lightning flashed. Thunder crashed. She hugged herself, trying to calm the mounting terror. Despite all her efforts, she'd never quite overcome the fear demon that clawed inside when the storms raged outside.

Hammer blows sounded from deep in the house, startling her. Grizabella cocked her ears toward the back hallway and trotted off to investigate. Meredith trailed after the cat, fisting her hands at her sides as she stalked down the hall. Who was banging inside the house? The sound seemed to emanate from the dark and dank basement. Grandma had refused to allow the girls to go down the narrow, rickety steps into the damp stone-walled room. She approached the closed door, wondering if that was the door she'd heard slam shut. Griz sniffed at the gap between the door and the floor and then looked at her expectantly. At least curiosity had replaced her caution.

The sound definitely came from behind the door. Meredith opened the door without giving herself time to reconsider her actions. The hammering continued for a few more blows, followed by silence. Griz trotted down the new wood steps, the scent of pine still lingering. Meredith followed cautiously down the solid treads. Racks of bottled wine lined the far wall. Shelves above low benches on the other walls she could see from where she stood held the necessary emergency supplies: jugs of water, canned goods, candles and matches, flashlights and batteries, and a manual can opener. Even a percolator and can of ground coffee stood at the ready. Meredith noticed the charcoal grill with a small bag of charcoal and lighter fluid tucked into one corner, a necessity for cooking outside should the power go out.

The tap of a hammer striking a nail echoed in the cellar.

"Hello? Who's down here?" She reached the bottom step and gripped the handrail, her longtime wariness of the basement only mildly subdued by the obvious renovations.

Sean poked his head, hair still dripping from the rain outside, around the corner of the wine-cellar wall. A large claw hammer rested easily in his massive palm. "Hey. Did you need me?"

"What are you doing down here?" She stepped to the cold cement floor.

Sean grinned and shrugged. "I just had to check to make sure all was right, while the storm was doing its thing. Do you like it?" He swung the hammer like a baton, catching it with his other hand.

Meredith scanned the wine cellar turned tornado shelter and then looked at him. "You did all this?"

"Yes, ma'am. Your grandma reckoned we needed a safe place to be, after them April twenty-seventh tornadoes swept through Alabama a few years back."

"But we're nowhere near where those storms tracked through." She paused, a ripple of concern shooting through her. "Right?"

Sean rubbed the back of his neck with one hand. "That don't mean we won't see any here, now does it. Tornadoes tend to be a might unpredictable."

Damn. She feared thunderstorms enough, but she'd tried to put the idea of a tornado threatening the area out of her mind. After living in Maryland for so many years, the frequency of tornadoes had no longer been a real concern. The difference in terrain between the rolling countryside of her adopted home versus the flatter valleys around Roseville also changed the probability of tornadoes forming and traveling where she might be impacted. *Double damn.*

"Yes, of course. Did you build the wine cellar too?"

"Yes, ma'am, about three years ago. Your grandmother subscribed to one of them mail-order wine clubs and needed a place to store the bottles." He leaned close and winked at her. "Them bottles arrived faster than she could drink the stuff, you know."

"Grandma joined a wine club. That explains the bottles of wine in the fridge." The wooden wine racks stared at her. They could hold eighty bottles, and nearly all the slots were filled. "Well, if we're forced to seek shelter, at least we won't be without calming influences."

Sean chuckled, waving a hand toward a table against the wall behind him. "Wine by candlelight too."

Several pillar candles huddled beside a large box of stick matches and a weather radio. A camping lantern and bottle of oil sat beside the candles. A pile of what looked like tool hangers lay in the center of the horizontal surface. Above the table a two-foot-square piece of Peg-Board waited for Sean to finish hammering in its supporting nails.

"You've made a huge difference from what I remember as a child, when Grandma forbade Paulette and me from stepping foot down here. But I've interrupted you." Meredith moved back, preparing to leave the close confines. Even though the room had been transformed from a damp, dark space into a welcoming shelter, the walls weren't far enough apart for her comfort. She took a deep breath and pushed it out. "I'll leave you to it, then."

"No need to hurry away on my account." Sean hefted the hammer, tapping it against one palm. "Take a look around. You might oughta make sure you know where things are, just in case."

Dread flowed down her spine at the idea of spending any length of time in the basement. The distant crack of thunder reminded her of why she'd be down here, and the dread deepened into a near panic. Darting a glance about the room in pseudo compliance with his suggestion, Meredith strode to the foot of the steps. "Come on, Griz. Let's leave Sean to finish."

Grizabella mewed as she joined Meredith, rubbing against her leg before trotting up the steps.

"You sure 'nuff have that cat trained." Sean used the claw hammer to scratch an itch on his thigh.

"More likely vice versa." Meredith started up the steps, amazed to be relieved to venture up and into the house despite the booming thunder and flashing lightning outside. She paused and looked back to where Sean's shadow lay across the floor. Such a small area to have seating for eight. She shuddered and then called back to the handyman. "Thanks, Sean, for all your hard work, but I truly hope we never need to use it."

The early morning storm cleansed the air and left

everything glistening when the sun appeared. Max turned off the ignition and sat staring at the old plantation home, seeing it as it might have looked in its prime. Antebellum homes spoke to something deep inside him. He liked all historic properties, truth be told, but he held a special fondness for those created during the flourishing times prior to the American Civil War. They reflected such optimism about the economy back then, about the future of this great country, and most tellingly about the people who worked and lived with hope for a prosperous lifestyle. Since that time, most homes no longer tried to be showcases, preferring practical styling and architectural features. Like what Meredith said she designed. The thought sent a shot of sadness through him, followed by a longing for the past elegance of homes. This plantation, having been the site of several military occupations and encampments by the Yankees, deserved to be safeguarded as a testimony to the history of Tennessee, let alone the country. He'd see to it if he had any chance of doing so. His appreciation for the past remained the primary reason he campaigned for countywide ordinances to preserve and protect the history of the county embodied by the old homes.

He slid from the truck and strode to the kitchen door, briefcase in hand. Meredith's expression last evening had been difficult to read, but he sensed she withheld important information about her intentions. Call it a gut feeling or instinct, but she was up to something. Given he'd been the one to submit the National Register application on her grandmother's behalf, he intended to ensure the property received its due.

He rapped on the door and waited, searching the expanse behind the house for any signs of the direction of her thoughts. All seemed as it had been. Stately magnolias and oaks stood watch over the house. The blooming azaleas and forsythia bushes punctuated the pastoral setting with highlights of red, orange, and yellow. He imagined the families who had occupied this home over the span of generations had spent a lot of time outside, enjoying the cool breeze and shade of the trees. Or at least, he would spend most of his time sitting in the gazebo with a good book and a glass of sweet tea or dozing in a hammock. Perhaps a loving wife and a brood of children working in the garden or playing ball in the yard. A sigh escaped. He'd welcome their interruption to his usual quiet solitude.

He turned at the sound of the door opening behind him. Meredith paused, briefly examining the screened door separating them, and then regarded him with wary attention.

"Max, what a surprise."

"I need to talk to you. May I come in?"

"Depends. What do you want?" She held firm to the door, a physical barrier to his entrance.

He swallowed his demand to know her intent. He must tread carefully or he'd scare her plans underground. "Coffee? And a chat?"

He could appreciate her torso through the door, but her tension appeared in the angle of her head and the searching gaze she pinned on him. Those enchanting green eyes, flecked with gold, watched him, sizing him up. Despite her virtual hedgehog exterior, he needed to understand her. In fact, he wouldn't mind spending more time with her. She was smart and attractive and alluring. But mostly she presented a puzzle he wanted to solve. After a moment she made up her mind and opened the door.

"I made some fresh joe." She waited for him to walk inside and then closed the door behind him. "But we don't have anything to talk about."

"I'm sure we'll think of something." He dragged out a chair and sat down while she poured steaming coffee into two mugs.

She carried them to the table and sank into the chair opposite. Long fingers wrapped around the cup, nearly obscuring the fading picture of two young girls sitting on a porch swing holding rag dolls.

"Is that you and your sister?" Max drank his coffee, the hot liquid nearly burning his throat. He hoped when she revealed her next steps his backup move would be unnecessary.

"Where?"

Max nodded at the mug, and she unwrapped her hands to peer at it.

"Wow. I'd forgotten about that picture." She shook her head and then gazed out the window for the span of two heartbeats before returning her attention to Max. "It was taken a long time ago."

"Where?" He stared at her mesmerizing eyes as they turned inward. So beautiful and yet so prickly. If she forced him to, he'd make her the test case for his proposed countywide ordinance. The one that prevented owners from making external changes to historic properties without prior approval.

"Out back on the old swing, the one we broke the next day because we pushed it to go too high." A tiny smile appeared on her lips, a faraway look on her face.

"You were what, six?"

She focused on him, pressing her lips together before moistening them with a quick flick of her tongue. A surge of desire shot through him, catching him off guard. He shifted to a more comfortable position before taking another swallow of coffee. The tiny movements of her fingers as she cradled the mug had him envisioning other actions of those hands. She stirred sensations and longings in him he'd never felt for anyone else. Which figured, given her glacial attitude toward him. That seemed to be his luck with women. The ones he found intriguing and attractive found him the exact opposite.

"I was five. Like I said, it was a long time ago." She covered the picture with her hands, and he had to force his eyes away from them to meet her gaze. "What did you really want to talk about? Not old photos, surely."

"You. This place." A different kind of longing filled him as he looked around the kitchen. He'd always wanted a fine home, but his resources were stretched too thin to bear such a treasure. Until he was promoted to senior partner at the law firm, which would happen once his proposed legislation to safeguard the county's history came to fruition. "Have you decided what you'll do with it?"

Her eyes chilled another degree, if that were possible. "Why do you care so much about what I do? What's your interest in this whole affair?"

He shrugged lightly. "Your grandmother loved Twin Oaks and all it represented. I'm hoping you'll honor her wishes."

A gleam appeared in her eyes as a slight frown drew down her brows. "Her wish was for me to inherit it. I've not seen anything in writing that expounded on that in any way, so I have no clue what you mean."

"Obviously, she wanted you to have it so you could keep it in the family. She knew you have the skills necessary to fix it up as it should be." He leaned forward, resting his arms on the table as he snagged her gaze. "You're going to keep it?"

"I told you before, I haven't decided."

"True, you did." He regarded her for a long moment, taking a sip of coffee to keep his mouth occupied while he considered her guarded expression. What lay behind that pensive façade? "As you make your plans, it should be comforting to know that once the state commission approves the application, you won't have to worry about any highway widening projects threatening to take or destroy Twin Oaks. They'll have to steer clear of your property."

"Maybe I'll rent it out. Or perhaps I should sell it. I really don't deserve it."

The frown deepened as she let her gaze slide out the window. He followed her glance, noting the gravestones jutting above the wrought-iron fencing in the distant shadows of the magnolias. He'd stood beneath them the cloudy day they'd buried Mrs. O'Connell. He missed the little elderly woman, her spunk, her intense desire to keep her family heritage intact. She'd wanted nothing more than to ensure Twin Oaks continued to be an O'Connell family home. He'd been one of many who had formed the long funeral procession from the Roseville Funeral Home. State troopers had stopped traffic along the route, out of respect to the deceased as well as to allow the snaking line of cars and trucks to proceed unimpeded to the plantation. The very place Meredith contemplated selling.

"Why would you say such a thing?"

Those emerald gems focused on him once more. Her long fingers twirled the mug in her hands, a slow, precise spinning of the handle counterclockwise on the table. "It's such a big place, one meant for a large family. Which you may have noticed I do not have."

He wouldn't let himself fantasize about those fingers surrounding anything else. Not for the moment. He needed to keep his wits about him.

He pushed the cold, empty mug out of his way. "Perhaps you should start your own family here then."

She jerked back in her chair, crossed her arms, and glared at him. "That's none of your business."

Ah, he'd struck a nerve. Her body language spoke volumes about the defensiveness he'd sensed earlier. From what did she protect herself? "You don't want to have a family?"

She scowled at him and flowed to her feet. "I have a lot

of work to do, so if you're done prying, I'll ask you to leave now."

"I haven't finished." He leaned back, assessing her expression. Testing her response like he would a witness in court. He'd wanted to know how she'd react to his questioning. Tense and unfriendly. But why?

"Yes, you have." She crossed her arms over her chest and nodded at the mug he'd pushed aside.

Well, she had him there. He cocked a brow and grinned. "Could I have some more? You make great coffee." At the sharp shake of her head, he effected a sigh and scraped back his chair. Some research seemed in order as to why she went from being a hedgehog to an irate porcupine. He'd learned all he could from her, apparently. Time to do some digging on his own. He nodded once. "If I've offended, please accept my apology."

"Done." She marched to the door, yanking it open. "Good day."

"I'll leave. But before I go, I want to say, we can agree on one thing. You and I both want what is right for Twin Oaks." He paused at the threshold and drank in her pretty features along with the wariness in her expression. "Rest assured I'll do all in my power to ensure Mrs. O'Connell's vision for the plantation remains intact."

"And what about my vision for it?" Meredith clung to the door with one hand and the opposite door frame with the other, preventing him from stepping back into the kitchen.

"As long as yours meshes with hers, we'll get along fine."

She blanched but didn't back down from the challenge. "Thanks for the warning. If you don't mind…" Her eyes sparked with resolve even as her expression closed.

"I don't know what you're planning, sweetheart…but I'm going to make sure you comply with your grandmother's wishes."

"You've done your job, Max." Meredith started closing the door, narrowing his view of her lithe body. "She'd be proud of you. Take care."

"I'm sure we'll run into each other again. Roseville isn't that big."

Once back in his pickup, he considered the woman watching him through the screened door as he turned the key in the ignition. He needed to find out exactly what she hid from him. If that meant dogging her very footsteps, day after day, month after month, until he found the answer to that question, well, then he was the man for the job. He grinned to himself as he pulled out of the driveway. He owed that much to Mrs. O'Connell, whether Meredith liked it or not.

Sunshine angled through the small windows of the attic, appearing almost smoky through the dust motes. Grizabella flinched each time Meredith swung the hammer and struck the screwdriver handle, its flat blade jolting the padlock hinge. She'd tried locating the key, with no success. How did that happen anyway? Were small keys like socks in the dryer, disappearing along with the hot air? She continued hammering with precision until the padlock finally sprang open. Dropping the tool beside the useless monkey wrench and crowbar, she grinned at the cat. She gripped the front corners of the trunk lid and paused, contemplating what might jump out at her.

"Finally I find out what the great secret is." She considered the calico positioned to one side of where Meredith kneeled before the trunk. "Ready?"

Grizabella flicked her tail and hunkered down to watch Meredith lift the heavy metal lid.

As sunlight fell across the open trunk, Meredith froze. The box was crammed full of yellowed, handwritten letters, a set of matching leather-bound books, and a three-inch vinyl binder labeled in elaborate typeface, O'CONNELL FAMILY TREE, brimming with sheets of paper. Curious, she picked up a packet of letters secured by a length of lace. Flipping through them, the dates reached as far back as the 1850s. She counted ten groups of letters, each measuring about three inches thick, spanning through the 1860s. Reading all of them would take ages, but her curiosity piqued when she noticed the set written between three O'Connells—two women and a man—shortly before and during the Civil War. Perhaps they were relatives sharing news of family. Her family, in fact.

Setting the letters aside, she lifted the binder out and carefully opened it so no pages escaped. Grandma O'Connell had apparently spent a great deal of time over the years pulling together genealogical research on the family. She'd identified their family back to when they immigrated to America prior to the Revolution. The concept of delving into the family tree, tracing the ancestral line, made Meredith's skin crawl. Historical research was more Paulette's gig, not hers. At least when her sister decided to focus and buckle down to work at anything. But no way would Meredith ask Paulette to apply her skills to the search. Not after their abortive dinner the night before.

Meredith looked at her grandmother's beautiful script handwriting, which flowed across the page, prompting Meredith's throat to close. Call her sentimental and perhaps a touch foolish. She held the very paper her grandmother had held years before. The sense of connection between them, their fingerprints layering upon the page, warmed her like a blanket. As she focused on the words, though, she grew more and more intrigued.

From her notes, Grandma had tirelessly searched for some reference to her husband's grandfather's sister. Grace

Abigail had disappeared from the family records in 1862, though Grandma had hunted for decades to find some hint of her whereabouts. Grace's sister, Edith, married a Confederate officer in late 1863 in Lexington, Kentucky. Interestingly, Grandpa's great-grandfather, David Joseph, known as Joe, had also served in the Confederate Army as a soldier. According to Grandma's notes, she'd discovered from the letters that when he came home after the war, he found Twin Oaks abandoned, though with every indication it had been the Union Army's campsite during the fighting. The specific reference provided the evidence needed for Grandma's application to list the plantation on the National Register.

Grandma O'Connell had documented the timeline of the fighting and troop movements from 1861 until the war's end. The Union troops had moved south from Roseville, Tennessee, to Huntsville, Alabama, in early 1862. Grandma had surmised that was the time frame during which the Union Army encamped at Twin Oaks en route. Grandma detailed the timeline of the many letters Grandpa Joe wrote to distant family members trying to ascertain where Grace, his favorite little sister, had gone, but he failed to locate her. He never gave up hope and even bequeathed her an interest in Twin Oaks in his will should she return.

How sad. Meredith closed the binder and pressed it to her chest for a long moment. Why would Grace have left without a word? Maybe she tried to defend Twin Oaks and the Yanks killed her? Or maybe she died of cholera and nobody knew who she was, a nameless victim in an overcrowded hospital? Most likely she died in one way or another, since she never came home. Meredith sighed, laying the book back in the trunk. She'd never know now. Not if her grandmother had been unsuccessful in her search.

Meredith had no clue where to even begin genealogical

research. She fingered the tobacco-leaf-colored letters, gently lifting another packet out of the trunk. Her family's history lay captured within the leaves of these pages. She trailed a fingertip along the short end of the folded letters, thinking about how much time and effort her grandmother must have devoted to digging into the O'Connell family past. No wonder she didn't want little hands digging through the trunk. She peered at the packet, contemplating the secrets hidden within the handwritten letters. Secrets she'd like to one day expose to light.

Griz rose up to a sitting position beside Meredith, her tail twitching, ears alert. Meredith glanced over her shoulder, listening. She heard footsteps on the floorboards below and tensed.

The steps stopped. "Hello?"

Meg. "Up here!" Meredith quickly replaced the letters and lowered the lid.

"Gracious, what are you doing up here among these old things?" Meg ambled into the room and let her gaze skim the contents of the dusty attic. Sean came up behind her, peering over her shoulder. "Wow, I need to get in here and clean this place up."

"Hey, Meg. Sean." Meredith stood and swept an arm through the air to indicate the attic at large. "My curiosity got the better of me. I've wanted to know what these old trunks hid ever since I was a little girl."

"It's all yours now, so have fun exploring to your heart's content." Meg's eyes widened when she spotted the replica of Twin Oaks. "Goodness, there's your old dollhouse. I remember the summer you and your dad put it together."

Not wanting to explore her personal family history and that particular sore point, Meredith diverted the conversation. She brushed off the knees of her blue jeans. Griz chose to strut out of the room, careful to avoid contact with their guests. "Did you need something?"

"Where did you want us to focus today?" Sean asked. "Inside or out?"

"Inside, definitely." She glanced at the trunk. "Can you take the trunk down to the sewing room for me?"

"Where did you want it?" Sean moved to do as she asked.

"Beside Grandma's favorite rocking chair, I think." Meredith stepped back while Sean hefted the trunk. "I want to read these letters Grandma studied, as well as the thick binder of genealogy research she did, to learn more about my family's history."

"Is that what's in there?" Meg asked. "Your grandmother spent a lot of time on some online genealogy site, but I didn't realize she'd documented it all. Of course, I'm not surprised, given how much she loved this place."

Sean lugged the trunk down the stairs, his steps heavy on the treads, though he didn't seem to have any difficulty with the bulk. The two women followed him. As Meredith placed her foot on the floor in the foyer, a light breeze chilled her arms. This drafty old house would be the death of her yet. She considered the front door, its solid wood firmly closed against any intrusion. She'd always been drawn to the front porch of the house. No matter the season or weather, the entrance lured her. She and Paulette used to play with their dolls on the front steps and beneath the immense columns. Before they'd started arguing over every little thing between them. Still, the porch held many happy memories from her summer visits. She took a step toward the locked door, a compulsion pulling her toward it and beyond.

"Where you going?" Meg asked, pausing in her progress down the hall. "Did you hear somebody at the door?"

Meredith shook her head as she turned toward the housekeeper and then glanced back at the wooden barrier. The impulse increased, pulling her toward the door. "No, but I thought I'd like to go out onto the porch."

"Come on, we've other tasks to tend." Meg motioned for

Meredith to join her. "Sean needs you in the sewing room. Right, Sean?"

His grunt sounded muffled.

"Okay, I'm coming." With a last longing glance at the door, Meredith strode toward Meg. She took a breath to clear the sigh forming inside, only to inhale the familiar sweet scent once more. She reached Meg in several strides. "Do you smell honeysuckle?"

"No." Meg regarded her silently for a long moment, brows furrowed. "Why?"

"Never mind." Meredith rubbed her nose with the backs of her fingers, trying to obliterate the scent. "It must be my imagination."

"Or your nose is better than mine." Meg entered the sewing room and headed toward a mussed, crocheted afghan on the settee's seat. She refolded the blanket and smoothed it into place. "Honeysuckle is really out of season, though."

"Exactly." Meredith stopped inside the doorway and surveyed the room.

Sean placed the trunk beside her grandmother's rocker. Meg had brightened the room, no cobwebs or dust visible anywhere. Fresh-cut daffodils and tulips in the crystal vase perfumed the spring air. The floorboards gleamed in the sunlight. Despite the faded and peeling wallpaper, a cheery atmosphere prevailed. Beyond the partially open window, the songs of birds blended into a symphony. She rested a hand on the back of the settee, the soft wool of the afghan recalling the image of her grandmother's hands working the crochet hook. No wonder this was her favorite room in the house.

"Maybe the scent comes from the potpourri I threw out this morning." Meg fluffed a pillow and replaced it on the chair. "I didn't notice it, but then I wasn't paying attention."

"The smell must be coming from somewhere," Meredith said, frowning. "And I'm going to find it."

Chapter Five

"I can't locate the source," Meredith said hours later. "I've looked everywhere."

"Don't fret. I'm sure there's a logical explanation." Meg finished polishing the kitchen countertop, all traces of mold removed from its gleaming surface. "Maybe in the basement? Or some little secret compartment beneath the floorboards. Folks used to hide things around the house, especially during the Civil War, to protect their valuables."

"Right, I'm sure somebody hid a supply of dried honeysuckle vines so they wouldn't be without after the fighting stopped." Meredith laughed and shook her head at her own sarcasm. "I doubt that."

She crossed to the table and flopped down where she could gaze out to the rear of the property. God, she was tired. She'd been all over the house, into closets and cabinets, poking behind drapes and doors. She'd opened stubborn drawers on dressers in several bedrooms. Nothing accounted for the sweet scent she'd pursued.

The family cemetery drew her attention, the magnolia trees showing the first signs of buds forming among the large waxy leaves. Azaleas huddled nearby, tightly furled petals hinting at the deep pinks and reds soon to be in full color.

Such a beautiful property, lovingly tended for generations, only to be handed down to her ungrateful care. She looked closer at the plants in the yard. What she didn't spot was honeysuckle.

Her grandmother had wanted her to inherit the family property, but Meredith had not been in touch with her for years. Why? She hadn't expressed interest in Twin Oaks since she was a little girl, building the dollhouse. At that time she'd dreamed of living in the manor and raising a huge family. Her childhood dreams included her version of Mr. Right: tall, handsome, creative, fun-loving, and intelligent. Together they'd make beautiful babies—at least three and hopefully many more—to fill the multitude of bedrooms with laughter and love. Maybe her grandmother remembered how she'd adored visiting the plantation. Obviously she'd kept the dollhouse all this time. Now Meredith had the real house, but no hope of the family. Rubbing her arms, she glanced at Meg.

"What would you do?" Meredith contemplated the panorama before her.

"About what, dear?" Meg came and stood beside her, resting one hand on the back of Meredith's chair.

"Would you live here, take on all this obligation, if you were me?" Meredith stared out the window, not wanting to detect censure in Meg's eyes. "Even if you knew in your heart you didn't deserve it and never could?"

Meg gasped and sat down. "Why would you say such a thing?"

Meredith shifted to regard the older woman. "Because it's true."

"I can't believe after all the time you've spent here, the joy you felt staying here, that you'd turn your back on your heritage."

"I'm a city girl now." As good an excuse as any other.

Meredith ran a hand through her hair, slipping the ponytail holder off with a sigh of relief.

"That's by location, not heritage." Meg gripped her shoulder and squeezed until Meredith met her eyes. "Your Irish blood will speak to you, remind you of the legacy the land represents. Both past and future for the O'Connell family."

"I haven't heard an Irish brogue in my head yet." Meredith grimaced. "Don't know that I want to, come to think of it."

"You know it's a matter of time. You'll always come home to the one thing that has bound this family and Twin Oaks together for generations."

"What do you mean?"

Meg leaned toward Meredith and pointed out the window, indicating an area to the right of the cemetery. "Have you forgotten the fairy tree?"

Meredith's eyes widened as she followed the direction of Meg's finger, finally sighting the old hawthorn standing alone in the middle of the meadow. She'd forgotten all about it. Or perhaps ignored it on purpose. The fairy tree. Her grandmother loved the ancient hawthorn and the myths associated with it. Despite the fact they only technically existed in Ireland, Grandma insisted on protecting the little tree as though it were from their ancestors' homeland. To her grandmother, the fairy tree symbolized the unity of the O'Connell family, across time and space, no matter what befell them. She claimed the tree alone protected the many generations of O'Connells.

She stared at the hawthorn. Roads had been relocated in Ireland because a fairy tree happened to grow in its path and the workers dared not harm it. Good men trying to provide for their families had died who had cut down a fairy tree. The tree's one mission, according to Grandma O'Connell, was to keep Twin Oaks safe from all harm. What should she do?

"I wasn't planning to cut down all the trees, Meg." She stared out the window at the little tree, wishing it and her grandmother's traditions away. No luck there, though. "In fact, I wasn't planning to harm any of the trees and bushes."

Meg sat down beside her and grasped Meredith's hands. "I can tell you're having a difficult time returning here."

Meredith leaned back in her chair, sliding her hands out of Meg's. Her choices had seemed so easy from the comfort of her apartment balcony. "I thought I knew what to do before I came."

"So you're having a time figuring out how to do what your Grandma wanted. Right?"

Meredith fiddled with the salt shaker. "From what Max told me, she wanted me to live here and keep this place as a home. To renovate it and maintain it the way she wanted. I don't know that I can do so."

"Why not?" Meg peered at her. "It's a lovely house; it merely needs some work to make it right."

"Roseville, to start. This family home, to finish."

"You don't want a family home?" Meg angled her head, considering Meredith for a long moment. "Or you don't want a family?"

"I had a family." Meredith gazed at Meg, seeing her as though for the first time. The memory of talks with Meg as a younger woman, taking time to listen to a young girl's childish heartache and disappointments, floated past her mind's eye. Meg had always been willing to stop mid-task to squat down and hug a young girl. Her caring eyes radiated laugh lines across her face. She was probably the only person in Meredith's world who would truly understand. Meredith took a deep breath and let it out slowly. "But it was taken from me."

Meg slowly nodded. "Your husband."

Startled, Meredith narrowed her eyes and gazed at Meg. "How much do you know?"

"Your grandmother told me about Willy." Meg grasped Meredith's hands again, squeezing twice before releasing them. "I am so very sorry you had to go through such a horrific time in your life."

"Nobody should have to experience that kind of grief." Meredith stayed mum about the other life lost in the attack. Only she and her doctors knew about the needle-sharp loss, and she intended to keep it that way. "I loved him so much it hurts to breathe without him."

Nodding still, Meg relaxed back in her chair. "When I think of the prospect of losing Sean, I imagine an immense black hole I'm falling into, and a huge knot forms in my throat so large I fear I'll choke on it. I cannot fathom my Sean dying, of him not being with me. I am truly sorry for your Willy."

"When I was young and built that silly dollhouse, I wanted nothing more than to have a large family to fill these rooms with laughter. Willy was the foundation of my dream coming true." Meredith looked around the kitchen, letting her gaze touch on the familiar stove, the tiled table, and the landscape pictures on the walls. A small aerial photo of Twin Oaks caught her eye, patchwork fields surrounding the large brick-and-stone building. A house, though not a home any longer. "Now I can't stomach the idea of living here without him."

"Meredith, your husband would never have wanted you to live in the past. He'd want you to find the strength to move on. Such strength comes from your family, and of course, from the land, Twin Oaks."

Meredith turned to look out the window at the gravestones visible through the wrought-iron fence surrounding the cemetery. Willy lay buried in a cemetery outside of Baltimore. She visited him frequently when she was home and not traveling on assignment, taking a single yellow rose to place on his grave. She fiddled with the ring he had placed on her hand years ago. She couldn't stay here when he waited for her in Maryland. The graves here held the bodies of people she did not know, would never know, in fact. But they were her family, so maybe she should spend some time learning who they were.

"Do you know who all is buried out there?" She waved toward the cemetery.

"O'Connells and others stretching back two hundred years." Meg stared out the window for a long moment. "Those who have lived and loved Twin Oaks as much as you and your family."

"It's so interesting to contemplate the many lives of people who lived here and cherished each moment only to end up below the ground." Meredith glanced at Meg and then stared out the window. "What does it all mean in the end?"

"I'm not sure I follow," Meg said.

"We each do our best with what we have but never know if it's the right thing." If she didn't stay, she'd be letting her ancestors down, no doubt. "All the striving and trying and failing and trying again while we live, and then after we die…" A cloud shaded the sunshine, chilling her so she wrapped her arms around herself. "We disappear from sight except for a piece of stone aboveground. Do you suppose it matters, once you've passed, where your body lies in order to be happy?"

"No, it's the soul that's important, not the human form." Meg folded her arms and considered Meredith. "Though perhaps where your body lies determines how your soul reacts to the act of dying. More importantly, the timing and manner in which a person dies probably affects how peacefully they rest. I do believe those who die before their time are restless souls looking for answers."

"Restless? You believe in ghosts?" Meredith sighed, unfolded her arms, and played with the salt shaker. Willy had died saving her life, an honorable death in his eyes. "Willy is buried in Baltimore. I know he's happy there since he's close to our home."

"I and Sean have made plans to be buried in Lynchburg when our time comes." Meg smiled wryly. "We've always enjoyed some Jack Daniels in the evening."

Meredith grinned and thumped the shaker onto the table before linking her fingers together. "You've thought ahead, I see."

"Do we really know what happens once we die?" Meg shivered and then laughed, the sound echoing in the room. "Ooh, someone must have walked across my grave. What maudlin talk for a pretty spring day."

Meredith looked outside at the white gazebo, its black iron trim in stark relief among the surrounding trees. Her grandmother had loved to sit on one of the Adirondack chairs in the shade and tell Meredith and Paulette about the fairies and their many antics. Unlike the happy and carefree fairies of many tales, Irish fairies tended to play tricks and wreak vengeance for perceived wrongs. While Meredith never wanted to confront angry fairies, she had to admit their dealings made for entertaining stories. The cloud drifted on and sunlight splashed down on the gazebo and surrounding yard, highlighting the tulips and daffodils nestled around the exterior and along the sidewalks.

"Let's take a walk up to the fairy tree and clear our heads. I haven't thought about the little tree in decades." Meredith stood and pushed in her chair before following Meg through the screened door. "I can hear Grandma telling us her wild tales now."

Being outside in the sunshine improved her spirits, a burden lifting from her shoulders. The house itself weighed upon her. She breathed in the sweet scent of the azaleas and the tang of the magnolias while the sun warmed her arms. They strolled across the gravel driveway to the flagstone path. A low stone wall separated the wide drive from the shady yet welcoming formal garden.

"My Sean has spent most of his time tending to these plants," Meg said, ambling along the large flat stones forming the winding path through the array of plants. "He loves working with the flowers, coaxing them to bloom and smell so sweet."

The neatly arranged flowers and bushes reached for the spring sunshine. Tall trees stretched out to provide intervals of dense shade. She didn't know much about plants, not like Willy had. He'd have been exclaiming over a rare flower or special shrub. A shudder of grief washed through her. Willy would have loved this place. His knowledge of landscape architecture would have sprung to the fore as he looked at each little green being and commented upon its uses and benefits. How the dying of the blossoms fertilized the future growth of the plant, the circle of life within the plant kingdom. A sudden idea made her miss a step. What if she created a memorial garden in his and the baby's memory?

"Willy loved horticulture," Meredith said, pacing beside Meg. "He and Sean would have gotten along fine."

"I'm sure they would've." Meg nodded and strolled on down the path. She tossed a smile over her shoulder. "Sean adores his plants."

They walked in silence for a few minutes, drinking in the surrounding sights and scents. Meredith considered asking Sean to design the garden she envisioned. She nearly queried Meg as to whether he'd be interested, only Meredith wasn't yet ready to share her vision. They emerged out the back side of the garden, through a low, wood gate leading to an immense grassy meadow. Wildflowers dotted the field. She could identify wild daisies and Queen Anne's lace among the pinks, whites, yellows, and purples sprinkled before her. They paused to appreciate the view. She shaded her eyes with a hand and scanned the field, noting the trees along the fence line in the distance. The fairy tree stood defiantly in the middle of the expanse.

"Your grandma loved to come out here until her legs wouldn't carry her this far."

Did Meg have to mention her grandmother at that exact moment? The stories surrounding the fairy tree had been a part of Meredith's childhood as much as Humpty Dumpty and Ichabod Crane. Myths and legends that her grandmother loved to tell. Way back when Meredith was a kid and bedtime stories were still important. Staying with Grandma for the summer months meant she and her sister heard many wonderful tales of adventure, ghosts, and myths about Ireland.

Meredith had let the memories of those stories fade as she grew older and more removed from this little piece of the world. Until this moment she had not considered them, not for a second. She'd moved away and moved on, reaching for her future and relinquishing the past.

"Did Grandma come here often?" Meredith walked into the field, avoiding the tiny wildflowers as best she could. She liked the way they graced the vista with their specks of color.

"Weekly at least." Meg paced beside her. "Until a few months before she died."

"Max said she died without warning, sitting in her favorite chair." White petals lay scattered about the tree trunk like pearls escaped from a necklace. "I hope it was painless as well."

"She looked like she'd dozed off, so I hope she felt nothing."

Meredith picked up a satiny petal and rubbed it between her fingers and then let it drift back to earth. "Did you find her?"

Meg's eyes grew misty as she considered Meredith. "Yes."

"I'm glad it was you who did." Meredith inexplicably

wanted to hug Meg but hesitated. She wasn't a hugger and hadn't been for years. So why did she want to hug this woman? She resisted the urge as long as she could. Compelled by something she didn't understand, she drew the older woman into her arms and gave her a brief squeeze. Meg's lips curved into a half smile as she moved away.

Meredith crossed her arms, feeling foolish mixed with a new sense of calm. That hug hadn't been solely for Meg's benefit, apparently. Maybe hugs were underappreciated. At least by her.

"I'm sorry you had to find her, but am glad at the same time." Meredith unfolded her arms and stuck her hands in her back pockets. "You were more than a housekeeper to her, I know."

"Over the years we became pretty good friends." Meg wrapped her arms around her waist. "She was good to me."

Meredith reached out to squeeze Meg's arm but stopped her impulse and shoved her hand back into her pocket. "I'm sorry I lost touch with her."

"She talked about you often. Followed your career through the articles in the magazines and sometimes the newspaper."

Grandma must have read the interviews over the years after Meredith had started her career as an architect. The trade magazines had taken an interest in her daring designs as well as the conservative mansions she'd created. News of the random shooting that devastated her life had made a ripple in the papers, though thankfully one quickly forgotten by the press. That kind of publicity ranked right up there with a root canal.

"I didn't know she read the trades." She prayed her grandmother understood her need to start afresh. To create a space in which peace and serenity abounded. Meredith started strolling back toward the gate.

"She knew all about your work to restore the nineteenth-century schoolhouse in Virginia as well as the upgrade to the Georgia plantation on the coast." Meg kept pace with her as they meandered across the grassy field. "She subscribed to anything related to architecture, in particular historical renovation and preservation. That's how she came across Max's name and his dedication to historical preservation of local buildings. She had a dream of renovating Twin Oaks to its original appearance. She expected you'd manage the effort too."

Meredith didn't slow her progress, but her heart sank. "She did?"

"She left you this beautiful property to maintain and preserve," Meg said. "You have the right skills to make her dream a reality."

Don't tell me that. Please. Don't. She kept walking, reaching the break in the stone wall. Thoughts of her grandmother's expectations and hopes collided with her grief and anger. Those emotions were the only ones she would permit herself to feel. She'd killed the other emotions within her, buried them so deep she feared they were untouchable. Guilt wiggled into her heart as she contemplated the clash between her grandmother's hopes and her reluctance to see them become reality. She had options but didn't know yet which way to turn.

Off to the side she saw the wrought-iron fence framing the cemetery. Speaking of burials. She changed direction and skirted the garden.

"What's the matter?" Meg hurried to catch up. "Where're you going?"

"I want to see who exactly is buried on this property."

"Your ancestors, of course."

Meredith reached the iron gate with its intricate latch, deftly squealing it open. *Gracious.* "Like fingernails on a chalkboard. I need to put some WD-40 on the hinges."

Meg chuckled as she rested her hands on the fence. "Not too many visitors come out here."

"True. After you." Meredith held the gate open, waiting. A flicker of uncertainty danced across Meg's features, suggesting a level of unease in the woman. "You're not coming in?"

Meg shook her head. "Nothing's changed in here since we buried your grandmother over there." She gestured to the left.

Grandma. Here. Meredith followed her motion, spotting the raw earth mounded underneath an immense maple tree in the far corner of the fenced area. A white marble headstone gleamed in the shadows. How had such a glaring detail slipped her notice? Meredith drew in a deep breath and let it out to the count of five.

She picked her way through the graveyard, careful to walk around the graves themselves like her mother had taught her when she was a child. She paused to read the headstones, noting they did indeed date back to before the Civil War. Most contained names of unknown people, presumably to be found somewhere on her family tree. Then she saw it. David Joseph O'Connell. Grandpa Joe. Born 1843. Died 1917. He was seventy-four when he died. She hoped he had a good life. A marble footstone marked the end of a space beside him.

"Is that an empty gravesite?" Meredith pointed to the area beside Grandpa Joe's grave. "Why does it have a footstone but not a headstone? Was someone supposed to be buried there?"

Meg leaned on the fence, peering at the spot. "Oh, yes. Your grandma said Joe wanted his sister Grace buried beside him if she ever came home. But she had disappeared while he was away fighting. Your grandma told me Joe tried to find her. Wrote to everyone he knew. He apparently never gave up hope she'd come home."

"I wonder whatever happened to her." Meredith

glanced at the grassy space, and then back to Meg. "Where did she go?"

"That's the mystery," Meg said. "Nobody knows for sure. Though, according to his letters, her twin sister, Edith, seemed to think she ran off with a Union officer. But why would Joe's sister be a Union sympathizer while he's off fighting with the Confederates?"

A shiver began in her lower back and worked its way through her until she shuddered. She folded her arms to still the tremor. "The war separated many families, pitching brother against brother, father against son. Why not brother against sister?"

Meg shook her head. "Your grandma didn't think so, based on what Joe wrote in his journal. He seemed to feel something bad had happened to her."

Another shiver shook Meredith as a chilly breeze wafted by, carrying a hint of sweetness. She wrapped her arms more tightly around herself to try to still the tremors. The fact of her ancestors' presence coupled with the trunk of genealogical research piqued her curiosity. She certainly wouldn't allow herself to act on an emotional level. Well, not an uncontrolled emotional level anyway. She stared at her grandmother's headstone, her thoughts awhirl. First she needed to know more about who had lived here, including more about what her own grandmother had learned through her research. Deep inside she needed to better understand what she had inherited. That wasn't emotional, that was logical. Honestly. She turned and made her way back to where Meg waited.

Meredith swung the gate closed behind her and started for the house. The calls would have to wait. "Time to explore the trunk's contents in more detail."

Long shadows draped across the trunk situated next to her

grandmother's chair in the airy sewing room. Thank goodness Sean had handled the heavy lifting. Having a man around had its pluses after all. Meredith held the first of many leather-bound journals in her lap. The binding warmed her hands, an illusion born by the sense of invasion she felt as she contemplated reading Great-great-great-grandfather Joe's thoughts and sensibilities. Would he have minded? She shook her head and opened the cover. He'd never know, so what did it matter?

Joe had returned after the war and immediately began a new journal. He had neatly written in the first page about choosing to document his life after the war, after peace had settled over Tennessee. The precise script called to mind her grandmother's handwriting. The art of cursive penmanship was losing prominence in Meredith's day-to-day world, what with most communication being by phone and typing on a keyboard. Back in Grandpa Joe's day, the quality of a person's penmanship distinguished them as educated and refined. Good thing she didn't have to compete on that level with her own scrawl. She read on.

Nov 5, 1863—Just got home two days ago to find the old home abandoned. I thought Grace would be here, having not heard anything from her to the contrary. I'll write to Edith today to see if she knows where our sister has gone.

Nov 6, 1863—Inventoried what's left, which didn't take long. Damn Yanks and maybe Rebs, too, carted off most everything they could. Even the good silver tea service. Wish I'd been here, but don't know whether I could've stopped them if I was. At least they left a few pieces of furniture so I have a bed to sleep in and chairs to sit on while I eat my supper. Though the plates and silver have all vanished.

Daily entries continued, with Grandpa Joe's cryptic yet insightful commentary painting a picture of the plantation's state of disorder and chaos after the war ended. Meredith sensed the pain and sadness of Grandpa Joe carried through the decades via ink upon yellowed paper. The very paper he had held in his hands. Again the sense of connection to the past flowed through her. Could feelings be transmitted through inanimate objects such as paper? Was that why the journal had warmth to its cover?

Nov 30, 1863—Heard from Edith she thinks Grace may have run off with a Yank officer to marry while I was away. Can't believe that. I suppose stranger things have happened, especially during this awful war. But for her to leave without talking to me first is difficult to swallow. Then no word at all after that. I do wonder if something or someone has hurt my little sister. I vow to continue looking until I know the answer.

Meredith laid her head on the lace doily fastened to the chair. What must he have felt when he came home to find she'd abandoned Twin Oaks without any word of explanation? To never discern her fate? Dealing with the loss of her own husband remained difficult even knowing what had happened, though never having a satisfactory answer as to why. She had closure, which Grandpa Joe never realized. She closed her eyes, putting herself in his place, trying to imagine the house through his eyes as someone who loved what was then a practically new plantation home and all it stood for. She'd loved visiting her own grandmother in this big old house, running up and down the stairs and from room to room as though at a grand amusement park filled with fun. And love. Always a sense of undying love emanated from the house's woodwork like the sweet perfume of a rose. Or perhaps honeysuckle.

The soft rustle of silk followed by the sound of light footsteps echoed in the hallway.

Meredith bolted upright, eyes flying open. She searched the room, looking for the source of the sound. "Griz? Is that you?" She put the journal on the chair beside her and stood. "Grizabella?"

Another rustle from the hallway. She moved slowly across the carpeted floorboards, hearing the telltale creak of her progress with each sneakered footstep. She held her hands out to the side as though to steady herself as she made her way across the room. In truth, she needed a sense of balance as she contemplated how she'd protect herself from this intruder.

"Who's there?" Meredith reached the arched doorway and peered into the hall. Nothing. She turned and glanced the other direction and then gasped when the sweet scent of honeysuckle reached her nose. Again.

Cold seeped into Meredith, and she shivered as she inched toward the front door, summoned and unable to resist.

Meredith crossed her arms, trying to still the beginnings of another shiver. What happened to the sun warming the house earlier? The shadows had deepened into near darkness within the house. The light switch was out of reach at the end of the hallway. Something compelled her to walk forward, urged her to open the front door, to reach for the knob and turn it. Her fingers curled around the tarnished brass.

A flash of light caused Meredith to look behind her. The door separating the hall from the kitchen stood open. Knocking soon followed on the screened door in the kitchen. Who was that? It didn't matter. First, she must go onto the front porch.

Meredith looked toward the bolted-shut front door. Her fingers tightened on the knob as she reached with her other hand to flip the deadbolt open. More knocking on the kitchen door was accompanied by the sound of Max's voice. "Meredith?"

Though fearful about what she'd find, she must see what waited for her on the other side. Max jiggled the kitchen door so hard it rattled as he ultimately jerked it open, his booted steps pounding through the house. She heard but couldn't turn around. She stared at the door, mesmerized by the tug of forces pulling her in opposite directions. She needed to open it but was afraid at the same time. She tightened her hold, fighting the compulsion building inside her. Sunlight broke through the clouds outside and streamed across the floor. Max ran into the hallway behind her, sliding to a stop.

"Damn it, Meredith, why didn't you answer me?" He grabbed her by the arms and spun her around to face him. He searched her face and then shook her once. "Meredith?"

She blinked and stepped back, her arms falling to her sides, hands tensed. "I'm fine. I think."

"What's going on?"

How did she explain what she didn't understand? She dragged in a deep breath, only slightly relieved she didn't smell honeysuckle. Flexing her hands to ease the bizarre desire to hit something, anything, she looked at Max as she blew her breath out in one big release. That helped. She did it again, the tension inside her giving way with the spent air. She searched her memory for why she stood in the hall feeling this deep-seated anger coupled with pain emanating from outside herself. More disturbing was the compulsion to unbolt and swing open the front door. To let someone in? Or out?

"I thought I heard something," she finally said. Was it the Lady in Blue again? She hadn't noticed anything, or anyone. She rubbed one arm, noting the chill in the air had gone. "But I guess I was wrong."

"You scared me," Max said, shoving his hands in his front jeans pockets.

"Did you forget something?"

"No, I just had a feeling something was wrong, so I came back." Max rocked onto the balls of his feet, and then back on his heels, a nervous boy in front of the schoolmaster. "To—to make sure you're safe."

"As you can see, nothing is amiss." Meredith turned and walked back into the parlor, not waiting for his reply or explanation. She needed to ensure the journal remained safely tucked away, out of sight of casual readers. Like Max.

Said man followed her, as she expected he would. His boots sounded louder and less tentative on the creaky floor than her sneakers. She stuffed the journal back inside the trunk and dropped the lid before looking at him. That's when she observed the vein in his neck pulsing beneath a clenched jaw. Big, strong man like him visibly shaken. Because of her?

"What's the matter with you?" Meredith took a step closer, and then another, searching his expression. Stubble shadowed his jaw in sharp contrast with his worried gaze.

"I'm glad you're not on the floor, writhing in pain, is all." With a rush of air he exhaled and then squatted, resting his elbows on his knees. He let his head drop down, his dark hair obscuring his face.

Nobody, not even Willy, had ever been as upset as Max currently was on her behalf. Her heart softened, allowing compassion to ease into her. This big, strong man had fallen prey to concern for her safety, concern leaving him tense and even a touch afraid. She liked that he cared about her even if his concern probably stemmed from the house's future. Meredith squatted in front of him. "Hey. Look at me."

In slow motion, he complied with her demand.

"I'm fine. Really." She touched his clasped hands to reassure him. She almost believed it wasn't for her own sake, kinda like the hug she'd given Meg to comfort her. Yet again she found herself wondering whether she was comforting or being comforted.

"Why were you standing in the foyer? Where were you going?" Max turned one hand over and snagged hers with his strong fingers. "You looked like you were under a spell."

"I did?" Should she tell him, or would he think her crazy? She stared at his manicured nails as he used his index finger to trace the outline of her ring finger, spinning the thin gold band as he stared at it. She didn't need him holding her hand, sending these unwanted sensations through her. Making her want him in ways she hadn't wanted any man in a long, long time. She should stop him. But it had been an eon since she'd permitted herself to feel, to let another help her feel anything. She met his questioning eyes. "I thought I heard something and went to check."

"What kind of something?" He studied her, intent on her every movement.

"That's the odd part." She hesitated to reveal the truth. "Don't call me crazy. Okay?" She waited for his nod before continuing. "It sounded like the rustle of silk and a lady's footsteps."

His expression didn't change as he looked at her. "These old houses have a language all their own, using creaks and thumps like words. What did you find?" He captured her other hand and pulled them both to their feet, mere inches separating their bodies.

"Nothing." He stood so close she could see a thin scar across the bridge of his nose. She imagined the air from their speech mingling in the space between them as she watched his pupils dilate, his gaze weighing on her lips. "Not even Grizabella."

"Maybe it was a stray breeze, touching on things and making them move." His gaze drifted up to her eyes. "Stranger things have happened, so they say."

She moistened her lips with her tongue. His gaze zeroed in on her mouth. "I don't think so."

He squeezed her hands and pulled her closer until her breasts brushed his chest, causing her nipples to bud. "Why not?"

"It's a calm day," she said, trying to prevent her breasts from remaining in contact with him but not willing to break the intrigue quite yet. After all, he hadn't done anything she didn't allow him to do. She was adult enough to control the situation. No problem. "No wind."

Without a word, he lowered his mouth to hers. She gasped against his lips—from the spark of the contact or from the sudden act?—and pulled back, severing the kiss. "Don't."

He dropped her hands and stepped back. "I thought you wanted me to."

She did, and she didn't. "I—You were mistaken." She scrubbed a hand over her lips and then shoved both hands into her back pockets.

"Was I?" He kissed her again, a simple press of lips on lips.

Her body thrummed from the unwanted, but not unpleasant, kiss. "It's not personal. It's that—"

"What?"

Damn, he was handsome. Stunning blue eyes searched her face. His strong jaw jutted closer to her, raising his chin as he studied her. His interest in her drew her to him, nearly causing her to gravitate toward him like a ball bearing to a magnet. Putting distance between them proved harder than she'd imagined. "I can't start a relationship with anyone."

"I see." Max tightened his lips and nodded once, letting her hands drop from within his long fingers. "My apologies. I must have misinterpreted your response."

His language had become lawyerly. No more mingled words to tantalize. Only distance between them. He shifted, and she tried to feel relieved as he easily accepted the change in her position toward him. That was what she wanted. Really.

"Other than your gut feeling, why did you drive back out here?" She strove to put space between them, emotionally and physically moving away from him. "You could have phoned. Don't you have other clients?"

"It wasn't far." He shrugged. "Since I'm here, I'll share

some fantastic news." He sat down on a chair, almost as though his legs wouldn't hold him, but Meredith couldn't imagine that a kiss affected him in such a way. He peered at her. "I heard from the Register."

"And?" A chill swept through her as she watched him carefully place one ankle on the opposite knee. Being on the National Register wasn't the worst thing that could happen, but it could complicate her aims.

"Twin Oaks is officially on the National Register of Historic Places."

Damn. "So?"

"It's fantastic. You should be thrilled." He put both feet on the floor and leaned forward. "Unless you want some apartment complex to buy out Twin Oaks?"

"No, of course not." She sank into the rocker and crossed her legs.

"Then why aren't you happier about this news?" He linked his fingers between his knees and stared at her, waiting.

"It's nice to be on the list, if you like that sort of thing." She hesitated, letting her attention drift to the window and beyond to the sunlit gazebo in the back. She'd take Grandpa Joe's journal and go sit out there for a while once Max left, enjoying the twitter of birds and the gentle warmth of the spring breeze. "But I'm thinking I may stay and make some improvements."

"Fantastic." His twining fingers stilled. "What sort of improvements?"

She dragged her gaze back to his captivating eyes and considered her response. Suddenly dreaded his reaction. "You don't need to worry, Max. I'm not planning to sell, and nobody will ever take this property from me."

"You haven't answered my question, and don't think I haven't noticed." Max rose and looked down at her from his towering height.

A blast of irritation made her tremble. Why did so many people feel like they had to know everything when in fact they only wanted the last word? The idea that Max would prove to be like her boss and her sister, always trying to "improve" on her ideas and plans fanned the irritation into resistance. She would deal with the property in her own way.

Max shifted his weight, drawing her attention back to the present. He stared at her where she sat in the rocker, slowly pushing it back and forth with one foot.

"My plans for Twin Oaks are not your concern so don't press me." She stopped the rocker and stood, reducing Max's towering advantage over her. "Thank you for checking on me. I'll be in touch if I should need your help again."

Max raised his eyebrows at her and then shook his head. "I'll leave if that's what you want, sweetheart, but we're not done. Not by a long shot."

Chapter Six

*C*innamon with a hint of cloves and nutmeg awoke her the next morning. Rubbing her eyes, her muscles protested her movements, almost as though she'd been in a battle the night before. She rested her arm across her forehead, realizing the only battle she fought raged within. Inhaling, she savored the combined spicy scent, saliva moistening her mouth in anticipation. Meg's breakfast buns had won awards at the county fair for decades. No need to fight her desire to feast on Meg's cooking. Pushing off the comforter, she swung her legs out of bed, her toes enjoying the coolness of the wood floor as she stood and stretched. Lacing her fingers together, she raised her arms above her head and angled left, then right. Sunlight flowed through the window, warming Grizabella where she lay in sphinx position, watching Meredith.

"Morning, kitten." Meredith lowered her arms to slip her robe on over her shorts and tee.

Griz slowly swiped her tail from side to side and blinked in response.

Meredith padded on bare feet to her suitcase and selected fresh undies, blue jeans, and a scoop-neck black tee and tossed them onto the bed. Humming the theme of the seven little dwarves, she made short work of changing clothes and then attended to her morning ritual. Griz accompanied her to the bathroom, dutifully checking out the room for any signs of intruders. Meredith finished brushing her strawberry-blonde hair, seeing the same sad yet determined gold-flecked green eyes looking back at her between the black spots on the mirror. Another task she'd need to add to her list: replace the mirror since the moisture in the air must have interacted with the backing and the damage couldn't be reversed. Griz rubbed against her leg, and then turned and butted her head into Meredith's shin. Meredith reached down and scritched the calico's side.

"Let me get my shoes on, and we'll head down to greet Meg." Meredith strode back into the bedroom, pulled on socks and sneakers, and hurried downstairs.

As she approached the kitchen, Meg was singing "You Are My Sunshine." She hesitated before pushing the door open, her hand trembling at the memories the song evoked. The sound conjured the futile hope of singing to her own baby. Meredith squared her shoulders and pushed on the door. She mustn't dwell on the pain of never being a mother. Not today. Despite her recent lapses, both at the family cemetery and then later with Max, she could not allow emotions to affect her decisions.

"Good morning, Meg." Meredith snagged a mug from the cupboard and poured herself some coffee.

"Mornin', Meredith. I think the buns are about ready." Meg opened the oven door and sniffed the heat rising from the resulting gap. "Smells about right." She opened the door all the way and, using an oven mitt, removed the cake tin filled with golden-brown buns.

"Smells great." Meredith sipped her coffee as Meg placed the pan on a hot pad on the counter.

Movement outside the kitchen window drew Meredith's eye. A car pulled into the gravel drive. Paulette emerged, dressed in bright-green shorts and white top. She popped the trunk and withdrew a backpack, which she slung in place before dragging a wheeled bag from the depths of the car. Slamming the lid closed, she started for the back porch.

"Damn." She sure didn't need whatever Paulette had in mind. The sight of the suitcase did not bode well.

Meg used a spatula to lift the buns onto a china platter, arranging them in a daisy pattern. "What's the matter?"

"Paulette's here." Meredith plunked her mug down, watching her sister pick her way across the gravel driveway to the back door. "I'd hoped she'd wait until later to make an appearance."

"She always had good timing where meals are concerned." Meg chuckled, laying the spatula down before crossing her arms. "At least she's not heavy as a result of that."

"Bully for her." Meredith moved to ease the door wide open before Paulette could pound her fist against the broken door. Max owed her a new one, without a doubt. "You're early."

Paulette grinned and dropped her bags inside the door. "You know what they say about being first to the party."

"No, I must have missed that memo." Meredith eased the door closed so it didn't fall and then retrieved her coffee and took a fortifying gulp. Crap, that was hot. She swished the liquid in her mouth, cooling it before swallowing.

"Maybe it's a bird thing then." Paulette waggled a hand in the air, shaking her head. "I've never been able to keep all those weird sayings straight. Coffee?"

Meg filled a mug and handed it to Paulette, who accepted it with thanks. "You may not remember me after all this time, but I'm Meg Williams, your grandmother's housekeeper."

Paulette grinned. "I definitely remember you, Meg. You always made the best breakfast buns. Why do you think I'm here?"

"Just pulled them from the oven too." Meg motioned to the table. "Have a seat, girls."

Reluctantly Meredith sank onto one of the chairs and studied her sister as she lifted a bun and took a bite. "You didn't come here simply for breakfast, now did you?"

Paulette shook her head. "Of course not, but it seemed like a good idea. Meg's cooking is much better than the old biddy who runs the B&B. You wouldn't believe what she made me for breakfast." An indelicate shudder shook Paulette's shoulders.

"Given you'll eat anything, I'm afraid to ask." Meredith bit into her bun and nearly moaned with the pleasure exploding across her taste buds. Cinnamon laced with spices mingled with sweet pecans and cranberries as the bread melted on her tongue. Nobody beat Meg's baking. Nobody.

"Burritos stuffed with fried eggs, hash browns, anchovies, and sour cream. Ugh." Paulette took another bite and sighed. "I recalled you telling me the Williamses were still here, so I thought I'd take a chance."

"What would you have done if all I had was granola bars?" Meredith couldn't stop the grin splitting her face, knowing the answer.

"Leave for better breakfasts somewhere, of course." Paulette grinned back at her, lacing her tapered fingers around her mug. The one with the fading picture of the two of them, but she didn't seem to notice. "Seems like old times, doesn't it?"

"In some ways, I suppose." Meredith swallowed a mouthful of coffee as she assessed Paulette. Did she care about the friendship they once shared? Or had their rapport been obliterated by the more recent skirmishes in their lives? Some glimmer in her expression reminded Meredith of her penchant for finagling all she could out of any situation. "But I'll say it again. I don't owe you anything."

Paulette raised calculating eyes to meet Meredith's steady gaze. "Of course you do."

No. The word echoed in her head. Meredith had given all she could possibly give. She thought of the many times she'd dropped whatever she was doing to answer a summons to extricate her from yet another scrape. Paulette thrived on trouble, landing in one predicament after another. And expensive predicaments, at that. Between her penchant for finding melodramatic and abusive boyfriends and her daring nature, she managed to lead anything but a dull life.

The luggage at the door caught Meredith's eye, and a chill crept through her. Surely she was passing by, on her way to her next adventure. Assuredly, she wouldn't be planning what Meredith dreaded most. She did not want Paulette involved in any of her plans, let alone her ideas for the plantation, no matter how much her skills could help. She'd started envisioning the garden and its features. She began to see herself living in the old place, learning more about her family and heritage. But not with Paulette as a sore in her neck. She'd do it her way and nobody else would dictate how. For once. She pinned her with a glare, one she hoped instilled fear into her selfish, conniving heart.

"What is it you want?" Meredith clutched her mug between two suddenly cold hands.

"Your welcoming smile because, sister dear, I'm moving in." She threw wide her arms, her expression revealing her knowledge of the bolt of horror racing through Meredith.

Meg clapped her hands together, her smile wide and happy. "How lovely for the two of you to have the opportunity to become reacquainted."

Grizabella chose that moment to hack up a hair ball beside her food bowl. Meredith understood the feeling.

"No, that's not possible." Meredith raised her mug to her lips with a trembling hand.

"Why do you say that?" Paulette bit into the fragrant roll, studying Meredith as her jaws worked like a masticating cow.

"Because, my *dear sister*," Meredith said with a strained smile, "I'd strangle you if you ever lived with me again."

Paulette chuckled, eyes steady on Meredith for the span of two of Meredith's finger drummings on the table. Glancing up, her eyes reflected her delight. "Don't let your lawyer lover boy hear you say that."

Startled, Meredith observed with a pang of horror Max's fist poised to knock on the back door. He stood motionless, staring at her with his stunning eyes. She liked the way his temples sported gray highlights against his dark hair, making him appear even more lawyerish. She pushed up from the table at the same moment Meg saw him and crossed to the door to let him in. Meredith paused, hovering between sitting and standing, until she sank back onto the seat and watched him greet Meg. When he sauntered inside, his presence filled the kitchen with life.

He loomed above her, broad shoulders, muscular arms, and a hint of paunch, likely the result of his love of moonshine combined with his less than active lifestyle. She caught a whiff of his aftershave and noticed his strong, clean-shaven jaw. Nothing marred the perfection of the smooth surface: no moles or dimples or even a cleft in his chin.

"Would you like some coffee?" Meg asked, breaking the silence stretching between them.

"If you have a bun or two to go with it." Max dragged out a chair and sat down at the table, his wide smile aimed at Meredith. "They smell too good to pass up."

Meredith bit her lip, not wanting to be antagonistic so early in the morning. Max's familiarity in her house set her teeth on edge. But then, he'd likely been here many times discussing the future of the plantation with her grandmother. She swallowed a sigh, masking it as a deep breath.

"Did you sleep well?" Max asked.

"What? Why do you ask?" She glanced at him, and then back to where she slowly spun her mug on the table, automatically calculating the degrees of the circle as the handle navigated the outer edge of the circular path between her hands.

"You're still learning the noises of the house, so I thought you might be having trouble sleeping. Especially after yesterday. Thanks, Meg." He grinned as Meg placed a steaming mug and a plate crowded with two of the largest buns in front of him.

"Eat up; that's why I bake." Meg smoothed her hands down the front of her yellow gingham bib apron.

"So, Mer," Paulette said, "are you sleeping well? You do look a little peaked, what with the beginnings of bags under your eyes."

Meredith frowned in Paulette's direction. She wouldn't dignify her yet again off-base observation with a response. Bags, indeed. She'd checked earlier, and no sign showed on her face of her late nights and too early mornings. Yet. "My sleeping habits are none of your business."

Paulette nodded. "As I thought. You're not sleeping again, are you? You should get a prescription for a sleep aid."

Whether she stayed awake counting the knotholes in the wood ceiling or the number of hoots echoed by owls outside was her business. Meredith shot her sister the look her mother had perfected, the one that froze small children in their tracks.

Paulette laughed. "Don't look at me in that tone of voice."

Why the hell not? How had her life spun so far out of control in such a short span of time? Meredith fumed at the way these people were pushing their way into her private affairs. Ever since Willy and their child had been snatched from her, she'd kept her own counsel. Ever since that night when she'd been about to tell Willy she carried their first child. Sitting in his pickup in front of his parents' home, she'd been startled when a man calmly walked up to Willy's side of the vehicle, demanding his wallet. Willy barely had time to raise a protective arm in front of Meredith before she spotted the pistol. Heard the explosion of the gun and the jolt of her husband as he fell across her. Followed immediately by the shaft of pain as another bullet entered her womb, stealing the life of their unborn baby. She had bled profusely, wailing at the pain and the desolation. Willy's parents had rushed from the house at the sound of gunfire. The man had vanished by the time the police arrived and the ambulance carried her to the hospital. After they'd stabilized her, she learned Willy died along with their baby. If only he had listened to her they would have stayed home and not have been in the wrong place.

Nobody could possibly understand the depth of her pain, the grief lingering in her soul. Her body recovered, of course, but the grief morphed into an anger so hot and volatile she'd considered relinquishing her contracts for designing and building houses in order to concentrate on the opposite: demolishing them, piece by piece. But she couldn't bring herself to go against Willy's desires for her to make her name as an architect. A builder, not a destroyer. She longed for the ultimate closure, to move on. Finally, she had struck upon a path forward. She'd add to the family plantation property to stand as a tribute to new beginnings, a place where people grieving for a loved one could find their individual serenity. Then, with any luck, she'd be free of this terrible weight pinning her to the past. But it was her plan and would be carried out on her terms.

Max chewed his breakfast, watching her. In another time

and place, she could absolutely find him interesting, and definitely attractive. Hell, she'd experienced both already. But not at this time and place. She needed to work alone to achieve her objectives. This project was a sole-source contract and she the only qualified person to effectively handle the details.

She leaned back in her chair, drawing her coffee with her. "Why are you here so early?"

"I'm intrigued to learn what you plan to do with Twin Oaks." Max swallowed a mouthful of coffee and then leaned his elbows on the table. "Will you perhaps make it a B&B and entertain folks who love historical homes? Or turn it into a hotel? Or, my favorite fantasy, make it your home?"

"Why do you care?" Meredith studied his expression. She drummed her fingers in a slow cadence on the table in an effort to steady her swirling thoughts.

"You belong here. Don't you feel it?" Max reached across the table and laid his hands on hers. "I can tell you fit like a tongue-and-groove floor."

"It's getting deep in here." Paulette rose from the table, scraping the chair across the floor as she gained her feet. "Meg, is there more coffee to wash down all this baloney Max is serving up?"

"It's not baloney," Max said, squeezing and then releasing Meredith's hands. "It's the truth."

She stood, taking her mug to the sink, which put distance between her and Max. Paulette, too, but mainly she needed to be outside the range of Max's radiant heat and magnetic vibes. "As it so happens, I do plan to stay, for a while at least."

"You're not staying?" Meg crossed her arms and blinked at Meredith.

"I told you I couldn't guarantee how long I'd be here." Meredith shook her head. She hadn't meant to be so bald about her short-term plans. But the horse was out of the barn. "That's my plan."

"How long before you kick us out again?" Meg shifted her weight from one foot to the other, her arms sliding down to wrap around her waist. "Have you decided that?"

Meredith didn't want Meg to have a meltdown right there on the kitchen floor, so she hedged. "I have not finalized the details as of yet, Meg. I'll be here for weeks, maybe a month or so anyway."

"Oh, well then." Meg relaxed her arms, allowing them to fall at her sides before folding her hands loosely in front of her. "It's not like you're abandoning us, then. We've plenty of time to change your mind, haven't we, Max? Paulette?"

"Right, plenty of time." Max stood and approached Meg. "With a little investment in time and money, this place will shine again."

"I'm in," Paulette said. "Twin Oaks is growing on me. The longer I'm here, the more I remember what a lovely property it is. Between us, we can make a go of it. I love the idea of a B&B, Max. That would bring in income, and we'd be keeping the place in the family. What do you think, Mer?"

"You've only been here a few minutes. You can't possibly have grown attached to it so fast." The thought of living here, with her sister sharing the house and Meg and Sean in the cottage, shot tremors through Meredith. Max, too, would be coming and going.

The scene played before her like a B-rated movie. It could not happen. No way. They'd make her march to their drummer. The mere idea caused her breath to catch and her heart to race. Bracing her hands on the counter, she dragged in deep gulps of air to steady herself. She relived the glint of the gun's barrel pointed through the window and the echoing blast before Willy's dead weight pressed into her. The idea of having a family home without Willy and their child caused her to shake from head to toe.

Max speared her with his intense gaze and then walked toward her. With each step he took, her heart raced faster and her lungs burned. Dark blotches appeared before her eyes, slowly shifting and blending.

"You know it's your destiny." Max stopped in front of her, though thankfully he didn't touch her. "Deep down inside, what we're proposing is what you really want."

The room spun like a whirlpool around her. The blotches obliterated the people grinning at her. "No."

Her legs gave way, failing to support her reeling self. Max caught her in his arms as all went black.

"That went well," Paulette said to Max. She shook her head and shrugged. "I've never seen her faint before. Can you carry her up to her room?"

"Good idea." He started out of the kitchen with Meredith passed out in his arms.

Paulette grabbed her suitcase and followed him up the stairs. "I'll just put my stuff away, and then I'll come check on her."

"No need." Max shifted Meredith in his arms, her head resting against his shoulder. "I can handle it."

"She's my sister." Did he think she didn't care? "I'll only be a minute."

"Suit yourself." Max disappeared into the master bedroom.

She raced down the hall to the large bedroom at the front of the house. Sunshine streamed through the two double-hung windows flanked by floral-print curtains. The twin beds faced the windows. Everything remained the same as when they stayed there over summer break so long ago. As if Grandma expected them to come back. Even the quilts she'd made them graced the beds. She sank onto hers, tracing Saturn's rings with a finger. She glanced up and froze. Her sampler still hung above her bed. She rose and went to it, examining the stitching. She'd prided herself on making them as even and tight as her grandmother's.

She had once wanted to become a fashion designer when she grew up. She loved the feel of quality fabric and enjoyed creating new dresses for her dolls. She'd imagined having fashion shows with runway models wearing her creations. Until her dad convinced her decorating houses would help more people. He'd been right, of course. She'd thought, by becoming an interior decorator, he'd be proud of her, and they would team up and work together. He'd build the houses, and she'd decorate them. Sadly, her dream hadn't happened.

She'd made such a blasted mess of her life. Pregnant and alone, worming her way into Meredith's life. Needing her in a way she'd never wanted. What she told Max was true. She cared about Mer because they were siblings. But also because they once shared a much stronger bond. She wanted their friendship back. Hell, she wanted a lot of things from her life. She finally had a new chance to make at least some of it happen. Maybe even pursue her desire to design clothing. First, she needed to wiggle back into Meredith's good graces.

Chapter Seven

A soft purr and meow tickled Meredith's ear. She blinked awake, Grizabella's whiskers brushing her cheek. Where was she? The last she remembered she couldn't breathe and Max's arms wrapped around her. Oh, that woke her up. She ran a hand down Griz's back and along her tail as the cat turned and strutted to the end of the bed.

"I'm glad you're awake." Max rose from the straight-backed chair now positioned beside the bed and shoved his hands into his front pockets. "How do you feel?"

Meredith pushed herself up to a sitting position, checking to ensure all systems functioned correctly. "What happened?"

"You fainted." He shifted his weight from one foot to the other.

"I don't faint." Yet she must have, or she wouldn't be in bed with no memory of how she arrived there. With Max hovering by her bedside like a worried lover. *Where had that thought come from?* Time to regain control over her own life and future.

"You did. I carried you up here so you'd be more comfortable."

Great. Not only had she passed out, but he'd had to lug her too-plump ass up two flights of stairs. Then put her in bed. She glanced down. At least he hadn't tried to change her clothes or anything. She still wore jeans and a tee. Small comfort but she'd take it.

"How long was I out?" She swung her feet to the floor and stood, grateful the room no longer spun and her lungs worked.

"A few minutes, maybe ten. Take it easy, though." He reached to steady her, but she brushed away his hands.

"I don't want to take it easy," Meredith said. "I want everyone to leave. I have work to do."

She started for the door of her bedroom. Grizabella minced in front of her, slowing her progress. Max took advantage of the delay and caught up to her.

"What kind of work?" Max asked, trailing behind her.

Right, like she'd reveal to him her plans so he could morph them into what he wanted. "Some research, if you must know. Go away."

"Maybe I can help you."

"Not likely."

"I want to help."

They reached the top of the stairs. She peeked at him, detected his curiosity and sincerity—and something more— and started down. She didn't want to define the mysterious twinkle in his eyes. "Is that why you showed up this morning? To help like you did yesterday, breaking down my door?"

"Of course not. But I do know who to call to start the necessary repairs and to find the right period furniture. That sort of thing." He shadowed so close she could feel his breath on her neck.

At the bottom, she spun around the newel post and it came off in her hand. She lovingly replaced it.

"I know where to get a period newel that would match

better than that one." Max waved at the offending acorn. "Look how it doesn't even fit properly."

"No, it's always been a part of the house since I was a girl." And made it with her own hands but she wouldn't open herself up for more criticism by revealing that fact.

"It's defective let alone corny." He frowned at her, the downward pull of his brows dimming the vibrancy of his eyes. "I can have it fixed."

"Really, there's no need." But she needed to free herself from this unwarranted debate. She needed water and privacy, in that order. "I told you I can handle my own affairs."

She pushed through the kitchen door and stopped, Max running into her before ricocheting back a step. Paulette and Meg busily washed the windows, crumpled newspapers polishing the old glass. In ten minutes they'd decided to deep clean the house?

"What are you doing?" Meredith eased into the room, memories bombarding her. Paulette always loved washing windows, had even fought to make it her chore.

"Helping you—actually, us—with our new abode." Paulette finished drying the window by the sink and paused to inspect her work. She rubbed one corner again and then flashed a smile at Meredith. "I love to view the world with wide-open eyes."

"You're not staying, Paulette." Meredith marched to the cupboard, retrieving a glass and filling it with cold water. "Let's be clear."

Her sister merely smiled and went back to work.

"Did you hear me?" The water cooled her tongue. "Paulette?"

"I'm staying because you need all the help you can get, and I need your hospitality." Paulette turned and shrugged at her. "I've got no job, no money, no nothing. I have nowhere else to go."

"She is your sister," Max said, grinning.

He poured coffee into his mug. Like he was planning to stay too. Which he wasn't. Meredith would make sure he realized how unwelcome his presence remained. Even though she had totally lost control of what was happening around her. In fact, looking back over the last few weeks, she'd lost control of her own actions the moment Max had contacted her about the inheritance. She'd have to make immediate changes in order to reclaim the direction of her future. If there were no place, they couldn't dictate how it would be used and by whom.

"Listen up, everyone," she said, banging her glass onto the counter, water sloshing onto the tile. "I'm a one-woman show, and I do not need your help to make the necessary changes I have in mind."

She tried to glare at the questioning expressions, but they didn't seem to feel threatened one iota. Perfect. She'd have to make them understand somehow. This situation simply couldn't continue. Shock and awe time.

"What intentions, precisely?" Paulette stared at her, arms poised at her sides, questions in her eyes.

What could she say to prevent their insistence on pushing her? Of correcting her every idea or thought? She drew in a breath and let it out on a sigh. "I'm going to establish Twin Oaks as a premier memorial park."

"Out back?" Max nodded as he folded his arms. "There's space out there."

Meredith shook her head, grief and anger twining into reckless ideas. "Here. I will take down the damn manor and return the site to a green field and build the memorial park in its place. Then you won't need to worry about the place ever again."

Damn. Where had that come from? But it wasn't her fault that they'd pushed and pressed her into a corner until she felt compelled to lash out like a cornered raccoon. She moved to lean on the kitchen counter, braced for the reactions sure to be aimed in her direction. She didn't have to wait very long, either.

"You cannot mean to do that." Rage echoed in Paulette's voice as her words hovered in the air. "You wouldn't dare."

Max glared at Meredith, outrage blazing from those gorgeous eyes. "What the…? Are you daft, woman? If this is why you want me to remove the protection from Twin Oaks, then forget it. I won't."

She glared at him, moving her hands to grip her hips. "You're my lawyer, and you'll do as I say."

"No, goddamn it, I won't." He rounded on her. "Twin Oaks means way too much to too many people for you to be allowed to go through with dismantling it."

"It's mine." A slow smile spread onto her lips as she regarded his blustering rage. "You can't stop me. The Register has no authority over me as the property owner, only developers and such."

"Not legally, perhaps." Max rested his hands on his hips, his torso narrowing the distance between them as he leaned toward her. "Morally you can't want to destroy your own heritage. What your ancestors fought and died for."

She cringed at the guilt shooting through her. Grandpa Joe had indeed fought and died to save his home. Max and Paulette had forced her hand. She couldn't back down now. "Nothing you say will change my mind."

"Something better." Paulette stalked across the floor to stand beside Max.

"I'm appalled and speechless." Meg stood with her mouth open, eyes accusing.

Well, what had they thought? That she'd let them run her life? Meredith squared her shoulders. If they wanted a fight, then so be it.

"I don't imagine you can understand this, but you don't

have to." Meredith speared each with her gaze. "Grandmother O'Connell left Twin Oaks to me, and me alone. It's my choice and my decision as to its future."

"You selfish bitch." Paulette glared at her. "Twin Oaks is my heritage too. What did Mom and Dad say about your *plan*, or haven't you told them yet? Grandma would never have left it in your care if she had any idea you'd destroy it."

"I'm certain you're right. I'm sure she'd never speak to you again," Meg said, her voice sharp as it cut into the family dispute. "Why would you want to do such a thing to a beautiful, historic home?"

"Explain your reasoning so we can try to understand your motives," Max said, crossing his arms and tilting his head. "I'm all ears."

"Yes, please do." Paulette mimicked Max's stance.

Confronted with a triad of accusers, Meredith resisted the temptation to turn on her heel and stride away. They'd probably chase her down and pry the reason from her. Maybe even tie her to a chair and torture her until she confessed the truth. One way or the other, they would eventually find out. She sighed. They deserved an answer of some kind, even if not the whole truth.

"Returning the property to nature will honor my husband and his life's work. That's all you really need to know."

"Willy never would have agreed with your intent," Meg said.

"Your husband?" Paulette blinked at her. "You want to bury Willy here?"

"No. Where'd you get that idea?" Meredith shifted her weight to one foot and considered Paulette.

"It's kinda the same thing," Paulette said. "Tearing down the house to plant grass is like digging a new grave for him."

"How did Willy die?" Max asked.

"Protecting me." The frown on Max's face cleared, replaced with raised eyebrows as understanding dawned.

"Oh, I see." Max's mouth screwed into a grimace. "You think destroying something beautiful and historic will make you feel better?"

"In a word, yes," Meredith said, snuggling her crossed arms tighter to her waist. "I'm glad you finally understand."

"I didn't say I understand," Max said, huffing out a disbelieving laugh. "I'd never understand harming one board of a historic property. I thought you cherished them as well."

"I don't understand, I don't mind saying." Meg frowned and stalked to where Meredith stood, feet braced as though for an attack. "What I do know is I'm ashamed of you."

"It's really very simple." Meredith cringed at the derision in Meg's voice as she noted the tension in the woman's frame. "This is a huge home waiting for the very family stolen from me. In order to move forward, I must restore peace here." She laid a hand over her heart.

Meg shook her head slowly, eyes trained on Meredith's face. "You won't have peace inside if you do such an awful act."

"You need time to think, to let nature take its course in the grieving process." Paulette moved to stand beside Meredith, one hand lightly resting on Meredith's crossed arms. "You don't need to destroy it immediately, right?"

"True. I did want to research more about the family who lived here, to understand the history of the plantation before I...um, enact my plan." Meredith unfolded her arms, effectively ending the contact between them.

"How do you plan to do that?" Max asked. "Pry each board loose and analyze it? God, Meredith, I can't believe you."

His hands flexed and tightened into fists, shooting images of boxers in their corners dancing through Meredith's mind.

He wouldn't hit her; physical violence wasn't his style. She forced her shoulders to drop into their normal position.

"No, Max. But Grandpa Joe's journals and letters and, of course, Grandma's research will hopefully shed some light on who lived here over the years," Meredith said.

Meg nodded. "The papers in the old trunk Sean carried down for you."

"So while you think about your next steps," Paulette said, "rather than summoning a wrecking ball, you could see what you can find out about Grace."

"Right," Meredith said. "And why did Edith go off to Kentucky and marry? It would be interesting to see if I can find the answer to that question too."

"Have you looked at the online genealogy research site?" Paulette asked.

"No, I've never used it, but Grandma did." Meredith hadn't had a moment to even figure out where she could access the Internet. "Meg, do we have Internet service here?"

Meg shook her head. "Not unless you turned the cable service back on."

Meredith looked at Max, striving to ignore the tension in his hands and his stance. "I didn't; did you?"

"No. Damn it, Meredith, I'm still stunned by your plan." Max shoved his hands into his back pockets and rocked onto his heels, glaring at her. "But if it will delay what you seem to consider inevitable for even a day, I'll call them right now."

"Once it's back on," Paulette said, glancing askance at Max, "I can help with the research. I discovered a lot about Johnny's side of the family, so I'd know where he came from."

"One day you'll have to tell me what happened between you and Johnny," Meredith said. "He seemed like a good fit for you."

"He gave me fits," Paulette said, a smile tugging at the corners of her mouth. "But, yeah, I'll tell you about him one day."

"So you're giving Twin Oaks a reprieve?" Max asked. "You'll not tear it down without notifying me first?"

He really did care about the old place. Or, worse, he wanted to control the situation. Meredith studied the tightly pressed lips and worried glacier eyes. "For now, but I haven't changed my mind, if that's what you're asking."

"*Gawd*. What do you want?" He strode closer to her. His eyes darkened to deep wells of worry. "What would it take for me to convince you not to do this?"

"You can't." Her throat constricted, making breathing difficult. "You're the one who made me decide to do it."

Paulette pulled the last article from her suitcase and placed it in the drawer. The old oak dresser held all her clothes with room to spare. She pushed on the drawer, but it didn't budge. She leaned against it, and finally it rubbed closed. She turned and scanned the room. Her room. It felt good to be home, if only for a little while. Above Meredith's old twin hung her cross-stitch sampler. Paulette sauntered over to examine it and smiled at the careless stitches. Meredith had never enjoyed the sensation of needle and thread in her hand. She'd rebelled about having to make the sampler, but Grandma insisted a girl should know how to sew. Paulette adored the slide of the needle as it pierced the fabric and then pulled the floss through with a slight vibration. Sewing created music in her hand.

If Grandma had left everything as is, then her diary should still be under the floorboard in the closet. She opened the door and pushed aside her dresses hanging inside. Two boards from the back of the closet, she pressed on the knothole and popped the third shorter one up. She reached into the dark space, trying not to imagine something grabbing her hand. Feeling around, she found the red clothbound book and drew it into the light. She stood and started to close the door again, but spied a large wooden box up high on the second shelf above her head. She blinked. Her samples. She stretched onto her tiptoes but couldn't reach the prized box of fabric scraps Grandma had supplied to Paulette from her sewing projects. Scraps that became dresses and blouses and skirts and tops for her Barbies. She wanted to take it down, but she couldn't reach it. She needed a chair.

She turned around and spied the only movable object in the room she could stand on. The desk chair. She'd used it before to reach her box. One more time wouldn't hurt. She hurried to it and rolled it to the open door.

Grizabella raised her head, eyes and ears pointed toward the front door. Meredith paused in reading, a frisson of anticipation brushing across her nerves. Was it the Lady in Blue? She sniffed but smelled only the cinnamon-scented candle burning on a small side table. The front door knocker banged twice, making the cat leap from her napping place and dash into the hallway. Meredith hurried after her to answer the door.

"Howdy and welcome to the neighborhood." A lanky brunette with heavy makeup blinked at her with hazel eyes that sparkled with mirth. The woman thrust a foil-covered casserole dish into Meredith's hands. "We haven't met yet. My name's Luanne Brashears. I'm your neighbor to the south of here."

"Nice to meet you, and thanks." Meredith held the cold dish, not quite certain what she should do with the gift. She didn't want to be impolite, but she also didn't want company. Would it be rude to not invite her in?

"I'm so glad you came to take charge of this beautiful plantation." Luanne smiled at Meredith even as she looked beyond her into the house. "Mrs. O'Connell set such store in your ability to polish this old place up like a new penny."

"You knew my grandmother?" Did everyone know Grandma? As well as her desire for Meredith to restore the plantation? Hopefully not.

"Sure. I stopped in now and then to bring her some veggies from my garden. You know you can never eat all the zucchini and peppers even a small patch yields."

"How kind." Meredith clasped the door, debating on how best to end the conversation.

"I'd love to see what you've done since you moved in. May I?"

Panic flared in Meredith's chest. "I'm sorry, but I'm really busy at the moment. Perhaps another time?"

Luanne blinked rapidly, cocking one hip as she contemplated Meredith. "I see. Well, sure. I don't mean to intrude."

That was code for Meredith had hurt her feelings. Not her intention, by any means. "I am sorry. I—"

A loud scrape upstairs preceded a muffled scream. Meredith gaped at Luanne as a second scream reached down the steps. Meredith plopped the casserole on a side table, and then they both raced up the stairs.

"Paulette?" Meredith called. "Paulette, are you okay?"

"Owww. In here."

Meredith steeled herself against the anticipated emotional onslaught and hurried into their once-shared bedroom. She focused on her sister, struggling to sit up on the floor. An overturned desk chair, its wheels spinning, lay on its side in front of the open closet. A quick glance inside showed a wooden box stuffed with various scraps of colored cloth nearly falling off the highest shelf.

"What were you doing?" Meredith helped Paulette to her feet.

"I found my old box of swatches and patterns." She checked herself over and then looked at Meredith. "I used to be able to balance on the chair, easy peasy."

Meredith frowned. "It's always been foolish to try to stand on a chair with wheels."

"Why did you want that old box?" Luanne asked.

Meredith blinked at the unfamiliar voice, having forgotten momentarily the woman had followed her.

"I'm sorry; I don't believe we've met." Paulette smiled at the stranger and stuck out her hand, and Meredith snickered at the non sequitur. "I'm Paulette O'Connell."

"Luanne Brashears, your southern neighbor." Luanne shook hands with Paulette. "Nice to meet you. So, why did you risk your neck?"

Paulette chuckled. "Over some scraps of fabric, I'm afraid. Dad always said it was a waste of time. I didn't realize it could be dangerous too."

"What?" Meredith strode to the closet and stared up at the box.

"You don't remember?"

Something in her voice made Meredith turn to scrutinize her expression. She found disappointment blanketing her features. "There's much I tried to block out from our childhood. Refresh my memory."

Paulette righted the chair and pushed it back to the small desk. Resting both hands on the back of the chair, she turned and regarded Meredith. "I dreamed of being a fashion designer, of one day having my own line of clothes."

"Like Coco Chanel." Meredith grinned. "I do remember now. You made clothes for your Barbie dolls."

Paulette shrugged. "I did."

"They were pretty too." Meredith considered her wistful

countenance, the tension in her hands gripping the chair. "You became an interior designer, though. So what happened?"

"In a word? Dad."

"Because it was a waste of time?"

Paulette nodded, knuckles white.

Meredith hurried to her sister, wanting to hug her but afraid of being rebuffed after all the rough water between them. "I'm sorry."

"You should ignore your dad and follow your heart," Luanne said, striding across the room. "After all, Meredith here did and look how successful she is. Your grandmother was so proud of all her accomplishments. And now she can apply her God-given talents to restoring this beautiful home."

Meredith gaped at Luanne, flummoxed as to how to respond without making things worse. How dare she say such a thing? Her comment made it sound as though Meredith was somehow better, more accomplished than Paulette. As though Luanne understood anything at all about her family and the right course of action regarding Twin Oaks. She let her gaze wander instead of piercing into the intruder. Only then she had to face all the reasons why she'd avoided coming into this room.

The quilts her grandmother had stitched still graced the twin beds with their matching wooden headboards, each featuring a raised, carved bouquet of flowers. The clusters of pink roses on the cream wallpaper desperately clinging to the wall had seen brighter days, but they still made her think she smelled their delicate perfume. Her first, or rather only, cross-stitch sampler of the alphabet and numbers hung on the wall, its uneven stitches a testament to why she did not attempt another.

"Luanne, is it?" Paulette recovered first. "Is there something we can do for you?"

"Oh no, dear," Luanne said, waving a hand as though

shooing away an annoying gnat. "I simply stopped by to bring my famous casserole to welcome you to the neighborhood."

"I'm sure we thank you for your thoughtfulness." Paulette managed to herd Luanne toward the door, drawing the intruder with her eyes and the motion of her body. "I'm sure you have other tasks you must attend to, as do we, so let me escort you to the door."

Meredith bit back a grin and tagged along. When her sister launched into her bossy-bitch mode, nobody could stop her.

"I see." Luanne scooted down the steps rather clumsily as Paulette hurried behind her. "Um, remove the foil and pop the dish in the oven for an hour at three-fifty, and you'll have a nice hot dinner."

Paulette opened the front door with a flourish. "Thanks again." Luanne hurried through the opening. "Bye."

Paulette leaned her back against the closed door and grinned at Meredith. "Whew."

"Impressive." Meredith crossed her arms and laughed along with her sister. The relief of being outside of the bedroom made her slightly dizzy. "I never knew you were so diplomatic."

An unladylike guffaw erupted from Paulette. "She was a nosy neighbor more than anything else. I can't stand them."

Meredith sobered. "She was right about one thing."

Paulette eyed her. "About your awesome talent?"

Meredith shook her head. "No. You really should follow your heart. It's not too late."

"It doesn't matter now." Paulette pushed away from the door and walked to the foot of the stairs. "I'll go paw through the memories associated with my childhood dreams, then donate the scraps to some quilting club or something."

Meredith watched her sister walk up the steps. So often some little thing a person said, whether thought through or not, directed or derailed the course of a person's life. Paulette's shoulders were rigid, her back straight, yet emotionally bowed from dreams abandoned after their father punctured them with a passing comment. If only she had a magic wand to wave in order to mend her sister's broken heart.

Chapter Eight

*A*nger can lead a person to say and do things they never thought possible. Including taking something lovely apart in order to create something even more rewarding. Or at least that was Meredith's hope as she began contemplating her next steps. She wandered outside to get some air after all the excitement.

Soon Twin Oaks would help her find the path to alleviate the pain. She finally had a course of action that would assuage her turmoil. She'd bury her grief through the catharsis of a fresh beginning by returning the once-beautiful but now decaying plantation to nature. Let the land heal her, as her grandmother had long ago told Meredith their Irish ancestors believed, though perhaps not in the way she meant.

First, she'd dismantle the manor one piece at a time, removing anything of value and selling it off to whomever had the money to buy it. Despite the building's grand scale, the house was too small to warrant using dynamite to implode. *Damn.* An implosion would satisfy on many levels. But she could visualize a nice, hot fire licking up the exterior. Yes, a fire would serve the purpose of bringing it down.

Studying the front of the house, she automatically categorized which pieces of the architecture were salvageable. One shutter clung precariously to an upper window frame. Ultimately, what could be saved didn't matter as much as how quickly she could do her job and subsume the grief into the ground. Hopefully, the inside decor didn't include any faux painting. She hadn't noticed any. Otherwise, much of the woodwork would prove worthless. She was in luck that the fireplaces had been constructed using real marble. She'd have to contact a local appraiser to determine the true value of any other items worth recovering from a historical perspective. Then salvage anything else for scrap that would help offset the cost of either the heavy equipment needed to take it apart or for hiring the guardian firemen to conduct a controlled burn.

Burning down the building in a controlled fashion tugged at her desire to contain the pain, to manage it and flush it once and for all out of her system. Perhaps afterwards she could breathe without the raw hiccup of intense grief snatching at her lungs. Maybe she'd be able to sleep in her half-empty bed without missing Willy like a severed limb, the ghostly ache never far from her mind.

She hardened her resolve. Emotional reaction must not sway her course.

She'd let an auction company take the furnishings and furniture. Then arrange for the dismantling of the house and outbuildings. Nothing would remain standing when she was finished returning the property to a green field.

While she and her sister delved into the genealogical research, she could start the process of taking the buildings down. It would take several weeks to make the necessary arrangements and have the right people do the right things to carry out her plans. Given the very real resistance from local historians and her own family, she'd likely have to allow extra time. She hated to draw this process out any longer than required, but she'd learned long ago to be realistic when setting the timeline for a project. Her reputation rested on her ability to carry through with the detailed plans. Once she'd set the schedule for a project, she had never missed her deadline.

She pulled a small notebook from her pocket and began jotting down tasks to add to her list. She'd have to contact the auction houses to arrange for appraisals, as well as the antique architecture firms to determine what they'd offer for the more unique decorative and structural appointments. The columns and the cornice pieces would be hot ticket items, certainly. Same for the hardwood floorboards and wallboards, at least those not faux painted to look like marble or a more expensive wood grain. And of course the old handmade bricks, made from the clay on site, may be worth the effort to clean and reuse, assuming they were still in good shape. Even the antique glass encased in the double-hung windows would be valuable.

Three weeks to dispose of the antique furniture. Another two to sell off the architectural antiques. Add on four more weeks to line up the necessary permits and equipment, as well as the manpower required to conduct the actual demolition. Altogether, no more than nine weeks she'd be forced to spend in the house, living among the many memories struggling to snag her attention. She'd originally hoped it would only take a month at most to make the transition from house to park-like garden, even though the garden part would stretch far into the future. But the takedown of the house must be done right in order for her to realize the inner peace she craved.

Max had tried to convey why the plantation house deserved to remain standing. Yet, once she'd dismantled it, once she'd filled in the stone foundation, once she'd converted the site to a park, then she would finally have peace. A rebirth from the death of the house. She'd bury the pain consuming her by finally putting to rest the dreams she and Willy had shared. At least she hoped so.

Then there was the emotional consideration she struggled to push aside. She moved away only to be dragged back to the very roots she'd tried to dig up and throw away, like some Irishman bent on removing a fairy tree only to find himself and his family cursed by the angry fairies. In order to follow through with her plans, she'd have to go against the O'Connell family's tradition of keeping the ancestral home and its property safe, like the Irish faithful protected the fairy tree to bring good fortune to the land and its owners. That would include razing it by a family member. Wouldn't it?

Willy's love of horticulture had spurred her decision to turn the old building into a park filled with living plants. Had her own ancestral ties to the land also informed the choice? She pictured a flower-lined path winding through a park-like setting. Memorial signs would indicate specific bushes or trees planted in memory of a loved one. Benches would be tucked into shady nooks where visitors could rest and enjoy the serenity of the park. The fairy tree would remain safe in its meadow, set apart from the formal garden paths, keeping its vigilant watch.

Max believed she belonged on the plantation but she couldn't for the life of her figure where he developed such a notion. She exemplified the fish-out-of-water kind of person. City life and its hustle and bustle, the honking of horns and wailing of sirens, spoke of living. Being surrounded by the sounds and smells of humanity suited her much more than country life, with its cacophony of silence punctuated by crickets and birdsong. Oh, and don't forget the damn roosters.

But times changed, and Twin Oaks remained her one hope for starting fresh and burying her pain and anger. To tear down the pain and build calm acceptance of her life. But what would Grandma have to say of her intent? Or even Grandpa Joe? Would they understand or condemn her sudden perhaps ill-considered decision? A shiver wiggled down her spine at the thought of their reaction. Maybe this once she should back away, but how?

Chapter Nine

*A*n owl hooted from outside the kitchen, dragging Meredith's attention from loading the dishwasher. She leaned onto the sink and stared out the window. The black, velvety sky sparkled with untold stars and a sliver of moon. She let her gaze slide back to the ground, touching on the white gazebo gleaming in the night.

The dishes could wait. She closed the door of the appliance and dried her hands on a towel. Flicking the light switch by the back door, she peered through the window. Yes, the fairy lights glowed across the ceiling of the gazebo. Hurrying, she strode through the house.

"Paulette, where are you?" She poked into each room she passed and then took the steps two at a time to the second floor and went down the hall where light peeked from beneath Paulette's door. She tapped twice before pushing it open. "There you are. Come on, it's a lovely night to sit outside and share a bottle of wine. You game?"

Paulette lay on her bed, her head propped on two pillows, a book open and resting on her tummy. She laid the novel aside and pushed to a sitting position, a grin on her lips. "If you insist."

Before long they rested beneath the mass of tiny white lights, an open bottle of merlot between them. The soft glow of a citronella candle flickered on the table. Crickets chirped in the background.

"I'd forgotten how much I enjoyed sitting out here," Meredith said, stretching her legs and crossing her ankles.

"Grandma had great taste in vino too." Paulette sipped the dark red liquid.

"Her latest interest, apparently." Meredith angled her glass, watching the candlelight dance in the reflection. She sipped, swallowed. "So, want to share why you came here? What happened to Mr. Perfect?"

The cricket symphony hushed in anticipation as Paulette sighed. "He's probably wrapped up in a parka somewhere in Alaska." She shook her head, peering into the darkness surrounding them.

"Really? Whatever for?"

"His dream job. Wildlife journalist for *National Geographic*. Ugh."

"I can't imagine you among the polar bears and penguins, anyway." Meredith chuckled. "You're too much a hothouse flower."

Paulette laughed. "You've got part of it right. First, there aren't penguins in Alaska. Second, you're dead-on about me needing a warmer climate. That's why I'm here."

"I thought you wanted to make me squirm." Meredith sipped her wine, imagining the crickets rubbing their legs to create their unique music like a symphony orchestra warming up.

"I love seeing you squirm, but that wasn't why I really came to find you." Paulette scooted back in her chair, sitting more upright. She leveled her gaze on Meredith, resting her wineglass on her tummy. "Truth be told, I missed you. Or more accurately, I missed our friendship."

"That was eons ago." Meredith looked away. Although

she longed for the closeness they once shared, she would never allow her sister to maneuver close enough to hurt her ever again. The emotional barrier she'd erected had to remain in order to protect herself from Paulette's barbs.

"Hm." Paulette twirled her glass slowly, the fairy lights glinting off the wine's dark surface. "We can't see the future."

"No, yet we both know the past."

"Do we?" Paulette cleared her throat, the sound harsh in the gentle spring evening. "I'm never certain I understand what happened, let alone the underlying meaning of events. It's like music, as far as I'm concerned."

Meredith focused her attention on her then, puzzled by the analogy. "How is music a mystery?"

Paulette waved her hand, palm up and open. "Music flows around me but is elusive, fleeting. I enjoy listening to it but don't entirely comprehend what it's trying to say."

"Not everything has to have meaning, does it?"

Paulette nodded. "Absolutely. People crave to know why things happen. Think about all the symbolism applied to everything. Even the clothes we wear are said to show the kind of person we are."

"Music is a different medium, though." Meredith sat up, her back pressing into the Adirondack chair. "The notes speak to me, share a mood and a feeling simultaneously that carry the meaning. Don't you hear the ambiance when you listen?"

Paulette slowly shook her head. "I don't think so." She shrugged. "But maybe some of that seeps into my subconscious."

"Even the crickets are sharing their mood, playing their sense of peace and joy."

"It's the soundtrack of their life, you mean?"

"Brilliant." Meredith nodded and stared at her sister. She'd never thought of each person having a soundtrack of music that reflected who they were during their lifetime. The myriad of tunes and compositions heard during momentous occasions as well as the day-to-day happenings, all combined into a tapestry of sound. "What would yours be?"

Paulette put her glass to her lips but lowered it without drinking. "Mine would include nursery songs and ballads as well as show tunes. And sewing." She lifted her wine and sipped.

"Sewing?" Meredith cocked a brow. "How is sewing a kind of music?"

"To me, the stitches are like notes. When you combine different colors and patterns, you achieve music."

"I can see that. Mine would be a blend of classical and new age with highlights of children's and R&B." She smiled, imagining the playlist she'd create for her iPod. "This is kinda fun, isn't it?"

"What about your sexy lawyer? What would his look like?"

Meredith tossed her head and laughed. "He's not 'my' lawyer, and more importantly, why would I care about his soundtrack?"

"Aren't you curious? He's such a hunk. I'm surprised you haven't snapped him up."

"Not interested." Meredith gripped her knee with one hand, balancing the foot of her wineglass on her other leg. Not much, anyway.

"Can I have him?" Paulette cut her a glance, her smile mischievous.

"Fine by me." The image of Max's laughing eyes played in her mind. "But you'll have to clear it with him."

Paulette chuckled. "Well, I'm not really interested in him, either. He'll have to figure it out for himself."

Meredith tapped glasses with Paulette. "To Max."

"And Grandma."

"Yes, indeed." Meredith drained her glass and then refilled it before hovering the bottle over Paulette's. "More?"

Paulette nodded, and Meredith poured. "Thanks."

Meredith considered her sister's pensive expression as she sank back against the chair. She wriggled into a more comfortable position. Took a sip. "So, since Johnny is out of the picture, what are your plans?"

"As in, how long am I staying?" Paulette stared at the liquid in her glass as it reflected the lights above. She shrugged. "As long as you'll let me, I guess."

Meredith worked her lower lip with her teeth, tasting the subtle fruity hints of the merlot. She wanted to be alone so she could enact her plan without interference. Yet Paulette displayed a vulnerability Meredith had never seen before. Curious. Was it the result of Johnny's uncaring dismissal of their relationship?

"I make no promises as to how long I'll be here myself." Meredith swirled the fluid in her glass. They claimed to be adults, so perhaps they could manage to survive in the same house for a few weeks. "But I suppose it's only right for you to stay with me for as long as I do."

"Thanks, sis." Paulette glanced at Meredith, a smile flitting across her lips. "I have nowhere else to go. Soon I'll have to find a job, but for now…thanks."

The crickets suddenly stopped their singing, and Meredith could swear she heard blues floating on the spring breeze. Impossible, of course. But then so was smelling honeysuckle this time of year. "I want us to try to be friends again. I know it won't be easy, and we're as likely to resort to fisticuffs as hug. But, well…what do you say?"

"Sharing secrets and fixing your hair? That kind of friend?"

Meredith nodded. "Yes. So do you know any?"

"Hairstyles?" Paulette's voice squeaked out her question.

Meredith started, surprised at the hint of alarm in her sister's eyes. "No, secrets."

Paulette swallowed and nodded. "Actually I do. But you have to swear to keep it to yourself. I haven't told anyone because I haven't decided what I'll do."

Meredith leaned forward, the stem of her wineglass gripped lightly between her hands. She had suspected Paulette hid something. Now she'd finally learn what. "I swear. Spill."

Paulette set her glass down on the table. She linked her fingers together over her stomach. Reclined against the white Adirondack chair, her skin glowed in the soft light. She turned to look at Meredith. "There's no easy way to say this. I'm pregnant."

"Oh." What could she say? Paulette hadn't married Johnny, only lived with him for the past four years.

"Exactly. Now I have to decide what to do with it." Paulette shot upright, shaking her head and frowning at Meredith. "No, I can't refer to this child as a thing, an 'it.' He or she was conceived out of love, even if that love has flown to Alaska."

"Will you keep the babe or put it up for adoption?"

"That's the million-dollar question."

Her sister had come to Twin Oaks, the family home, because she needed family to help her through this new challenge in her life. Meredith gazed at her, imagining how she'd feel if in her shoes. The need for loving support, not recriminations, would be first and foremost on her list. "Whatever you decide, I'll be here to support your choice. I'm glad you're not considering an abortion."

"For me, that's not a choice."

"Your fall earlier. Are you sure you're okay?"

"I expect so." She rubbed her hands over her flat stomach. "Everything seems fine."

Meredith rose and went to her sister, pulling her to her

feet. "I'm here for you." She gave her a long hug, feeling her sister's deep breaths within the embrace.

"Thanks, little sis." Paulette was the first to flop back in her chair. "Just, please, don't tell Mom and Dad. They'd freak."

"Double-dog swear. They're far away, at any rate. You don't have to let them know anything until you decide which direction to take."

Paulette smoothed a hand over her abdomen. "I'm only eight weeks, so nobody can tell by looking at me. I have some time to decide how to proceed. Now it's your turn."

"For what?" Meredith asked, puzzled.

"A secret. Surely you have one?"

Only one, which she'd never shared with anyone. Meredith looked at Paulette's expectant gaze and sighed. "I do. I've never told a soul."

Paulette's gaze intensified, eyes glinting in the fairy lights. "That's the best kind. Spill."

"I was pregnant when Willy died. The same man who killed him also killed our baby. Willy never even knew he was going to be a dad." The words rushed from Meredith's mouth.

"Oh my God, Meredith." Paulette gripped her hands together as her eyes flew wide open. "I'm so sorry. I—I didn't know."

Meredith shrugged. "Nobody knew." She drew a deep breath and let it ease from her chest. "Now it's no longer a secret, which feels good."

Paulette reached to squeeze Meredith's hand. "Thanks for trusting me again."

Meredith sank back on her chair and picked up her glass. "Should you have had wine tonight, knowing you're with child?"

"Recent studies have shown a glass now and then won't hurt." Paulette fingered her glass but left it on the table. "Thanks for letting me stay."

"You can help me try to unravel the mystery of Grace's disappearance. You said you know something about the online genealogy site, right?"

"A bit."

"Tomorrow you can start searching for whatever you can find. I'll keep reading the journals and letters for clues."

Paulette lifted her glass and leaned toward Meredith. "To family."

"And to uncovering the truth." Meredith clinked glasses, the ring of crystal punctuating the cricket symphony.

"Truth about?" Paulette asked.

"What really happened to our great-great-great-aunt."

A sliver of moon appeared through the sliding glass doors leading onto Max's tiny balcony. Streetlights added their luminescence to the night sky. He sat in his leather recliner, a legal brief spread across his lap. The lamp on the end table to his right cast light across the ignored pages. Distracted, he gazed out the doors to where a small plastic table and single chair occupied the balcony's square inches.

The pages in his lap contained important details about the limitations he had to work within for a new trust he needed to complete. He picked up the next page. Stared at the sentences. Yet his brain refused to absorb the words. Meredith's face floated in his mind, obliterating the letters and their meaning. Her voice echoed in his ears, tantalizing and seductive. Despite her desire to raze Twin Oaks, she drew him in a way no other woman had ever before. He reread the sentence, but nothing stuck. Screw it. He flung the pages aside and stalked to the kitchen.

He poured a glass of Macallan scotch and adjourned to the fresh air outside. Standing at the railing, he surveyed the established neighborhood lying quiet so late in the evening. Maple trees stood outlined by the streetlights, sporting new leaves on their skeletal limbs. Few cars drove past on the street below as he grasped the metal rail with one hand and sipped his drink. Fantasizing about that woman had to stop or he'd never be promoted to senior partner. The promotion would enable him to afford a historic home of his own. Her intent to destroy the very thing he longed to possess rankled deep in his chest, at odds with the desire spearing through him when he thought of her voice, her long legs, her strawberry-blonde hair he'd love to plunge his hands into. And her eyes. My God, they mesmerized him. She'd turned his world upside down the moment she'd stepped into his truck. Her mysterious ways coupled with her beauty and intelligence made her a dynamite package. One that may well blow up in his face.

The ringing of the phone drew him back into the apartment. He stared at the caller ID for two rings before answering.

"Hi, Rhonda. What's up?"

"Hey, handsome. I was sitting here, all alone, thinking about you. How about I come over for a nightcap?"

Her feline purr slid through the phone, curling into a lump in his stomach. Rhonda Sommers had been a mistake from their blind date, arranged by Sue, three months before. He should never have trusted his secretary to set him up, but he'd been feeling low and in need of some female company. When they'd met for drinks at the Hideaway, with her white-blonde hair, red-painted talons, and low-cut blouse leaving little to his imagination, he could tell she was not his type. What had Sue been thinking, fixing him up with the likes of her?

"Sorry, but I'm working tonight." Or at least trying to. He swirled the dark amber liquid in his glass, watching the play of light as it shone through the scotch.

"It's so late. I'd have thought you'd be relaxing by now." Her voice hardened a degree.

She obviously suspected his disinterest. Maybe at one point in his life he'd have found her offers intriguing, even welcome. But not now. Not after Meredith had entered his life. "Listen, I appreciate your call. But I have to go."

"A rain check?" A wisp of hope laced her question.

"Rhonda…" He hesitated. How did he let her down easy?

"Fine. Have a nice life." The line went dead.

He stared at the silent phone for a long moment and then hung it up. Any other man would adore the buxom blonde he'd so easily brushed off. He envisioned Meredith's entrancing eyes laughing at him. He could envision her swinging a sledgehammer to knock down the walls of the old plantation, or worse, lighting the fuse to blow it up. He cringed at the image. Twin Oaks had been his favorite place, and he'd find any excuse to visit Mrs. O'Connell so he could soak up the historical atmosphere. He swigged a mouthful of scotch and let it burn down his throat, eating away the bad taste the images in his head evoked.

Figures. He finally found the woman of his dreams, and she'd turned out to be his worst nightmare.

Chapter Ten

Roseville's streets thronged with cars and pedestrians. Meredith shut the car door and then waited for Paulette to emerge from the passenger side. The cozy town surrounded her like a strait jacket. She trembled at the feeling.

They crossed the square, heading for Golden Owl Books and Brews. The bookstore had occupied the 1860s-era brick building as long as Meredith could remember. The three sisters who ran the thriving business had diversified over the years, adding in a variety of attractions and merchandise to keep the townsfolk flocking through the doors. Flyers on the windows announced open mic nights featuring local artists to share their talents. A yellow kiosk in one corner enabled people to buy and download books from a variety of publishers.

"What are you looking for again?" Meredith asked. "I thought we had enough books at home."

"A book on the county history, one published fairly recently, might provide some new clues." Paulette tucked her clutch purse under her arm. "Grandma's are so old they're practically worthless."

"I'm sure they have some useful history in them,"

Meredith said, pushing open the door. A bell jangled above her head. "But a newer one may be worth the investment. New facts may have come to light, with any luck."

"Hmmm, it smells wonderful in here." Paulette paused inside the door and scanned the crowded bookshop.

"It's the bakery. All the cinnamon and cloves and apples." Meredith drew in a deep breath, savoring the aromas of fresh bread and spices. "What a brilliant idea these ladies had to include fresh cinnamon rolls."

"I'll be in the local history section." Paulette pointed to the sign indicating the area and strode toward the back of the store.

Meredith considered her next move as she surveyed the bookstore. She wanted to discover what kinds of books existed that could shed light on the census and how to interpret them. But first, she needed to stand there and merely experience the atmosphere. She inhaled, cataloging the mingling scents, detecting paper and ink as backdrop to hot coffee and cinnamon. In one corner, a small stage waited for the next open mic participant. The sisters opened the Golden Owl two nights a week to let people read from their writing or perform a musical number. Those evenings only, they also featured a wine-and-cheese party as extra incentive for the locals to attend. The bell over the front door rang every few moments, announcing customers coming and going.

Tables sat scattered throughout the shop, laden with books or calendars and other related products. Handmade jewelry crafted by local artisans hung on tall stands dotting the floor space. An open balcony featuring tables and comfortable chairs ran around the upstairs walls, leaving an airy feel in the center. A rack of greeting cards, advertised as designed by locals, hugged the wall under the stairs, a postage stamp kiosk beside it. Beyond, a small table and chair waited for the correspondent to fill out the card, put a stamp on it, and then slip it into the mailbox outside the front door of the shop.

The bell jangled, and Meredith ducked her head when Sue sauntered in. She didn't need to run into Max's legal secretary, knowing whatever Meredith did and said would be shared with the man himself before she'd even pulled into her own driveway. In fact, the fewer people she ran into, the better. Meredith made her way to the stairs and quickly climbed to the second story where the other nonfiction reference books resided.

Wandering past the array of books, Meredith searched for titles that sparked her interest. So many topics, she should have gone to the library instead. Only, she'd have to sign up for a library card. She'd rather plunk down money than have everyone know what she was reading. Finally locating a book claiming to be able to analyze census records, she turned to seek out Paulette.

"Find anything?" Meredith stopped beside where she stood with her nose inches from an open book.

"What? Oh, um, yes." A red blush infused Paulette's neck, spreading upward to blaze on her cheeks.

"Such as?" Meredith leaned closer, trying to read the title of the hardback.

"It's nothing." She slapped the book closed and hugged it close to her chest, hiding the title completely from anyone passing by, including Meredith.

Meredith smirked. "What are you up to? It's not porn, is it?"

Paulette's blush deepened. "No, of course not." She glanced around and then angled the book so Meredith could read the title.

"*Making the Right Choice*? What's it about?"

"Hush. It's about what we talked about last night." Paulette's eyes narrowed. "Don't say it out loud, or I'll have to exact revenge on you."

Meredith laughed. "Don't worry. You're secret's safe. But what about the local history?"

Paulette flapped a hand and grinned. "Oh, that." She pointed to a thick volume laying on the table beside her. "This seems like it will be interesting to read and helpful to boot."

Meredith was about to reply when a hand landed on her shoulder. She spun and beheld Sue, her arms laden with several romance novels and cozy mysteries.

"Hey, Meredith, how are you?" Sue shifted the books to clasp them more firmly in her hands. "Is this your sister I've heard about?"

Meredith performed the introductions, all the while wondering why Sue had made such an effort to seek her out. "Looks like you've found some good stories."

"Yeah, I hope so." Sue glanced at the spines of the books and then peered at Meredith. "I want to tell you again how happy I am you've inherited Twin Oaks. Your grandmother was loved in these parts, and while she wasn't able to manage the upkeep, now you can. She had such high hopes for what you will do to help the place shine again."

Stunned, Meredith shrugged, unsure how to respond. Had Max told her of the plan to transform the plantation into a memorial park? What did she know?

"Grandma always spoke highly of the people of Roseville," Paulette interjected. "I'm sure she'd agree this is a friendly little town. All the wonderful historic properties, so lovely and cherished."

Paulette's wide-eyed innocent look weighed upon Meredith. Another dig. Why wasn't she surprised?

"Yes, she loved it as much as any of us." Sue smiled, her eyes crinkling at the corners. "I don't have long, but I did want to share that I've been touting your talents to the other townspeople. Everyone is anxious to see what renovations you'll bring to the plantation, what with your architectural background and all. It's so very exciting."

"Don't get your hopes too high," Meredith said but then regretted her words at the look of puzzlement on Sue's face. "I mean, I wouldn't want to disappoint if my efforts don't hit the mark."

Sue guffawed and swooped a hand through the air. "You're so funny, Meredith. We all know from the papers and mags how famous you are for your architectural genius. I can't wait to see your plans."

"She's still working on them." Paulette stepped closer to Sue and smiled, though her mouth appeared tight, holding back a terrible secret. "We've got to finish our shopping as we have a few other stops to make on our way home. Will you excuse us?"

"Oh, sure." Sue glanced at her watch. "Goodness, Max will be wondering where I've gone. See you both later." She waved as she hurried away.

"Thanks. I never know what to say." Meredith ran a hand down her arm, trying to calm the agitation inside caused by the reminder of how the townspeople would react when Meredith carried out her plan. The earlier guilt blossomed into blatant existence. But she never backed off a commitment. Did she? No, she never had.

"I'm not about to let anyone know your scheme." Paulette grabbed up her books and herded Meredith toward the checkout. "And definitely not while standing in the Golden Owl. A riot may erupt."

Meredith allowed Paulette to shoo her to the register, where she paid for their books. Once back outside on the sidewalk, Meredith drew in a deep breath as her eyes adjusted to midday sunlight. "I'm glad to be out here where nobody will accost me about my inheritance."

"Well, except for Max." Paulette nodded in the direction of the courthouse and moved toward Meredith's car. "You coming before he gets here?"

"Damn." Meredith scooted to the driver-side door,

unlocking the vehicle with a press of a button on the fob in her hand. "Let's go."

"Meredith, wait!" Max strode down the sidewalk, looking vital and handsome with the sun glinting on his hair and reflecting in his dark glasses. Beside him an elderly woman hurried to keep up, her gray hair in soft waves about her face, her figure trim and petite.

"Too late." Paulette opened her door but didn't step inside.

"Hi, Max." Meredith pulled her door wide, indicating she didn't intend to stay long.

"I wanted you to meet my aunt, Genevieve Wilson. Aunt Jenny, this is the fabulous architect Mrs. O'Connell told you about years ago."

"You're Meredith?" Jenny reached out a hand. "Nice to meet you at last."

"Thank you. Did you know my grandmother well?"

Jenny smiled softly. "Not really, though we did enjoy a good glass of wine together now and again. She told me about how you'll improve Twin Oaks, make it better than it has ever been before. I can't wait to see the renewed place."

"I hope it meets expectations." Her stomach had become home to a million agitated butterflies. Her heart sank. What now?

"Such vision you must have for what the gorgeous place will look like." Jenny sidled closer to Meredith and grinned up at her. "I'm sure you'll do wonders."

"Yes, she has grand plans for Twin Oaks. Hi, I'm Paulette, Meredith's sister."

"Pleased to meet you, my dear." Jenny nodded at Paulette across the roof of the car. "Will you be helping Meredith with her plans?"

"Indeed, I will." Paulette crossed her arms, the open door a barrier between her and the small party standing on the sidewalk. "She'll need my help to finish the interior."

Meredith squinted at Paulette, wondering what she meant. Paulette knew there'd be no interior decorating happening at Twin Oaks. At least as things currently stood. Unless… Meredith kicked herself for even thinking of changing her mind. But the thought persisted.

"That's lovely, dear. I'm sure she's glad to have the help. It's such a big place, isn't it?"

"Yes, ma'am." Paulette grasped the door and started to pull it toward her.

"We've got to go," Meredith said, preparing to ease into the car.

"I'll see you around," Max said, catching Meredith's eye. "We have some unfinished business, you and I."

"Call me, and we'll figure out a time to meet." Meredith slipped into the car and closed the door. Paulette followed Meredith's lead, practically slamming her door closed. Max motioned for Meredith to open the window.

Max moved to the driver's window and leaned down to peer into the car. "I'll be in touch."

Meredith nodded, not trusting her voice. Shifting into gear, she eased out of the parking spot and headed back to the plantation.

Meredith's car merged into traffic and quickly out of sight. She seemed rather evasive when Max had mentioned their unfinished business. He intended to make sure she never carried through with her horrifying scheme. But how? She had all the skills and knowledge to do exactly what she planned. Somehow he had to convince her to change her plan.

A worrying thought crept into his mind. He'd caused her to make the decision. How? What could he do to undo the damage? Or at least prevent her from following through on her intent.

He strolled back to his office, exchanging casual greetings with the people he passed. Aunt Jenny had left him to meet her book club inside the Golden Owl. He enjoyed small-town life much more than the city life where he'd attended Harvard. Here he knew many of the people he passed on the street. In Cambridge he'd walked anonymously through the town, ignored and alone. The sense of belonging he experienced in Roseville made him want to burst into song, an urge best left to his piano playing rather than inflicting his voice on his neighbors. He lifted a hand in greeting to the postman and opened the door to his office. It felt good to be accepted for who he was.

"The council chairman wants you to call him as soon as possible," Sue said in way of greeting. "Did you see Meredith?"

"Okay, and yes." Max grinned and closed the door.

"I'm thrilled for her, aren't you? Her efforts will be rewarded." Sue handed him a yellow note. "Here's the chairman's number."

She didn't know the half of it, how lucky Meredith was. Her plan galled him all the more as a result. "I'll be in my office."

He dropped into his leather executive chair, leaned his elbows on the mahogany surface, and scoured his face with his hands. *Think, damn it. There has to be a way.* Raising his head, the yellow slip of paper snared his attention. Of course. He snatched up the receiver and dialed the number.

Ten minutes later he had put his own plans into play. He'd arranged to move up the vote on the legislation so she would be prevented by county ordinance from destroying the historic building. He sat back in his chair, content he'd done all he could for now to save the plantation. His only worry was if his best was good enough.

Chapter Eleven

The stack of Grandpa Joe's journals caught Meredith's eye as she strode into the parlor. She'd taken a quick break to refill her lemonade. Who knew reading was such dusty work? She'd removed each journal and placed it carefully on the folding table she'd set up for the purpose. She wanted to know exactly what she was dealing with in the trunk. The journals now sat in chronological order, spanning forty years, from 1863 to 1903. Then there were all the letters to go through, which was more difficult as not all the writing was as easy to read as Joe's. She wished she'd spent more time training her eyes to decipher handwriting, and would have if she'd ever thought she'd need such knowledge.

She put her glass on the end table and turned her attention to the trunk, its lid sitting open and inviting. She peered inside and lifted a handful of letters, neatly grouped by a length of ribbon. A tug and the lace slipped off. She shuffled through the stack, sorting them by date as she went. In her hands resided living history, the words and emotions of those who had gone before. She placed the stack on the table beside the journals and reached back to the trunk for another set. Once she had all the letters out of the box and sorted by postmark date, she sat down in her grandmother's favorite chair to catch her breath.

Paulette sauntered into the room, tall and lanky, no sign of her pregnancy yet showing. Meredith remembered the inner joy she felt when carrying Willy's child. Did Paulette rejoice at carrying Johnny's? She looked pale, as though in pain. What did she need now?

"Yes?" Meredith reached for the top journal, resting it in her lap as she waited for her to say something.

"I've been digging into our ancestors' past on that genealogy site." Paulette sank into the other rocking chair and rested her head on the doily. She closed her eyes with a sigh. "So much to sift through, I've got a migraine."

"Did you learn anything helpful?" Meredith turned her attention to her sister even as the stacks called to her. But perhaps what Paulette had discovered would enhance understanding a detail she'd otherwise consider insignificant. She tried to be patient, but the urge to reach for a journal, to open the book and delve into Grandpa Joe's words again, pressed on her nerves.

"The 1870 census shows Edith O'Connell married to Anson Bigbee and living in Lexington, Kentucky. He apparently was a doctor and lived in town. They had a couple of kids."

"None of which helps us find what happened to Grace." Meredith gripped the edges of the journal in her lap. "Where else can we look?"

"Hmmm, I can't think with this blasted headache pounding into my skull." Paulette laid a hand over her eyes.

"Do you need anything?" Meredith asked, sitting up. She studied her sister's expression, searching for any indication of illness or distress. "Maybe you should go lay down for a while. Pregnancy changes how your body reacts to stress."

Paulette let her head loll to one side, and then the other.

Then she slowly opened her eyes. "No, I swallowed my meds for it. I'll be fine shortly."

"But you're pale," Meredith said, gripping the gooseneck handles in preparation to stand. "Should you be taking medicine without asking a doctor or pharmacist at least? You're not going to faint on me, are you?"

"I appreciate your concern, but I'll be all right. I did call the doctor's office Meg suggested for my, er, sore ankle. They okayed me taking my migraine med. I have an appointment in two weeks." Paulette pushed to her feet. "What are you up to?"

"Good. I'm still reading through Joe's journals, looking for anything Grandma may have missed." Meredith flopped her head against the chair back as the immensity of the task loomed in her mind. "But she was so thorough, I have little hope of actually finding something she missed."

"Need help?" Paulette lifted a leather-bound book to examine Grandpa Joe's writing. She opened the cover and then looked at Meredith. "If we work together, this will go faster."

"No, thanks." Meredith retrieved the journal from Paulette's hands and carefully replaced it on the stack. This job had to be hers alone. "If both of us only read parts, we may miss some important link."

"You simply don't want to share the fun," Paulette said. "I get it. You still don't want me here. But I ain't going anywhere."

Ever since Paulette had moved in two days ago, the tension in the house had eased somewhat. They were slowly making some kind of peace between them, but they had a long road ahead. Meredith had been surprised when Paulette had chosen to occupy the bedroom they'd shared as kids. Nothing could induce Meredith to sleep in that room again. The fun and love they'd shared while playing in the sunny room had been replaced with animosity and dissension over the ensuing years. Their relationship had gone south so long ago, Meredith no longer recalled what had started the decline in trust and caring between them. She could only hope the path they trod now would lead them to a better, if guarded, relationship.

"It's not that I don't want your help," Meredith said. "Why don't you see what else you can find online about Edith and her husband? I haven't found much in the journals about them except Joe seemed to think Grace once had an interest in Anson."

"Why did he think that?" Paulette rubbed two fingers against her right temple.

"Grace wrote to Joe about having an argument with Edith about Anson." Meredith flipped open a journal and turned pages until she found the entry. "Here. He says, 'Grace had been misled by the attentions of Colonel Anson Bigbee, and she vowed to protect Edith from his underhanded manipulations of her affections.'"

"Ooh, do you think the evil colonel was playing them off each other? An antebellum love triangle?" Paulette picked up another book and opened it, skimming its pages.

"Did they do that then?" Meredith slowly closed the journal lingering in her hands.

"Do what?" Paulette stopped turning pages to look at Meredith.

"If two sisters fell in love with the same man," Meredith said slowly, "how might the man react?"

"If he's anything like Johnny was, he'd lap it up." Paulette tapped a finger on the page. "And if he were as 'underhanded' as Grace seemed to think, then he might even play up his advantage. Get the two sisters to engage in a good old-fashioned catfight over him."

Her sister may be on to something with this line of reasoning. Leave it to her to dream up such a dastardly plot. "What if Grace tried to warn Edith away from this colonel, and Edith thought her sister wanted him for herself?"

"Kinda like we fought over Brandon when we were teens?" Paulette asked, a smile appearing on her lips and in her eyes.

"Man, he was cute, wasn't he?" Meredith shook her head at the memory of the tall, black-haired teen with laughing gray eyes.

"Yummy to look at," Paulette added, her smile fading. "But I wish we hadn't gotten so carried away about him."

"Hm?" Meredith searched her memory and came up empty. "What do you mean?"

"You know…" Paulette zeroed in on Meredith's expression.

"No, I don't." What was she talking about? A sinking feeling made her queasy as Meredith tried to follow Paulette's thinking. "Talk to me."

"You're going to make me say it, aren't you?"

"Paulette, I have no idea what you're talking about." Meredith crossed her arms, more to have something to do with her hands than anything else. "So you're going to have to say something."

Paulette raked a hand through her hair and winced. "Damn headache." She paused and exhaled. "Fine. Brandon must have been what caused this rift between us. I see that now."

Meredith blinked at her sister as she tried to dig the facts from her brain. "I don't think we fought over him, did we?"

"Not overtly," Paulette said, worry lines on her forehead.

"Then what?"

"I knew you liked him more than me, so I didn't pursue my feelings for him."

"I didn't like him much, not enough to go with him," Meredith said, perplexed. "Besides he was older than you, so Mom would have had a fit if I'd dated him."

"You mean, I could have? Damn, I wish I'd realized that before now."

"Is this what you think caused us to fall out with each other?" Meredith cocked her head as she searched her sister's expression.

"Probably." Paulette shrugged. "I can't believe I've carried a grudge against you all these years for nothing."

"You thought I wanted somebody I didn't even care about. For that I'm sorry." Meredith stared at her sister, the memory of all the years of bickering and tension between them flowing past like a fast-forward movie. "I didn't know what had happened between us."

"Come here." Paulette struggled to her feet, grabbed Meredith's shoulders, and dragged her into a fierce embrace.

Such anger between sisters over a man. A man who was replaced by each of them with better men. Meredith still didn't know what actually occurred between Paulette and Johnny, why he'd abandoned her, but she did know Johnny was an improvement over Brandon and his little boy ways.

Meredith eased from the hug. "Imagine if we had really both loved Brandon how much antagonism we'd have endured between us. Could be what happened between Grace and Edith, you think?"

Paulette bobbed her head in agreement. "No wonder Edith ran off to Kentucky to get married."

"But what happened to Grace?" Meredith paced away from Paulette, energy bursting inside at the relief flooding her. Finally she and her sister could begin to put their troubled relationship behind them, though she had no illusions it would not take time for all the hurt and negativity to dissipate. "Maybe she ran away before Edith and Anson did the deed?"

"But why leave Twin Oaks if Edith was leaving?" Meredith paced around the parlor. "And without telling anyone where she went?"

"Good questions." Paulette laid the book back on the pile.

"Without answers." She strode from the window to the rocking chair, then from the rocking chair to the door.

"I'll go dig around online while you keep reading." Paulette tapped the stack of letters.

"The mystery seems to grow deeper all the time. I do hope nothing tragic happened to Grace."

"We may never know exactly what did transpire," Paulette said. "After all, that was over 150 years ago."

Meredith inhaled in preparation to reply and caught a hint of honeysuckle and the sound of blues on the cool spring breeze.

The day had started out bad and went downhill from there. Max paced his office, rolling a pencil between his fingers. First, while playing his favorite classical piece, he'd snapped a string on his baby grand—whoever heard of the seemingly impervious metal strings breaking?—and had to call in the piano tuner to have that fixed. Then Sue, his usually unflappable legal secretary, spilled her coffee all over the draft of the legislation he needed to proof by noon. The county council was set to meet in ten days to vote on his proposed ordinance placing restrictions on the use and modification of historic properties. State law required the draft legislation be in the hands of the county councilmen at least seven days prior to the vote. When Sue tried to print a new copy, the damn machine decided to give up the ghost, so she had to race over to the Quick Printer down the street. Time was running out before he had to leave to meet yet another obligation: the lunchtime rehearsal for the county high school spring concert.

If Sue's grandson hadn't been selected to perform a trumpet solo, Max would never have become involved. But how could he refuse to play when the usual accompanist had been called up and sent to Bagram? If the young woman could do her duty for her country, then Max could damn well do his for his county. He'd been hitting the old ivories every morning before work to prepare for his debut performance. No way would he embarrass Sue's grandson by messing up the energetic jazz band piece.

He paused his perpetual motion at the window. The sun shone on the small town of Roseville he called home. Finding this position had been a dream come true. At forty-six, he'd reached most of his goals in life: stable home, stable career, stable friends. Only one achievement had evaded him: a wife and family. He'd simply never met anyone with whom he could envision settling down and raising a gaggle of kids.

Until now. Meredith, with those amazing eyes and luscious figure, intrigued him. Smart. Driven. Talented. Yet under the professional surface, a river of tension and grief flowed. She fit at Twin Oaks so neatly, he understood exactly why Mrs. O'Connell had selected her to inherit the place. Meredith could restore the plantation to serve as a shining example of the antebellum era in the county. Her education, experience, and contacts all combined to afford her the skills and abilities necessary to accomplish seeming miracles to uninitiated historical architecture lovers like him. But somehow he needed to help her see a different path forward that didn't include her current intent. A path including him.

"Here you are, boss." Sue interrupted his musings by hurrying into the office and setting a small stack of pamphlets on his desk. "While I was there, I had them bound."

Max moved to his desk and picked up the top copy. Flipping through it, he said, "Perfect. I'm glad you did."

"It's a more finished product, which will hopefully

translate into the law being passed." Sue automatically straightened the neatly stacked files in the inbox. "You grabbing lunch before or after the rehearsal?"

"After." His stomach turned over at the thought of food at this point. Best to wait until his nerves settled a bit.

"Jeremy is thrilled you agreed to play, by the way." Sue moved a pen from its wayward place in a pencil holder to a cup sporting a set of matching blue pens. "He wouldn't have this opportunity without your kindness."

Max swallowed, his throat dry. "Glad to help." He checked his watch. "Speaking of which, time to head over to the high school. Don't want to be late for my first time."

He'd committed to doing this concert, but at certain moments he regretted having volunteered to play. What if he messed up? Would folks equate such a faux pas to his law practice? Not being able to play with teens meant he was unprepared to compete with the big boys in law? He mentally shook himself. *Get a grip, man.*

"Have fun." Sue trailed him out of his office and across hers to the front door.

He opened the door and nipped through it, soon covered by sunshine and the weight of the eyes and opinions of his town.

Chapter Twelve

Grizabella stalked into the attic, little squeaky meows announcing her presence to Meredith, who rose to brush off her jeans. Nearby, two stacks—one of books and one of newspapers—evidenced her efforts for this morning. She'd grown tired of reading the letters, trying to decipher the elaborate script while at the same time figuring out who the people were that Grace or Edith or Joe mentioned.

"What's up, Griz?"

The cat rubbed against Meredith's shin in response.

Meredith hefted the stack of newspapers and carried them toward the door. She looked back at Grizabella. "Are you coming?"

The cat sat down and licked one paw.

"Suit yourself." Meredith went down the stairs. Suddenly, Grizabella raced passed her, leaving Meredith chuckling at her quixotic feline.

She shifted the weight of her load to carry it a little more easily and finished traversing the steps. After depositing the stack with the recycling on the back porch, she returned to the attic to retrieve the books. She'd decided to donate the tomes to the historic society in town as most of them were very old, even antique. She bent to scoop up an armload but dropped them in a heap. When she reached to retrieve them, she noticed a piece of paper jutting from between the pages of one black leather-bound book. Pulling the book from the pile, she carefully slipped the yellowed paper from between the pages. She unfolded it. A letter. From Grace.

September 3, 1861

Dear Joe,

I only have a minute to dash off this note to you before the kind lieutenant said he must leave for Huntsville and the mail train there. Your kindness and attention to my petty desires is most appreciated. Thank you for remembering to send my favorite perfume all the way from Atlanta. If you hadn't spoiled me last year with my first bottle of Midnight Honeysuckle Rose, you wouldn't have needed to bother to make the purchase and have it delivered to me. Take care to return to us in one piece, and we will endeavor to also keep Twin Oaks in one piece until your return.

Your adoring sister,
Grace

Meredith read the short letter twice. Midnight Honeysuckle Rose. *Honeysuckle.* Her legs folded beneath her, and she plunked onto the floor. Grace's perfume had honeysuckle in it. What an odd coincidence.

Now where had she heard there are no coincidences in life? What did it mean, then, that her ancestor's perfume included the same scent as the mysterious odor she smelled in the house?

Folding the letter carefully, she tucked it inside the cover of the top book and picked up several to carry downstairs. She couldn't believe there had been another letter, one her Grandma must have missed in her previous research efforts. She started down the stairs again, her thoughts moving at lightning speed. What if she'd not noticed the bit of yellowed paper? She may never have known about the perfume. Were there other letters tucked inside the books?

She hurried to the parlor and set the small stack on the coffee table. One by one she lifted each book and riffled the pages. Disappointed, she found nothing. But there were more books still in the attic. She took the stairs two at a time.

She was disappointed yet again, though. None of the books held any other tidbits tucked inside. Not even a pressed flower. She carried the rest of the books to the parlor and added them to the pile.

"What are you doing?" Paulette paused in the open doorway, a laundry basket propped on one hip.

"Getting ready to donate these old books." Meredith waved a hand in the direction of the stack.

Paulette dropped the basket to the floor with a *whump*, walked to the table, and lifted one of the books. She opened it, scanned the title page, and then looked at Meredith. "Why? This one was Grandma's."

"So? It's only an old book lying around collecting dust. Who cares if it was read by somebody we know?"

"Really, Meredith, sometimes you, who love all things historical, make no sense." Paulette returned her attention to the book in her hands, carefully turning the pages. "Grandma made notes throughout this one. I wonder if she did in any of the others as well."

Meredith froze. Why hadn't she thought to look more closely? She hated to admit it, but having her sister around helped her in ways she hadn't expected. First the genealogical research, and now by preventing a huge mistake. "Let me see."

"Oh, now you care." Paulette quirked a brow as Meredith snatched the book from her.

"I'd looked through them for any slips of paper, after I found a letter from Grace to Joe tucked inside one." She flipped through the pages, her grandmother's lightly penciled commentary piquing her interest. She glanced at the cover, noting the title. These weren't just old books, but rather more local histories. Setting the book to one side, she grabbed up another and began searching through it.

"Glad to help." Paulette picked up a red leather-bound book and read through it. "At least my coming here hasn't been all bad."

Meredith paused in her reading. Paulette was right, for once. Having her around hadn't led to strangling her as she'd feared. "Seems like old times, doesn't it?"

"I wouldn't go quite that far down memory lane." Paulette replaced the book she'd been reading and shot a lopsided grin in Meredith's direction. "But maybe we can work together for a change."

"Depends on what your goal is, because if it conflicts with mine, then it won't work." Meredith closed the memoir in her hands and picked up the next book. It was apparent her grandmother had kept them for a precise reason, one she wasn't altogether certain of yet. "I'm hoping Grandma's notes will help me figure out what happened to our missing great-great-great-aunt. Then I can get on with the rest of the plan."

"Damn it all." Paulette shook her head and frowned. "I still think you need to reconsider your scheme. Destroying our heritage—this elegant, historic building—won't bring back Willy. Didn't he love architecture as much as you? Would he really want you to go through with this harebrained idea?"

Meredith slowly stacked the last book, trailing a finger along its cover as she tried to recall Willy's face. She could make out the general outline, but the details had faded like an old photograph. His features in her mind's eye had blurred, leaving behind only the trace of his image. Her gaze saw through the mental vision and lighted upon Grandma's rocking chair.

The very chair where her grandmother had sewn for years, decades. The arms of the chair had served as pincushions at times, holding a threaded needle between projects. Meredith walked over to the chair and sank down on the plush seat. The graceful armrests had been carved in the shape of a goose's neck, a long bill touching the base of the throat to form handles. Those handles were worn from Grandma's hands resting upon them. Grandma had rocked her own children to sleep sitting in this very chair. She pushed back and set the chair into motion. Grandma loved to rest in this chair, telling her grandchildren family stories of generations past. The plantation house and surrounding acres had been a character in each of them as the family members in the stories changed over time. Stories that reached down to when Meredith's own parents were young and lived in the house.

The light reflected off the gold band she still wore. The one Willy placed there to symbolize their love. Until death. An undying love had ended abruptly. She fingered the ring with her other hand. She sighed, knowing it was time to move forward.

Paulette cleared her throat. "Well?"

"I hear you, but…" Meredith looked at her sister and swallowed the lump in her throat. "What else can I do?"

Later that afternoon Meredith wandered into the kitchen to fetch some cold lemonade. She retrieved a glass and poured the pale yellow liquid into it. The sweet, lemony scent made her mouth water. Paulette walked in as Meredith set the pitcher onto the table and lifted the glass to take a sip.

"Guess what?" Paulette sashayed to the cabinet and grabbed another glass, plunking it down beside the pitcher.

"I give." Meredith took the hint and poured lemonade into the waiting vessel.

"I called our folks." Her smile was not camouflaged by the sip Paulette took from the glass.

"You did what?" *Oh no. Not now.* Meredith didn't need more visitors in the midst of everything else. She scraped a chair out and flopped onto it.

Paulette set her glass on the table and let her grin show. "Mom and Dad were thrilled with the idea of coming back for a long weekend. They'll be here this afternoon."

"I can't believe you would do such a thing. I knew it was a mistake to have you stay." Meredith slammed a hand onto the kitchen table, making the salt and pepper shakers as well as the stems of daffodils in the cut-glass vase do a little dance. "I'm trying to clear out the house, not inhabit it. This is my house, and you're not entitled to invite anyone over to stay. Got it?"

"It's our folks; why can't I?" Paulette stared her down.

"B-because it's not your decision to make. Damn it, Paulette." She rubbed a hand over her face and then shook her head at her sister. She didn't want to admit it, but she'd thought of doing the same thing. A grin twitched onto her lips. "Besides, I was going to call them."

A smirk flitted across Paulette's face. She walked to the fridge and peered inside, the cold air rushing across the kitchen floor to cool Meredith's bare toes. Retrieving an apple, she pushed the door shut and turned to face Meredith.

"I'm glad you agree it was a brilliant idea." Paulette took a bite of the red fruit. "After all, we haven't all been together in ages."

Meredith refused to feel guilty about that fact. She'd tried to gather her family together years before, but between Paulette's continual financial shortfall and her parents' globetrotting, a family reunion had proved impossible to orchestrate. Well, until now. Maybe it wasn't such a bad idea after all. Dad had contacts in the recycling world who would likely love to snatch up the marble fireplaces and the solid pine floorboards, if nothing else. Her mom, too, would know which antiques were worth auctioning or donating. Yes, Paulette did have a pretty good idea in seeking their help.

"We'll need to clean another room upstairs for them to use." Meredith pushed up from her seat. "I'll see if Meg has time. Can you check the grocery status? I may need to make a run to Edna's."

"Will do. You'll need to stop at the liquor store as well. After all, we must have plenty of whiskey for Dad and wine coolers for Mom too." Paulette moved to the pantry and pulled the door open. "Oh, we'll need potato chips and mixed nuts. You know how they like to snack."

"Didn't I say this was a bad idea? They'll eat us out of house and home." Meredith shook her head, but a smile found its way to her lips. "I don't care if it will be good to see them again. It's still a lot of work to make ready for them. They can be so demanding and all."

Paulette threw a smile over her shoulder. "I knew you'd come around."

"Don't get any other bright ideas without telling me first, okay?" Meredith dialed Meg's phone number.

"La-la-la, I can't hear you," Paulette sang, her head stuck back in the pantry's depths.

When Meg answered, Meredith relayed her request and then hung up the phone. "Meg will be here in a few minutes. So what else do I need at the store?"

Between the two of them, they made a quick grocery list. Meredith grabbed her purse and keys. "I'll be back shortly. While I'm gone, can you straighten up the double parlor? We'll need more seats when our folks get here."

"Aye-aye, Captain." Paulette mock-saluted as Meredith walked out the door.

The drive into Roseville seemed to pass in a flash. Along the way, the fields boasted neat rows of corn or cotton.

She'd not paid much attention on previous trips, but the green of the crops seemed bright and clear. The cloudless blue sky appeared nearly as intense as Max's eyes. She sighed. She simply did not need to be thinking about him. He was nothing but a kink in the wrecking-ball chain.

Edna's wasn't very busy this early on a Thursday afternoon. Steering her car into a parking spot near the entrance, she locked her door and headed inside, grocery list pinched between fingers and thumb. She snagged a buggy and started making her way up and down the aisles. As she turned at the end of the pasta-and-sauces aisle, Max waved to her.

"Fancy running into you here," Max said, joining her. "I was about to call you too."

"Shouldn't you be in court or something?" Meredith placed a jar of marinara sauce in the buggy. "It's the middle of the day."

"I had an appointment at the high school." Max picked up a box of spaghetti noodles and added it to Meredith's buggy. "You'll need some of this to go with the sauce."

"Thanks. But is something wrong at the school?" Meredith fidgeted as he did the guy thing; the once-over when a man meets a woman. She hadn't bothered with changing from shorts, tee, and flip-flops or pulling up her hair. She squirmed inside, feeling exposed and vulnerable under his scrutiny.

"Not a thing." He grinned, seeming to understand he made her uncomfortable. "We had a rehearsal, and I thought of you. I was going to call you to invite you to a concert tomorrow night. Unless, of course, you'll be busy tearing down Twin Oaks."

"Shhh." Meredith darted a glance about her, assessing how close other ears may be. "Don't say that out loud."

Max cocked a brow and smiled. "Why? Ashamed of yourself?"

"I don't need the whole town knowing my business."

"So, if you're not otherwise occupied, want to hear some good music with me?"

"You mean, a date?" She wished she'd taken at least a little time with her appearance before dashing out the door. Not that she really cared what she looked like, given she wasn't in the market for a man. Still, she liked to put her best foot through the door first.

"No, just a friendly evening out with a large group." Max shifted the basket in his left hand to his right. "The high school choir and jazz band give a spring concert, and it's tomorrow and Saturday nights. Want to come hear them? They're really good."

"My parents are coming into town today from Memphis, a surprise visit, so I'm not sure I can get away."

"Bring them along. Paulette too." Max snagged a bottle of grated parmesan cheese and put it in Meredith's buggy.

"Good catch, I'd have forgotten that." He added things to her buggy with the ease and familiarity of a married couple. His action seemed natural and right despite the apparent oddity of it. Meredith studied the boyish grin on Max's face, an expression of anticipation and expectation. He'd invited not only her but her entire family, most of whom she hadn't seen in ages, to a concert. A family outing, how quaint. "I'll see if they'd like to, but don't count on it."

"You may enjoy the accompanist." Max shifted his weight, bringing him closer to her. "I'll be on piano."

"You play? I'd never have guessed." Meredith looked at him with new interest. "What kind of music are we talking about?"

"My favorite is classical, but of course the choir can't sing to that." He leaned toward her conspiratorially. "So I've had to agree to play pop tunes and songs from favorite musicals mixed with some R&B."

"No hip-hop?" She stepped to one side to let an elderly

woman pass. The additional space between her and Max enabled her to breathe again.

"Sadly, no, but I am going to accompany an up-and-coming trumpeter in the jazz band. Sue's grandson." Max closed the distance between them. "Please try to come. The concert is the highlight each spring."

His cologne reminded her of hiking deep in the woods, earthy and tangy combined. His eyes seemed to reflect the sky she'd seen on her drive into town. And that mouth, God, what a kissable mouth he had. Heat rose in her cheeks at the memory of their brief intimate moments together. Resisting with all her being the sudden compulsion to touch him, to repeat their kisses, Meredith shrugged. "Why not? It might even be fun."

The windows sparkled after Paulette's and Meg's cleaning frenzy. Meredith turned her car into the driveway. The front double doors stood wide open. Hopefully, the cat was taking her afternoon nap and thus stayed inside. Paulette emerged onto the porch and waved. A chill swept through Meredith at the thought of standing on the front porch. She'd nearly forgotten the intense compulsion to open the door the night Max had burst into the house. Was Paulette having the same experience? She drove around back and parked the car and then gathered up the grocery sacks.

Grizabella met her in the kitchen with a plaintive meow. Seeing her shot relief through Meredith. But the doors needed to be closed before the front-declawed feline ventured outside. Dropping the bags on the counter, Meredith strode through the house. As she drew near to the open doors, she saw Paulette placing a folding chair beside a small table and a matching chair. Dragging the doors closed behind her, she stepped cautiously onto the porch.

"What's going on?" She folded her arms against the sudden chill sweeping over her.

"Folks should arrive soon, and I thought it would be fun to wait for them out here." Paulette opened her arms wide, encompassing the expansive yard and fenced lake, the drive reaching to the highway a quarter mile away. "Like old times."

"All this reminiscing…" Meredith let her gaze travel across the span. The grass needed cutting, and the gravel drive could use more stone. A flock of mallard ducks floated on the water. The immense trees evoked memories of hide-and-seek and baseball games. Yet her senses tuned to the cool spring air surrounding them.

Paulette sank into one of the strapped chairs and crossed her legs. "I love this view."

"Yes, it's stunning." Meredith gazed out over the yard for another moment and then sat in the other chair. The groceries could wait a few minutes. She crossed her ankles and tried to relax back against the green and yellow vinyl straps, but a deep-seated tension knotted her insides. Something was off, but she couldn't put her finger on it. She inhaled but didn't detect the sweet scent she'd come to expect.

"I've always wondered," Paulette murmured, snaring Meredith's attention, "whether you ever saw her."

"Who?" Meredith wrapped her arms around her waist. She suspected she knew the answer to that question, given recent sightings.

"It's silly, actually." Paulette blew out her breath, making her bangs lift and fall.

"Go on."

"When I was much younger, I used to have dreams about this beautiful yet sad woman."

"In a blue ball gown?" The chill inside Meredith threatened to rattle her teeth.

"You too?" Paulette's expression intensified.

"At least I'm not the only one." Relief eased through Meredith, but it raised a bigger question. "Was it a dream or—"

"A ghost?" Paulette asked. "I don't know. Either way, I've always been drawn to this porch and this view. There's something compelling about being here, in this spot. But also a sense of expectation, like waiting for a loved one to return home. You know?"

"Yes, I've been compelled to be out here before as well." She chuckled, releasing nervous energy. "I don't understand why sometimes I feel anxious and angry."

Paulette sprang to her feet. "Me, either. Maybe it's these giant columns calling to us. Trying to lend us some of their solid strength."

Meredith shook her head. "They're hollow, so no luck with that hope."

Paulette peered up the height of the columns on each side of the porch steps. "They look so wide; they must be."

"When I built my replica of Twin Oaks, Dad told me about how they made them. They were built in pieces and shipped here from up north. The cost of creating and shipping solid columns would have been prohibitive. That's the only thing I was required to compromise on in my dollhouse. I had to make them from dowel rods because Dad said it would be easier even though not accurate."

Paulette approached a column and examined it. Then she used her open palm to smack it once, and then again. "This one sounds solid."

Meredith sighed. "You don't believe me?"

In response, Paulette moved to the next column and smacked it as well. "Solid, definitely."

Meredith shook her head as she rose to her feet. "Nope. Sorry, but Dad said so. He should know, what with being in construction and reconstruction."

"Even Dad's not right all the time." Paulette smacked each, with the same result.

Meredith moved to the last one. "Here, I'll prove it to you." She raised her hand and smacked the column. But instead of the same sound, Meredith's hit didn't echo like the others had.

"What did you do different? Here, let me." Paulette sashayed to where Meredith stood. She raised her hand and smacked the column.

"Why does it sound deeper?" Meredith searched her brain for a plausible reason but came up empty. No way would they have built only one solid column. She eyed the structure standing twenty feet tall and three feet in diameter. The concept of trying to move such a heavy and cumbersome object over land via wagon or even train was mind-boggling.

The crunch of tires on gravel had them both turning to scan the yard to the mouth of the driveway. A steel-gray SUV pulled slowly up the stone road.

"They're here." Paulette skipped down the steps and hurried to meet the car.

Meredith glanced at the odd column, the chill inside spreading when she smelled honeysuckle. She tore herself away and went to greet her parents.

Chapter Thirteen

"What happened here?" Tall and broad, the gray-haired man assessed the exterior of the house, fists propped on his hips as his head swiveled up, down, left, and right.

"Nothing, Dad." Meredith strode up beside Brock O'Connell. "Yet, anyway."

"Darling, you know how he gets," Dina O'Connell said, emerging from the gray SUV.

"Hi, Mom. You look great. Traveling the world suits you." Meredith hugged her mom, her robust frame comforting.

"I do love being free to come and go," Dina said.

"What are you going to do about this?" Brock said, brows drawn together, accusing finger pointed at the sill board resting on the stone foundation.

"What are you talking about?" Paulette asked, peering at the building. "I don't see anything wrong."

"He's talking about the fact that the lower boards are beginning to rot and should be replaced." Meredith walked to the foundation on the side of the house and pointed to the evidence. "See here. The wood is warped, probably from a leak somewhere along the joint between the rock foundation and the siding."

"I have my tools in the truck." Brock marched up beside her. "Do you have the boards, or should I go into the lumber yard and pick some up?"

"You just got here. Don't worry about it, Dad," Meredith said. "It won't matter in the long run."

He turned puzzled eyes to look at her. "Why would you not want to fix it? If we do it quickly, the damage will be minimized."

"Take off your construction hat, Dad," Paulette said, bitterness in her voice. "She's planning to raze the place."

Meredith shot her sister a look she hoped would shut her up. She hadn't wanted to reveal her intentions quite so soon after her parents arrived. Rather, she'd wait until they'd had a chance to catch up on what was happening with each of them. A chance for Meredith to help them follow her precisely ordered, logical plan.

"Raise it up? It's already built." His frown deepened. "I'm confused."

"Not raise up," Meredith said, her words measured. "Raze flat."

"The hell you say." Her dad's brows rose so high, she was surprised they stayed attached to his face.

Her mother gasped and stared at her as though Meredith had lost her mind. How could she make them understand? She hadn't seen them in person for years, and now that they were here, they learn that their architect daughter intended to destroy their family home. They hadn't been here for five minutes and already the tension shimmered in the spring air.

"What do you mean, raze it?" Dina asked slowly. "You cannot possibly be serious."

"Sadly, she is." Paulette opened her palms to the spring sky. "She feels that returning the property to nature will help her move on, to overcome the grief and pain of losing Willy." Paulette crossed her arms, a familiar gesture by now. "Not that I agree with her, but there it is."

Paulette, of all people, had come to her rescue. Sort of.

Her father recovered first, snapping his mouth closed into a flat line. "You've obviously lost your mind, young lady. I don't care what you think you're going to do. I'll not allow you to destroy our family's heritage."

"Unfortunately, Dad, it's hers to do with as she wishes," Paulette said, frowning. "The lawyer dude, Max, said so. The will didn't specify any limitations for what she could do with it. Not that he agrees with her ideas, either."

"Max?" Dina asked, focusing on Paulette. "He's the lawyer? Good."

"You know him?" Meredith shouldn't be surprised, but somehow she'd thought they wouldn't stay in touch with who was who in the small town of Roseville.

"Of course. Mother spoke very highly of him." Dina shook her head, tears loitering in the corners of her eyes. She swiped them away and drew in a ragged breath. "Mother is probably rolling over in her grave at the very idea that you'd even consider—I can't even say it. How could you even contemplate such a thing? Do you realize what you'd do to this family with your selfish actions?"

"I'll contest the will, that's what I'll do," Brock fumed. "This can't happen. I should be the rightful heir, and no court in the land would deny me."

Looking at it from her family's viewpoint, Meredith would feel the same way. But from inside, where the black hole of pain and loss waited to be filled in, like the rock foundation of this house, she couldn't see any other way to end the journey through grief and move on. If only there was another way.

"Speaking of Max, he's invited us to the high school concert tomorrow night." Maybe changing the subject would help. She hoped. Three pair of eyes blinked at her. "He's playing the piano." As if that explained her reasoning perfectly. She sighed at the unbelieving stares aimed in her direction.

"Changing the subject doesn't make it go away." Paulette glared at her. "You'll have to face the fact nobody agrees with your atrocious plan."

"Nobody has offered another way to handle the grief I carry inside like a cancer, either." Meredith shrugged. "I've delayed my plans because I want to solve the mystery of great-great-great-auntie Grace's disappearance. But it's only a delay, not a cancellation."

"Who's Grace?" Brock asked, pacing. "Who the hell cares about her?"

Meredith summarized what she had discovered in the journals and letters thus far. "I don't believe she left willingly, but that's a gut feeling more than anything else."

Could there be a connection between the occasions of the honeysuckle scent floating on the air and the fact Grace used to wear a similar perfume? After all this time, how was it even a possibility? She kept mum on her speculations. Her family already thought she'd become daft. Why give them more ammunition?

"Why don't we go inside?" Paulette suggested. "Meg should have your room ready. We can gather in the double parlor after you settle in and have some lemonade and discuss all this."

"Okay with me, but don't think we're letting little Miss Demolition Expert off the hook regarding her intentions. Delayed or not." Brock stomped over to the back doors of the truck, pulled them open, and withdrew two large suitcases and two matching smaller ones.

Looks like they plan to stay awhile. Meredith sighed and shook her head. "Fine. I'll meet you inside in a few minutes. First, I have a little mystery I'd like to solve."

"Another one?" Brock asked. "What this time?"

"Before you arrived, we discovered one of the columns

sounds different when we bang on it. Any idea, Oh Construction Guru, why?" Meredith cocked her head to one side as she puzzled in her mind over possible reasons for the column to not sound as hollow as the others.

"While you two work on that," Dina said, snagging her bags from Brock's lax grip, "I'm going in. I haven't seen Meg in ages."

"Let me carry one for you." Paulette took the heavier suitcase and led the way inside.

Meredith started toward the front of the house, Brock trailing behind her, still carrying the two remaining suitcases. When they reached the porch, he dropped them with a *thud* onto the floorboards. "Show me what you mean."

Meredith walked to the farthest column and banged on it. "This one has a nice ringing sound." She moved to the next column. "As does this one and the next." She demonstrated to him as she spoke. "But this one on the end is different. It doesn't echo as much."

She pounded on the last column, and the sound died away like a muted note on a piano. He pursed his lips in thought as he repeated her experiment with each column, finding the same result.

"Interesting. I wonder if there's something in there. Maybe an animal crawled inside?"

"How would an animal find its way in?" Meredith examined the exterior of the column from bottom to top. "It's sealed at the bottom, and there's a cornice at the top to seal it off up there as well."

"But maybe the top of the cornice wasn't always sealed."

She gazed at the ornately decorated top of the column. "What if the cornice is hollow as well? Could something fall through it and into the base, do you think?"

Brock shrugged. "It's possible, I suppose. Does it really matter?"

Meredith hugged herself, trying to fend off the chill sweeping through her. This odd column held a clue to the mystery of Grace's whereabouts. The thought entered her mind as a fact. How did she know? Cold air brushed her legs, raising goose bumps on her skin. "Do you have your jigsaw with you?"

"You want to cut it open?" Brock stared at her, eyes wide yet again. "You really have lost your mind."

"A little hole." Meredith unwound her arms from her waist. She approached the column and with one finger drew an imaginary rectangle. "Merely twelve by six inches. Not big enough to compromise its integrity, but enough to see if there is anything inside."

Max had returned to his office after depositing his few groceries at home. His need to know all he could about the mysterious Meredith compelled him to close his office door and open his laptop. His search yielded an array of links that had taken a while to sort through. He reread the *Architecture Chronicle* article slowly, understanding dawning. Meredith's husband, William "Willy" Reed, had been killed by some guy over the astronomical amount of twenty bucks in his wallet. The shot that killed the renowned landscape architect preceded one that struck Meredith in the stomach. She'd been rushed to the hospital, her life at risk due to the amount of blood she'd lost. Willy died at the scene.

He lowered the lid of his laptop computer and sank against the cushions of the leather sofa in his office. She really did want to bury the past, but demolishing Twin Oaks wouldn't help her move on. Closing a door on painful events instead of burying them allowed one to live without ever truly forgetting.

He'd unearthed a plethora of articles in various professional journals and national newspapers touting her fresh and innovative designs. She'd blueprinted everything from bungalows to mansions for billionaires. She'd been the belle of the building industry. Until her husband of three years, at the prime of his life, was killed in cold blood by some punk who was never brought to justice.

Max clenched his hand into a fist and beat it rhythmically on the lid of his laptop. One and two and three. He'd like to find the bastard and bring him before a judge for the pain and grief he'd caused Meredith. She did not deserve to have her life's dreams and plans uprooted in such a horrific way. Damn lowlife. Because of delinquents like the creep, Max focused on noncriminal cases. He lost his temper each time he contemplated the damage caused by unthinking, uncaring people.

Every crime came back to one point. People hurt each other, and the injured party demanded recompense. Maybe monetary penalties. Maybe revenge. Maybe, like Meredith, to lash out against expectations to create a new path for her own life.

That being the case, he could help her find a path. Help her walk away from the pain and focus on tomorrow without destroying yesterday. She possessed too much talent, spunk, and integrity to turn her back on her creative endeavors in order to destroy others' works. Helping her would also provide him an excuse to spend more time with her. To know her as an architect instead of a demolition expert. As a beautiful, evocative woman instead of an angry, prickly widow. He'd relish the opportunity to be with her more often, speak with her about ways to deal with the grieving process. She'd occupied his thoughts long enough. In fact, he'd follow up on her suggestion.

He set aside his laptop and strode to the calendar blotter on his desk. His scribbled notes bespoke of the many irons he had poked into various fires. He grabbed his pen and added "start dating Meredith" on the first night of the high school concert. He'd begin with asking her out to a private place. He tapped the pen against his chin. Assuming she'd agree to go with him, of course. He laid the pen down and picked up the desk phone, dialing her number from memory.

"Hey, Meredith, can you talk?"

"I've got a minute."

"I'll keep this brief. Would you care to join me for dinner after the concert tomorrow night?

"I, uh… Over here, right about there. No, a little to the left. That's it. Sorry, Max, what were you saying?"

"What's going on?" Max stilled the pen, intent on hearing the scraping and shuffling in the background on Meredith's end.

"Just a little investigative demolition, nothing to worry about."

"Damn it, Meredith, we talked about this." Max cringed. "You're not already taking Twin Oaks apart, are you?"

"I'm merely trying to solve a little mystery. Nobody will ever know. Dinner tomorrow would be okay, I guess. We can talk about the Register and what you're doing about it."

That would be a very short conversation. He'd done nothing about removing the house from the Register because in the long run it made no difference. If Meredith wanted to destroy the house, she had the legal right to do so. At least for another ten days or so. But he hoped to help her see how immoral such an act would be. How taking it apart would not put her life back together again. Either way, time was draining away faster than he liked, and he had to do something to try to plug the drain.

"Fine. Meet me in the music room after the concert, and we'll go try the new steak house—the one with the deck overlooking the river."

"Perfect. I'll see you then." Her voice grew distant, and

right before the line went dead, Max heard her say, "You could cut there…"

"Why does it matter so much to you?" Brock walked up to stand beside Meredith. He peered at her. "You're shivering. Are you cold?"

"A little. But I have to know." She slipped her phone back into her pocket, choosing to put off contemplating Max's motives for asking her on a date. *A real date.* And she'd accepted without thinking, without considering being alone with the man. Her resolve must have tripped, but she could do something about that. "I can't explain, but I know there's something relevant inside."

"Come here." Brock wrapped his arms around her in a bear hug. "You're chilled. Let me help you go inside where it's warm."

She shrugged him off and shook her head. "Please, Dad."

He gazed at her a long moment, and then slowly nodded. "One small hole, that's all I'm agreeing to do."

Without another word he sauntered in his loose-hipped way down the steps and to his vehicle, where he retrieved his jigsaw and attached the battery pack. Before long he had the thin blade ready to pierce the exterior skin of the column. Meredith stood to one side, trying to quell the shivers racing through her. The whir of the small engine obliterated the sounds of the birds and the insects as the saw bit into the wood. Once the rectangular hole was outlined, Brock stopped the blade. The sudden silence shocked her ears. Her father laid down the saw and carefully pried the inset out of the column.

He peered inside. "There's something in there all right." He waved her closer.

Meredith approached cautiously and leaned down to

look into the hole. Though dimly lit by the incision, she made out the glint of what appeared to be very tarnished silver and a pile of dusty blue fabric. The same color as the dress worn by the Lady in Blue. She inhaled and nearly vomited when she smelled the sweet scent of honeysuckle and roses.

"No." It couldn't be. The terror a person would have endured in such a place made dark spots form before her eyes. No way could this happen. Could it? She placed a hand against the column to steady her quaking knees while tears streamed down her face. "It's Grace. It has to be. But how did she end up in there?"

Chapter Fourteen

Gravel pinged the underside of Max's truck as he steered the vehicle into the driveway of Twin Oaks. Slowing to avoid damage to the paint, he tapped a staccato rhythm on the steering wheel. Meredith's voice had quavered and then steadied when she'd phoned him several minutes after he'd invited her to dinner. The mystery she'd been working to solve apparently involved bones and a dress and a silver tea service. In one of the impressive columns standing sentry for generations. She'd wanted to know what they should do, and he'd told her to leave everything in place. He'd made a call to the county sheriff and the medical examiner's office to relay the findings. The officials should be arriving shortly to collect the remains.

He parked beside a steel-gray Lincoln Navigator, a beautiful piece of machinery that made his mouth drool. He darted a glance back at his own F-150 XLT, fully decked out but not nearly as elegant as the SUV. Maybe when he made senior partner, he'd trade in his pick-'em-up truck for something more refined. But he liked his truck. He hurried to the back door. He knocked on the doorjamb, avoiding the door itself since he had forgotten to locate the hardware needed to repair the frame. But he'd tackle the job first thing Monday.

He knocked a second time and then let himself in. "Hello?"

Footsteps hurried down the hall toward him. He crossed the kitchen, reaching the door as Meredith pushed through it.

"Max." Meredith's expression danced before him, her eyes alive in a way he'd not seen before. Their intensity drew him in; he could gaze into them forever. "Can you believe it?"

"It does stretch the imagination." Her beauty stretched his credulity as well. He heard his heartbeat in his ears, pulsing like the rush of a river heading toward a falls. Her lightly freckled cheeks glowed with excitement, eyes animated, lips perfectly shaped for kissing. So he did.

When his lips met hers, she didn't protest. Her eyes closed for a moment before flying open. He didn't end the press of their lips for another heartbeat. When he did, a flick of her tongue moistened her lips, first upper, then lower. He smiled, a deep sense of peace emerging inside. "I needed you."

"Max…"

He stopped her words with a finger laid to her mouth. "Hold that thought. Now you have a hint of what I plan for later. So tell me, what's this about a body?"

"Remains, definitely. Looks like human bones to me. Especially since there's a dress. And jewelry, I think." She gripped his arms and stared at him with wide eyes. "Oh my goodness, it's the blue dress both Paulette and I have seen in our dreams since we were kids. How? What's going on?"

"That's what I'm here to help figure out, sweetheart." He reached for her hand and squeezed it. "I'm with you every step until we know who it is who ended up buried alive in that place."

"It's so Poe-like, isn't it?" She shuddered. "How dreadful for the poor woman. I can't bear to think what she went through."

"Don't torture yourself, Meredith." He lifted her chin with one finger. "The sheriff and the ME are on their way. They'll help us sort this out."

"Come on, everyone's in the main parlor."

"Everyone?" Max followed dumbly. Stunned first by the vibrant beauty leading him through the hallways to the front right of the house and then again by the intensity of the kiss they'd shared. Voices drifted down the hall toward them. Who, exactly, was everyone? Meg. Paulette. Sean, perhaps? Who else? Meredith's luscious hips swinging in front of him with each step distracted him momentarily. What was that country song? The "Badonkadonk"? Fit her motion perfectly. They stopped, and he glanced into the parlor.

She paused at the doorway. "Hey, look who finally deigned to honor us with his presence."

Her family sat chatting among themselves until they noticed Max behind Meredith. They stared at the pair for a moment before Brock stood and crossed the room to shake hands. "Max, how have you been?"

"Good, good." Max returned the greeting, feeling the strength of the hand gripping his own and glad he'd been exercising his fingers on the keyboards. Otherwise, the handshake would have crippled him.

"Max called the authorities." Meredith moved into the room and perched on one of the matching flowered settees positioned to face each other. "They should arrive soon. What do we tell them?"

"We'll show them what we found." Brock resumed his seat in one flanking overstuffed wingback chair, waving a hand at an identical chair across from him. "Max, have a seat."

Max sank onto the chair. "Right, and the ME will collect the remains."

Meredith looked shocked. "What? Why?"

"They have to verify no crime has been committed and the remains aren't Native American." Max rubbed his hands on his pant legs.

"But we know who was buried alive in that awful place." Meredith glanced at Paulette. "Don't we?"

Paulette shrugged. "No, we don't know for certain." She shivered. "I can't even let myself contemplate dying in such a way."

"What all did you find in there?" Max relaxed against the chair, crossing one ankle over his knee. He looked at Meredith. "What makes you believe it's Grace?"

"The blue dress, mainly." Meredith twined her fingers together and shoved her hands between her knees as she darted a glance at Paulette. "And the honeysuckle."

"Honeysuckle?" Max asked.

Meredith chuckled. "It will sound nuts to you all, I'm sure." She took a deep breath and released it slowly. "I read that Grandpa Joe sent her perfume with rose and honeysuckle essence in it. If she was buried alive in the column, and thus has been haunting Twin Oaks ever since, it would explain why I smell honeysuckle so often. Wouldn't it?"

Max blinked and sat up straight. "Haunted? You think Twin Oaks is haunted?"

Meredith nodded, her hair flowing around her excited eyes, dancing against her chin. "It explains everything. Seeing her ghost. Smelling her perfume. The inexplicable desire to go to the front porch, right where her bones waited to be discovered."

"But, Meredith, you can't believe in ghosts." Brock stood up and slowly paced across the oriental carpet boasting bold reds, blues, and golds. "Nobody believes in spirits these days."

"That's not true, Dad." Meredith rose and caught hold of her father's arm, bringing him to a standstill. "Lots of folks believe in them, including me. There are many unexplained phenomena in this world."

Brock patted Meredith's hand resting on his arm. "If it makes you feel better, honey, then believe what you will."

Did ghosts exist? Many times in his own life, Max had experienced an unexplainable occurrence. The feeling of being watched. An inexplicable coincidence. Motion caught out of the corner of his eye, but when he turned, he saw nothing unusual or that could explain what he had imagined. Objects seemingly relocating themselves when he wasn't looking. But ghosts? Gremlins? Borrowers? Or simply a faulty memory?

Meredith shook her head and laughed. "You don't have to agree with me, Dad, but I do firmly believe the dress in the column belongs to Grace and that she wanted me to find her. But what I don't understand is how she ended up in the bottom of it with Grandpa Joe's missing silver tea service tied to her waist with ropes."

"You didn't tell me about the ropes." Max ran a hand over his chin. "We all know people hid their valuables during the war to protect them from the Yankees coming through…"

"You think she was trying to protect the silver?" Paulette asked.

"Most likely. The Yankees encamped on the front lawn in 1862 en route to capture Huntsville." Max tapped his fingers on the armrest.

"But she couldn't have lowered herself into the column," Dina said. "She'd need help."

Meredith sprang to her feet, snapping her fingers and drawing everyone's attention. "Edith."

"Wonder if Anson helped as well?" Paulette jumped up beside Meredith.

"Oh! What if the future husband and wife convinced Grace to deposit the silver in the column for safekeeping and then left her there?" Meredith mused.

"Dropped her?" Paulette said, horror lacing her voice.

"Even if the rope merely slipped from their grasp," Meredith said, "if it were a crime of opportunity and not premeditated, they would still be guilty of abandoning her to a dreadful fate."

"Whoa. Slow down." Brock ran a hand through his graying hair. "How would they expect to retrieve the silver once it was at the bottom?"

"The same way we did. Cut it open." Meredith roamed the room, from end to end of the carpet and back again.

"It seems so drastic." Dina stood and laid a hand on Meredith's arm, stopping her daughter's pacing. "I can't imagine being desperate enough to resort to such measures."

"I know; it gives me the willies to contemplate." Paulette shuddered to prove her point.

"People were desperate during the war." Max scanned the faces gazing at him expectantly. "Everything the Rebels believed in, worked for, and then fought for was at stake. So many died fighting their own family, it's hard to fathom."

A knock on the front door interrupted Max's explanation. As Meredith hurried to answer the summons, Max noted the others in the room had fallen silent, waiting. Perhaps worrying about what all of this meant to them. To the future of Twin Oaks. Had Mrs. O'Connell known about the ghost? She'd never mentioned it to him, if so. Would he have believed her, or thought her nutso? What of Meredith?

After the sheriff and ME left with the skeleton and clothing, including pale blue silk slippers, Meredith hunched in a folding chair, elbows on knees, and stared at the enlarged hole in the column. They'd been forced to widen and deepen the opening in order to remove everything. Meg had carted the tea service and jewelry to the kitchen to polish them. The authorities allowed the items to remain at Twin Oaks, since even if a crime had occurred, based on the style of the dress and the maker's imprint on the silver service, it had occurred so long ago the perpetrators had also died by now.

Poor, poor Grace. Stuck in a vertical tomb, in the dark, alone. Left to die by her sister and the man they both loved. Or at least, that's the story that made the most sense. The worst part of the situation was nobody would ever really know what caused Grace to be trusting enough to venture into the column. What might Edith have told her to convince her to be lowered into such a dark place? Especially with the "manipulations" of Anson that Grace had commented upon to Grandpa Joe.

What if Paulette had been Edith? Would Meredith have trusted her? Could she trust her now?

Meredith reclined against the back of the chair, crossed her arms, and surveyed the valley beyond the six columns. The road cut through the fields at a fair distance from the porch. Grace's cries for help would not have been heard unless someone chanced to approach the plantation. During the fighting, an improbable event except for the duration of the troop occupations. With no food or water, she wouldn't have survived more than a few days. Days filled with terror and no hope of rescue, joined with the knowledge her sister left her to die.

She rubbed a hand on her cheek. No matter how much conniving Paulette managed, Meredith would never allow harm to befall her. She held no ill will against her sister. She simply needed to protect herself from barbed comments at her expense. To keep Paulette at arm's length. They'd get along fine that way.

The Adirondack chair creaked when Paulette settled onto the wooden seat. She set her cold glass of lemonade— already sweating from the high humidity—on the small table beside her and opened her old diary. This volume started when she was thirteen and spanned until age sixteen, according to the dates in the front cover. She started reading, reliving the troubled, angst-ridden years of being a teen. The multiple crises of a young woman in hindsight appeared as nothing compared to her current predicament.

Unmarried and pregnant with no good job prospects. Johnny, the one man she thought she'd spend the rest of her life with, no longer in the picture. Nobody beating down her door asking for her unique decorating schemes for their houses. Her vision tended to be eclectic rather than traditional, a hindrance to pleasing clients and thus to receiving payment. A baby, growing inside, depended on her. As a result, the cries of unfairness and confusion in her diary seemed petty in comparison.

She flipped a page and read the entry where she'd admitted to her diary she liked Brandon. How unfair that Meredith should like him first, so Paulette must relinquish him. A love triangle not unlike their ancestors. She closed her eyes, hearing the birds twittering in the trees, while imagining the intense emotions at play between Grace and Edith. Affairs of the heart and the associated emotions wouldn't have changed very much over time. People fell in and out of love, hurting each other in the process. The depth of the pain of losing a lover would always be in direct proportion to the duration of the relationship. Thus, she still smarted from Johnny's departure, though not as much as she might have if he'd been more demonstrative with his feelings for her.

Despite the fact she carried his child, she was better off without his lukewarm love, if she could call it such. He'd supported her in many ways, but for him, emotions stayed buried inside. Not to be aired in public, or private for that matter.

She sipped her drink, letting her gaze drift across the

yard. The caretaker's cottage, its cheery exterior surrounded by flowers and bushes, stood snugly against the edge of the open area behind the house. The rear porches, one on each floor, of Twin Oaks stood in shade so deep the country rocking chairs and sturdy tables on the first-floor porch were barely discernible. The upper porch held no furniture, the floor being the site where Meredith and Paulette slept on many hot summer nights. Sunlight sifted through the gathering clouds beyond the house, hinting at foul weather rolling into the area.

Paulette turned the page and stared at the drawing she'd made so many years ago. Two young women, each wearing a flowing prom dress, designed with colored pencil. The classic lines of the skirts reflected subtle tailoring that would make the fabric float and swish with each movement. So long ago she'd allowed her one real dream to fade into nothing more than distant memory.

Closing the book, she leaned her head against the tall back of the chair. Now what should she do with her life? All her schemes failed. She'd been reduced to coming begging to Meredith for housing, feeding, and even buying her books. She had nothing but a widening girth to show for the years she'd spent with Johnny.

She'd taken the first step by worming her way back into Twin Oaks. At least she had a welcoming roof over her head, unlike the cold atmosphere of the B&B. Here she could breathe, think. Her next step was to continue mending the rift between her and Meredith so they never ended up like Edith and Grace. They'd come to the brink, with their verbal sniping at each other and pushing each other farther and farther away. At least they'd not harmed the other physically. The emotional hurt would eventually ease with care, along with time and love.

Meredith needed to heal from the loss of her husband, which would also take time and love to manage. While

Paulette couldn't agree with the demolition of this beautiful house, she grasped the extent of Meredith's pain if she'd been driven to the point of even considering such a drastic measure. Paulette's sadness stemming from missing her boyfriend paled to the depth of grief stewing within Meredith. But she could help her sister work through this time in her life, to see a future without having a gaping hole inside.

She rose, gathered her things, and walked across the yard toward the kitchen. She had barely enough time to help Meredith prepare for her big date with Max.

Chapter Fifteen

The Navigator pulled into the high school parking lot; one of hundreds of other vehicles bringing families and friends to enjoy the annual concert. Meredith tugged on the bodice of the wrap dress Paulette had insisted she wear. She rubbed a hand across her neck to relieve the irritation of the unfamiliar fabric. She hadn't packed any dresses when she left Maryland, being more comfortable in jeans and a polo shirt, or shorts and a tee, than in a skirt and heels. Paulette flatly forbade her to wear such a casual outfit when it came to a first date with a handsome lawyer. Even if said lawyer was Max.

"Here we are." Brock shifted to park and killed the engine. He opened the door to slide out of the truck. "I haven't been to a concert like this since Paulette was in choir. When was that, seventh, eighth grade?"

"Try tenth." Paulette opened the driver's side passenger door and carefully stepped down from the SUV onto the pavement.

"I didn't think it had been so long." Dina emerged gracefully from the front passenger seat.

Meredith pulled the snug skirt as far down as she could and then opened the rear passenger door and turned

189

sideways. The asphalt seemed to be three stories below her high heels. Hopefully, she wouldn't twist an ankle as she maneuvered out of the high vehicle.

"That's right." Brock closed Paulette's door. "She sang a solo too. 'I Feel Pretty,' wasn't it?"

"Yes, from *West Side Story*," Paulette said. "Dang, that seems so long ago and yet not."

Meredith stepped onto the running board and then to the ground, clutching the door's armrest the entire time. After both feet were steady on the pavement, she dared to let go and step back to close the door. She pulled on the silky fabric. Maybe she should have put on a long coat. Though the weather was muggy enough, she would have likely been too warm. She glanced at the darkening sky, the sun approaching the horizon. At least the threat of storms had lessened.

Once they'd all located the auditorium and found seats, she gratefully sank into the hard-backed cushioned chair.

"How do you walk in these things?" Meredith tugged on the strapped sandal, trying in vain to loosen where it dug into her ankle.

"You must have fat feet." Paulette gracefully sank into the seat beside Meredith. "If you'd brought your own, you wouldn't have this problem."

"I don't own shoes like this for a reason." Meredith gave up and relaxed against the chair. Around her, people greeted one another, milling about as they located seats.

"What's that? You like feeling dowdy?"

"Funny." Meredith scanned the auditorium. Folding metal chairs and black music stands sat arranged into a semicircle on the stage. To the back right of the chairs stood a row of drums and other percussion instruments. In front of the stage, three rows of risers waited for the choir. "I prefer having the means to run should the need arise."

"Paranoid, are we?" Paulette angled her head and

glanced at Meredith. "Nobody messes with me, so I don't worry about it. And if they did"—Paulette pointed to the stiletto heel of one shoe—"this would find a home in someone's foot. Just sayin'."

"Look, here comes the jazz band." Brock motioned toward the stage from where he sat next to Meredith.

The student band filed onto the stage, dodging the empty chairs and stands as they took their places. The brass instruments caught the spotlights and reflected them to the crowd. The woodwinds gleamed as the boys and girls sat waiting for the conductor to take the podium.

The choir flowed across the front of the stage in their robes, pale green for the women, black for the men. They arrayed themselves across the risers, carefully lined up so they divided neatly into their sections: soprano women on the left, alto women next, then tenor men, and finally bass men on the far right. Meredith had attended enough of Paulette's concerts to know how the choir was arranged. Indeed, her love of music stemmed from those events so long ago, when she'd watched her performing. Meredith's pride for her talents had never wavered, but Paulette's own sense of self-worth seemed to have faltered in recent years.

Max walked onstage with a tall young man, presumably Sue's grandson, Jeremy, carrying a trumpet tucked under his left arm. Meredith appreciated the way the black-and-white tuxedo accentuated Max's physique and classic features, even from this distance. He shook hands with Jeremy and then turned to sit at the grand piano. Once Jeremy reached his place with the rest of the brass section, the conductor and the choir director strode onstage, took a bow, and then assumed their places in front of their charges.

The school principal, Mr. Burnett according to the program, hurried to the microphone and waved for silence. He gave a short welcome speech and then turned the program over to the musicians. First, the choir sang a medley of show tunes, followed by a series of popular songs that had the audience singing and clapping. Meredith remained quiet, waiting to see if her sister would join in. She was disappointed when Paulette sang along, though not with her usual gusto. The choir finished their portion of the concert with a salute to local history by singing a set of folk tunes that originated in the county.

After the choir filed off the risers and out of the auditorium, Meredith's anticipation heightened as Max flexed his fingers and the band warmed up their instruments. The lead oboe played a concert A and the rest of the band tuned to it. The sound of the sole note pulled together the entire array of instruments into a single harmonious unit, if only for the span of a long breath. Max had told her they'd play a mix of compositions, but the feature was Jeremy and Max playing a duet for trumpet and piano. A scout from Juilliard waited to assess Jeremy's talent. Max had sounded nervous as he'd relayed that tidbit of information, his voice quavering ever so slightly as his fingers ghost played the piano on the table like a variation of air guitar. The audience grew quiet as the conductor stepped onto the box at the front of the band, tapped his baton on the music stand before him and, after ensuring he had the attention of both Max and Jeremy, lifted his baton.

The first riff captivated Meredith, transporting her to a place she could no more describe than taste. A place where she floated, not sitting or standing, not touching anything but the emotion contained within the ephemeral notes. The trumpet and piano complemented and contrasted at various points, but always in such a way as to weave a world unto its own. The interplay between the two musicians amused and challenged her ears. Jeremy performed techniques she marveled upon. Subtle and varying sounds and textures to the music evoked an immense appreciation for the skill necessary for this young man's performance. Max's hands flew across the ivory keys and then attacked the keyboard before playing around with a humorous tone that contrasted perfectly with the beefier character of the trumpet. When the last notes faded into silence, applause exploded throughout the auditorium. The audience rose to their feet in a surge of enthusiastic congratulations. Pride flooded Meredith as she clapped and whistled her appreciation of their performance.

Max and Jeremy accepted the acclaim, bowing to acknowledge and thank the audience for their praise. Then Jeremy invited the band to stand, and the audience erupted into louder applause. Minutes elapsed before the conductor motioned for Jeremy to lead the band backstage, signaling the end of the concert.

"Wow, I didn't know high school concerts were so wonderful." Paulette gathered her purse and wrap, slipping it around her shoulders effortlessly.

"I want that piece in my life soundtrack." Meredith slid her purse strap onto her shoulder and tried to stiffen her ankles to keep from twisting or, worse, breaking the joint. "They were fabulous. Especially Jeremy and Max. I'd never guess he could play like that."

"Jeremy?" Paulette winked at her. "Or Max?"

"Max, of course." Meredith shook her head, a grin forming on her lips. "I told him I'd meet him at the music room, so I should go."

"Are you ready for this?" Paulette asked.

"As ready as I'll ever be, thanks to you." Meredith tapped her with a fist. "You bullied me into not canceling and dressed me up to boot."

Paulette smirked. "What are sisters for?"

Brock touched Meredith's arm. "Max is giving you a ride home after dinner, right? If not, call and I'll come pick you up."

"Thanks, Dad. He's supposed to bring me, but I'll let you know if I need you. Mom looks dead on her feet. Why don't you all go on? I'll be fine."

"If you're sure?" Brock asked.

Once her father herded her mother and sister out of the auditorium, Meredith waited a minute longer for the crowd around her to disperse. Her ankles throbbed. She didn't want to take anyone else out if she tripped. She made her way from the auditorium and down the hall to the band room, careful to dodge the rambunctious and boisterous teens as they laughed and hurried around her.

Stopping out of sight of anyone inside the room, she jerked and tugged until the formfitting black dress settled in the right places. She should've never let Paulette, with her slimmer figure, persuade her to wear this snug-fitting dress. And the shoes. She hated wearing stilettos, but how could she wear the ubiquitous "little black dress" without them? Still, the rhinestones edging the sole sparkled with each movement of her feet. She did love shiny things. She'd have sighed, but she couldn't draw in a deep enough breath.

Despite her reservations, she entered the music room. After a moment she spotted Max at the back, standing with the conductor in conversation. He smiled and nodded at something the man said before noticing her. His intent gaze snagged hers and wouldn't let go. From across the large room, his essence connected with hers, informing her they breathed the same air. He said something to the man at his side. A quick nod and he walked toward her, each step bringing him and all he represented closer to her.

They were going out. On a date. Her first date since Willy died. Her heart thudded in her chest, echoing in her ears. Max drew nearer, larger as he approached. She wanted this. She really needed to face the music, pun intended, and move on. Besides, she deserved to find some kind of happiness again. Why not with Max? She'd been attracted to him despite all her protestations. She forced a deep breath and then a smile to her lips.

When he stopped in front of her, he grasped her hand and led her from the room. "Jeremy's technique has improved immensely this year."

"Who?" That was not what she expected him to say. She let him lead her down the hall, though she struggled to walk without wobbling. The hem of the dress slowly inched up her thighs with each step.

"Sue's grandson, the trumpet solo tonight." Max squeezed her hand. "I'm glad you and your family chose to come."

"I enjoyed all of it, but your duet drew the most applause." She used her free hand to tug the hem back down as they turned and walked toward the exit doors.

"You're too kind." Max stopped inside the glass doors, the neon red from the exit sign above their heads casting an unearthly glow on his cheekbones and nose. He smiled, his gaze roaming her face for a long moment. "You're so beautiful and smart and talented, all rolled into one lovely package."

"No, I—"

"You shouldn't argue the point. I know what I see when I look at you." He placed a finger on her lips and then followed it with a long, searching kiss.

An explosion of sensation flooded her body, sizzling through her veins like a sparkler on the Fourth of July. Leaning into the kiss, she closed her eyes and moved her hands up his arms until they wrapped around his neck. God, he tasted wonderful. His tongue teased hers, sparking forgotten needs in her core.

When he ended the kiss, he followed it with a series of light pecks on her lips, reminders of the main event they'd shared. She opened her eyes, and the usual vibrant blue of his eyes had deepened. "I've been waiting to do that all night."

"Why is that?" Meredith moistened her tender lips, and his gaze zeroed in on her mouth. A giddy sense of power flushed through her. She'd experienced that kind of rush with Willy, and the return of the power made her fuzzy inside, unsure of the present, let alone the future.

"It doesn't matter." Max took her left hand, wrapped his strong fingers around hers, and lifted her fingers to his kiss. "I'm glad you're here with me. Shall we go eat?"

She nodded, mesmerized by his gallant act. She saw the moment when he noticed she'd removed her wedding band. Her finger seemed naked without it, but the time had arrived for her to take the ring off and put it in her jewelry box. He pushed open the door and stepped out into the cooler spring air.

He paused on the sidewalk. "Ready? I'm parked over there."

She followed the motion of his free hand and saw his pickup, obviously recently washed and waxed, gleaming in the parking lot lights. She nodded, afraid if she spoke, she'd ask him to take her home with him instead of to a restaurant. She was hungry, all right, but not for food. Her body sang from his kiss, her emotions abuzz inside. Before she knew it, she was ensconced in the passenger seat of the truck, seat belt in place, as he shut the door and made his way to slide into the driver's seat. He grinned at her as he reached to secure his own belt. After lowering the windows to allow the cooler air into the stuffy interior, he laid a hand on hers and squeezed.

"It's been quite a few days, hasn't it? First finding the body and now the concert, I mean."

"Yes. I appreciate all you've done to help figure all this out. I don't know what I'd have done without your expertise."

"We make a good team." Max studied her expression. "You have the technical skills and experience, and I have the legal covered."

"Right. We could rule the world," Meredith said. He laughed along with her.

"I'm glad you agreed to see me after the concert, Meredith." He kissed her lightly. "I hope you'll let me get to know you better."

"Paulette told me it's time for me to try to move on from the past, to start looking to the future." She searched his eyes, looking for understanding. "I'm trying, in my own way."

"Let me help." He traced her jaw with a finger, pulling her chin around so he could lift it to his kiss. He leaned in and pressed his lips to hers for a long, lingering moment. "It'll be my pleasure, my lady."

The close confines of the cab lent a sense of security to the entire experience. Meredith allowed herself to respond, even closed her eyes to enjoy the sensation of his lips, and then his tongue playing with the tip of her own. A low moan began at the base of her throat and worked its way up and out into the night. She'd missed this more than she'd ever admitted to herself. The interplay between a man and a woman. If bones really could melt, then hers were doing so. Max's grip on her chin increased, and the kiss deepened.

"Hey!"

Meredith jerked back at the deep voice yelling through the darkened window. Echoes of a previous night reverberated in her memory. A yell. A demand. A gunshot. Panic swelled in her chest. *Not again.* The silhouette of a man appeared at the open window, the parking lights framing his outline and casting his face and features into deep shadow. A glint of metal shone in his hand. Terror, sharp and clear and white-hot, lanced through Meredith. A scream tore from her throat as the man raised his hand. Max turned to the stranger to say something, but the metal flashed in the light as the stranger moved. Spots formed before her eyes as another scream seared her throat, and then the night descended upon her.

"Meredith? Meredith, honey…"

Blinking awake, her eyes were blinded by the high parking lot lights above. She squeezed them closed against the intrusion and then slowly opened them. Max hovered above her, one arm supporting her shoulders while his other hand cradled her jaw.

"What happened?"

"You fainted." Max kissed her lightly. "Jeremy startled you, I think."

"I don't faint." Meredith pushed herself upright in the seat. Jeremy stood outside her open window, the light illuminating his worried expression.

"Seems to me I've heard that before." Max chuckled. "But if you say so."

"I'm sorry, Miss Reed. I didn't mean to scare you." Jeremy leaned in closer to the window, and Meredith zeroed in on the set of car keys in his hand.

"I—I'm sorry I freaked out." She shook her head. She obviously hadn't put the past behind her as far as she'd like. The terrible memory lingered too close to the surface for comfort. "I didn't mean to scare you, either."

Max leaned closer to Meredith, reminding her of Willy's dead weight falling onto her. She pulled away, biting her lip to refrain from crying out.

"What did you need, Jeremy?" Max asked across Meredith.

"I came to th-thank you again for accompanying me." Jeremy smiled, unaware of the tension inside the car. "You rocked the keyboard in there. And got me noticed by the scout from Juilliard. A full scholarship!"

"Fantastic news." Max high-fived Jeremy in front of Meredith's nose.

Jeremy noticed Meredith flinch and backed up a step. "Anyway, I wanted to tell you that. I'll see you next week. G'night." He touched a finger to an imaginary hat brim and then disappeared into the pools of light and shadow.

Max peered at Meredith. His eyes gleamed in the dark, reflecting the sodium lights' glare. "Ready for that steak?"

Was she? Traces of fear drifted in her soul. Her heart beat against her chest. She swallowed, but the lump of terror remained lodged in her throat. She couldn't do this. What if someone attacked Max and he died in her lap? What if she attracted bad luck, leaving a string of dead lovers behind her? A shudder pulsed through her. She couldn't handle continual grieving as her future. Couldn't do that to Max, or anyone else.

"Hey, what's the matter?" Max tightened his arm around her shoulders, pulling her closer to him. "You're chilled."

She stiffened, knowing this couldn't go on. She must make him see this simply would not work. "Max, don't."

He looked at her, stricken. "What?"

"This." She pointed to his arm and then leaned forward, indicating for him to remove it. "I'm sorry, but this can't happen."

He slowly withdrew his arm, reaching for her fingers. She shook her head, and he gripped the steering wheel with both hands instead. "Talk to me. I thought we had the beginning of something between us. I thought…"

His words trailed off as he looked away, staring across the now empty parking lot.

"I wanted it to work, even hoped I had managed to do like you wanted and put the past, including my husband

and child, to rest so I could move on the way I know Willy would have wanted."

Max whipped around, stared at her, his mouth a thin line. "Child?"

"I don't talk about him." She explored the anguish on his face. "It's too painful."

Max's grip on the wheel eased, though it didn't release entirely. His fingers flexed and tightened rhythmically, reminiscent of his earlier performance, as he stared at the brick building before them. "Should I feel honored by your secret?"

"Perhaps. I'm telling you because you need to understand why I can't see you again." She waved a hand in front of her helplessly. "Not like this."

He regarded her then, his attitude hard and a touch angry. "I don't understand. Explain."

"I wanted to try to be a couple with you, but this little fiasco proves that won't work. Wanting something and being able to have it are two entirely different things." She laid a hand on his arm, feeling the tension in the knotted muscles beneath the long-sleeved cotton shirt. "You've helped me realize I must stick with the program, follow the score, and not start improvising midway."

A frown appeared between his brows, his eyes quizzical. His fingers drummed the steering wheel, the sound humming between them. "What exactly does that mean?"

She took a deep breath and held it before slowly exhaling. "Take me to Twin Oaks. Tomorrow I'll pull out my to-do list and begin checking off items."

"But I thought—"

"It doesn't matter, Max. I won't live in Roseville or anywhere nearby. I don't belong here and never will. It's time for me to wise up and take care of what I need to do."

Max slapped the heel of his hand onto the steering wheel.

"No, Meredith, you cannot go through with demolishing Twin Oaks."

"I have to; it's the only way." She stared out the window instead of at Max. Knowing how deeply he cared about historic properties made her path all the more difficult to navigate.

"I'm going to stop you. You've obviously lost your mind and can't be relied upon to make a rational decision." His glare pummeled the back of her head. "Look at me."

When she turned to face him, she gasped at the anger etched into every line of his face. "You can't stop me, Max. It's my property to do with as I choose." She folded her arms, as much to quell the tremors his expression induced in her as to raise a protective barrier.

"I've moved up the county councilman's vote to Monday, and then we'll see who can do what."

"You're going to sic the law on me? How? You said the draft hasn't even been read, let alone be ready to go up for a vote. Get real."

"I am. You're a fraud, you know. You sell yourself as an architect, a lover of building and creating things, when in fact you're nothing but a conniving destroyer of all things precious, including your own family and your family's heritage. If I weren't such a gentleman, I'd leave you here to fend for yourself." He turned the key, and the engine roared to life. "As I *am* a gentleman, I'm taking you home."

Meredith popped open the door and scrambled as quickly as she could from the truck, reaching back in to snatch her purse off the seat. "No, thanks. I'll walk if I have to."

She wobbled in her high heels and then marched as best she could to the sidewalk. She stepped up carefully to turn and glare back at him. Except he wasn't in the truck but stomping across the parking spaces toward her, the driver's-side door ajar. She dug into her bag and withdrew her key chain with its dangling canister of pepper spray. Clutching the tiny can infused her with a sense of control over the situation. But Max's demeanor and glare challenged that notion as well. She wished for flat shoes and better self-defense training as he drew nearer.

"I'd never leave anyone, including you, stranded at this time of night. Now get back in the damn truck, and I'll drive you home."

"No. I'll call my dad."

"And have him think I'd treat his daughter like a hitchhiker to be left alongside the road? No thanks." He grabbed her hand and tugged. "Come on, don't make me carry you."

"You wouldn't dare." She yanked on the skirt, the image of being slung over his shoulder like his cavewoman in a bad movie playing in her head. If so, her lack of pantyhose could prove embarrassing indeed. Not that anyone else was around to see. In fact, she was alone with this irate man looming over her. So strong and tall, with killer eyes. Unease worked through her at the intense gaze he leveled upon her.

"Wouldn't I?" He stepped closer, his fingers flexing in preparation for whatever he had in mind. "Don't push me, Meredith."

"You're not seriously going to drag me into your truck and force me to ride with you? You're not that Neanderthal." She readied the spray nozzle, only to fumble both her purse and the canister to the ground when he took another step. Never mind the purse, he acted as though he seriously would haul her up and carry her off. "You wouldn't."

A growl emitted from somewhere deep in his throat. "Watch me."

His powerful hands grabbed her waist and hoisted her onto his shoulder. The air whooshed from her lungs when her solar plexus hit his shoulder bone. Meredith soon stared in surprise at the pavement passing beneath his black leather shoes as he strode back to the truck, cursing the entire way. He kept one arm clasped between her waist and her derriere, pressing her stomach tight against him in the most annoying manner.

"Put me down!" She kicked out, trying to force him to comply.

In response he tightened his grip on her waist and trapped one leg with his strong hand. "No. I'm taking you home whether you like it or not."

She struggled more, pushing at his back with both hands to no avail. "You monster. I can't believe you'd do this."

"Believe it, babe." He yanked open the passenger door so hard it bounced back and hit her in the shoulder.

"Ow! Damn, you're nuts."

"Watch your head."

She rubbed her shoulder for a split second before gasping as he dumped her onto the truck seat. Startled by the abrupt stop, she didn't understand what had caught Max's attention at first and then realized her skirt had bunched around her waist, exposing her black lace-edged panties to his hungry view. Which he was taking full advantage of.

"Are you done ogling?" she asked, seething inside.

"Nowhere near." He pushed her legs forward in the truck and slapped the door closed and then leered at her through the open window. "But a gentleman wouldn't take advantage of a damsel in distress, so I'll just keep the image in my mind while I take you home."

She hiked her hips and yanked the skirt, hidden stitches popping, back down into place, enjoying the strain on his face as he tried to avoid watching her actions. She snatched the seat belt and clicked it home. "If you insist. But don't leave my purse on the ground."

"Yes, my lady." He marched back and snatched the offending objects from the ground and handed them through the window. Then he strode to the driver's side and hopped in, slamming his door closed. "I'd never expect anything from you except more of the same."

"If you mean more trouble, then you've got it." Meredith slipped the pepper spray back inside her purse, wishing she'd had the opportunity to show him how much trouble she could be.

Chapter Sixteen

$\mathcal{A}$ puff of dust whooshed into the air when Meredith thunked the wire dress dummy down beside the stack of boxes she'd carted from the attic to the second-floor landing. She dusted her hands off, relishing the dirt falling to the floor. It felt good to finally return to her plan. The first step being to sort out and organize what hunkered in an attic replete with all those pesky memories. Resting her hands on her hips, she admired her work. Boxes decorated with crayon and stickers piled in one corner, reminiscent of days gone by. Plastic tubs filled with craft supplies towered in another corner of the landing. The mannequin stood in the center, lording over its underlings. Next up, the old furniture, an assortment of chairs and side tables, coat stands, and who knew what else. She hadn't bothered to look into most of the boxes and bags, not caring about their contents.

Back in the attic, Meredith surveyed the changes she'd wrought to the space. Dust bunnies huddled together along the baseboards, now easily visible without all the clutter. Pale sunshine angled in through the windows. She grabbed up a chair, one crossbar dangling, and lugged it down the stairs. With each step she gloried in the sense of achievement, of making good on her threat to Max. All the way home the night before, she'd fumed about being manhandled and carted about like a sack of potatoes. He didn't credit her with the brains and dedication to see her aims through. Well, he'd soon find out.

"What on earth are you doing?" Paulette emerged from her bedroom. From the stomping of feet as she approached, she was angry too.

"Following through with my plan." Meredith set the chair down beside the mannequin, bumping it slightly, causing the wire figure to teeter and then rock back into place. "Finally."

"I can't believe you're doing this." Paulette marched down the hall and stopped by Meredith's elbow. "I thought you'd delayed until you understood what happened to Grace."

"Right. Now I know, so I can proceed. I called Sammy's Salvage, and they should be out here this afternoon to cart away whatever is valuable."

"No. Way." Paulette grabbed Meredith's arms and shook her. Literally. "You really have lost your mind, you know that?"

Meredith stepped back, shaking off the punishing hands. "What is it to you, anyway? You never cared about this place while Grandma was living. Why now that she's dead? Tell me that."

Paulette cut her eyes away, and then back to glare at Meredith. "Maybe I want a little more time to be with family."

"You?" Meredith laughed. "That's funny. You've stayed as far away from family as you can get."

"So have you." She barred Meredith's attempt to stomp back up the steps. "You who think you're better than any of us because of your high-brow education."

"I do not. Step aside." Meredith tried to move her sister over so she could pass. "I've got work to do."

"No." Paulette pushed her back, twisting an ankle as she

wrestled to keep Meredith from moving away from her. "Ouch!"

"Let go." Meredith pried at Paulette's fingers. "Get off me!"

"You've never listened to me. I'm telling you now. You've made me care about Twin Oaks and I won't let you destroy it." Paulette pulled Meredith closer and then slapped her hard across the face. "Grow up, little girl."

Meredith gasped and then swung her open hand toward Paulette's jaw. Paulette ducked and spun, connecting her open palm to Meredith's cheek. They squared off like bantam weight boxers, assessing their abilities. They circled, looking for an opening. Meredith's blood surged with anger. Her sister always had the uncanny ability to pluck the nerve strings to create discord. Today proved no different.

"Damn you! You don't care about this place any more than I do. We just care about it in different ways. I don't want to hurt you, especially since you're expecting. Now get out of the way and let me finish what I started." Meredith fisted her hands on her hips and glared at her sister. "Stop trying to get yourself hurt and let me past."

"Bitch. I'm not letting you do this." Paulette assumed a ready stance, pumping her fists before her like the defending champion. "Bring it on."

The two women eyed each other, and then Paulette moved in, slapping at Meredith. She ducked and danced away. Paulette dodged in for a quick openhanded slap, a glare thrown in for good measure, and then retreated out of reach.

"Let it go." Meredith ducked as Paulette swung at her. "You'll never win this."

Paulette jerked left to cut off Meredith's attempt to rush past her. "I have to." She circled, slowly sidling toward the stairs leading up to the attic. She stopped when her body blocked the way up the steps. "You can't get away with your dastardly plan."

Meredith hooted. "You make me sound like some evil plotter to your *Perils of Pauline* character."

"Exactly." Paulette pushed at Meredith's shoulders, sending her backward several steps.

"Pauline was always the one in trouble, like you."

Paulette's brows dove together with each of Meredith's steps toward her. "Yet, she always won in the end."

"Not today." Meredith closed on Paulette, fury boiling inside. "Just remember you started this."

Huffing and puffing, Meredith glared at Paulette. She needed a white knight. Someone like Pauline's. Or that cartoon do-gooder who bungled his way through saving the damsel in distress. The image of Dudley Do-Right floated into her mind's eye, and she chuckled.

Paulette bristled, fists tight on her thighs. "What?"

"Where's Dudley when you need him?" Even the name made Meredith smile, then laugh.

Paulette grinned. "With his red-and-blue Canadian Mountie uniform and that huge jaw?"

"Your hero."

Meredith started laughing and couldn't stop. Her legs gave out, and she slid to the floor, lying on her back as the guffaws shot from her mouth. Tears pushed out of her eyes, and she brushed them away. Paulette, too, doubled over as she laughed, stomping one foot on the floor in her hysteria.

Running steps sounded from below, pounding up the stairs. Meg, her hair tousled and her cheeks red, came to an abrupt halt at the top, Dina right behind her.

"What in the name of heaven is all this ruckus about?" Meg asked, treading carefully to the landing.

Paulette straightened, wiping the last of the laugh-induced tears from her face. "This." Paulette indicated the piles surrounding the group of women. "She's seriously fucked up."

"Paulette." Dina shook her head as she took in the scene before them.

"She is." Paulette hunched her shoulders, reminding Meredith of how she'd acted when caught doing something she knew she shouldn't.

Dina directed her famous mom look at Paulette, the one that froze grown men as well as little girls into a pillar of guilt. Paulette muttered something unintelligible and stared at Meredith, thus avoiding the remnants of the incapacitating gaze.

"Now let's begin to act like ladies instead of roller-derby queens, got it?" Dina looked at each of them in turn. "What's this really about? Who wants to start?"

Meredith's heart clenched. Here they go. Reveal time. She pointed at Paulette but stayed mum.

Paulette narrowed her eyes, her right foot tapping the floorboards. "Sis, here, wants to ignore the fact that I don't want her to start over…"

Meredith gaped at her, one eyebrow raised, her heart racing. She'd never expected that to emerge from her sister's mouth. How could she not want Meredith to find some semblance of peace after all the tragedy of the past? "You don't?"

She shook her head. "Let me finish my sentence, will ya?" After Meredith nodded once, Paulette pressed her lips together briefly and then plunged on. "I don't want you to start over if it means you must obliterate our ancestral home. It's ours now, a grand old home to cherish and care for. Not destroy."

"Meredith, what have you to say in return?" Dina patted her fingers on one elbow, eyebrow quirked in question.

"I—" Meredith stopped, unsure what to say. "I don't think I can live here. It's overwhelming and confusing."

She let her gaze wander around the space now crowded with an assortment of boxes and furniture. Traces of previous years, days, lives. Representing a time before all the pain began in her life. When she'd had fun and found joy in her days. Back when she'd loved to play dress up and ride her scooter, build with blocks and real building materials. Constructing buildings and bridges made her happy from her childhood years up until the random attack.

But then the attack was random, wasn't it? Nobody could predict a young man would become so desperate as to steal twenty bucks and kill a man to do so. In some ways, she pitied the guy. How did he sleep at night knowing he'd murdered a man over such a small amount of cash? Not that it mattered anymore. She'd always miss her husband, always wonder about their unborn baby. But that didn't mean she must turn her back on all the good times she'd shared with them and the rest of her family.

She considered Paulette, the only sister she'd ever have. They had their differences and conflicting life goals, without a doubt. Paulette's unborn child would need a home and a family to love her. Meredith understood the protective spirit of a new mother. Could they work out their contentions? Was it possible for her to find a different way to assuage the grief festering like an infected wound? She'd thought amputation of the affected part, her heart, was the answer. But now she wasn't sure. Maybe having a partner to sort through all this junk would ease the burden in more ways than one.

Feelings experienced decades before shimmered in her conscience. Another day or two wouldn't matter, would it? "I—we need to at least sort this out so we know what we have, right? Those things we don't need or want. Then we can decide, together, what to do with the rest."

"Oh my God, really? Thanks, Mer. You won't regret this." A grin sparkled in Paulette's eyes. She closed the distance between them and linked arms with Meredith.

At her touch, a sense of familiarity spread through Meredith. "Let's go up together and see what's what, then. 'Kay?"

Hours later they'd sorted through the remainder of the attic's contents. Along the west wall, all the furniture stood stacked, with the assortment of boxes and trunks lined up along the north wall. Rubber and plastic tubs of Christmas decorations and other seasonal goods rested against the east wall. Along the south wall, to the right of the attic door, the random open boxes of books and photo albums waited to be carted down the steps. Meredith fingered the spines, feeling the dimpling on the leather covers, the raised lettering on the professionally bound tomes. So many fascinating titles piqued her curiosity. One photo album snared her attention with its black crumbling pages bound by a string looped through the cover and the pages and tied to secure the package. She slid it from the box and plunked down cross-legged on the dusty floor, engrossed by the words printed with an elegant hand on the cover in gold ink.

"What's that?" Paulette folded her legs into a sitting position beside Meredith and peered over at the book. "Wow, is that what I think it is?"

"Yes, the O'Connell album prior to the breakout of the Civil War." She traced the lettering with her index finger, the smooth, fluid feel of the ink still tantalizing, evoking a sense of time standing still.

"Open it. Let's see what they looked like." Paulette reached to do so, and Meredith stopped her hand in midair.

"Careful, the pages are falling apart. I'll do it." She slipped a finger between the cover and the first page and gently lifted.

Inside, photos were held in place by little slits in the page, the corners tucked into the crumbling paper, barely clinging to their places. Most of the people and places held no meaning to Meredith, but she slowly turned the pages. Black-and-white photos of serious men and women stared at her.

"Look, is that the girls and Grandpa Joe?" Paulette

pointed to a formal portrait taking up one entire page.

Meredith examined the image of two young women, not more than teens, attired in hoop skirts and elaborate hairdos, flanking a young man seated on a hard-backed chair. The ladies each had a hand on one of his shoulders and, as was customary in formal portraits, grim expressions, as though they'd had their photograph made at gunpoint. Below the photo script handwriting faded into history. She strained to make out the cursive, lifting the album to angle it in the soft light of the attic. A chill raced through her, goose bumps rising on her arms as a gust of wind slammed the door beside them. Both women jumped, the album sliding to the floor.

Meredith gasped and then frantically searched the attic with her eyes. She sniffed the air and forced her shoulders to relax. "She's here."

Paulette's eyes widened before she too cast a frantic gaze around the attic. "How can you tell?"

"Honeysuckle. Don't you smell it?" She hugged herself against the air blasting her bare arms.

Paulette sniffed cautiously and then gasped. "Yes. Damn, it's cold in here."

The rustle of silk accompanied the soft pad of footsteps. Grace appeared across the room, sequins glinting in the shadows. A gust of wind flipped the pages of the album lying on the floor in front of them. Meredith scooted back, afraid if she touched the whirring pages, they'd create a hurricane of dust and photos. The dust bunnies swirled along the baseboards like maniacal whirling dervishes. Finally the wind ceased and the pages settled. Meredith sucked in a breath and let it out slowly.

"Holy cow." Paulette shook her head as she gazed on the photo staring up at them.

"What?" Meredith peered closer. Instead of magnolias marking the site, twin maple trees stood shading the cemetery. A stone wall in lieu of the current wrought-iron fence surrounded the large rectangle of grass, a picket gate closing off the family graves from the outside world. But even with those differences, the layout of the graveyard remained. More importantly, the cluster of people dressed in dark clothing stood next to Grandpa Joe's grave. She searched the bottom of the page and found the caption: Joseph O'Connell, 1917.

"Grandpa Joe's funeral." Meredith lifted her gaze and looked around. She gazed at Grace and then studied the photo again. Evidently, Grace wanted her to be aware of Joe's funeral. "Why did she want to show us this?"

"I can't imagine." Paulette squinted at her. "Is she trying to tell us something?"

Meredith shrugged. "Grace? Tell me what you want me to do." Meredith kept her eyes on the spirit, waiting, hoping for a response and dreading it simultaneously.

Paulette shook her head as she stood and then suddenly spotted Grace waiting patiently, a soft smile on her face. "She's here."

Meredith nodded, questions flying through her mind. "Maybe she's trying to tell us there are no happy endings after all. We just die." Meredith stared at the photo. Only a few people really. Eight. Eight people cared enough to attend their great-great-great-grandfather's funeral. How sad.

"Sure there are. Happy endings are different, though, for each of us." Paulette hugged herself as Grace slowly dematerialized.

Meredith gaped at Paulette as if she'd grown two heads. "What do you mean? Surely you don't believe in happily ever after endings? You of all people?"

Paulette inclined her head and studied Meredith for a long moment before resting a hand on her stomach as though she'd suddenly experienced a flock of butterflies inside. "Of course I do. I have to believe that no matter how many roadblocks and how much grief I endure, eventually I'll find a way to be happy. I may even find a man to be happy with."

"See, this is why I read nonfiction more than fiction. There's no fantasy factor about the perfect man or woman, the perfect relationship, the perfect anything."

Paulette laughed. "How sad is that? Of course, even in love stories nobody's perfect, and thus no relationship is perfect. It's about finding a way to communicate, to share, to be together. That's what ultimately creates a happy ending. What was your favorite book the summer you turned twelve?"

"I don't know." Meredith hadn't thought about storybooks in ages. "Why?"

"You used to read this one book over and over." She stared at her, a smile spreading on her lips. "Don't you remember? *Lassie, Come Home*. Now that's a happy ending."

Meredith had cried and laughed and worried her way through the story of the dog who had to find her own way home to Timmy and his family. The collie had to overcome obstacle after obstacle, but nothing stopped her from returning to her home and the family that loved her.

Another icy blast whipped through the attic, even though the windows remained shut. The pages of the album whipped closed with a resounding thud. The back cover stared up at them, a silent witness to the strange occurrence in the attic.

Meredith rubbed her hands on her arms to warm them as the air slowly returned to its normal temperature. She tentatively sniffed the air and exhaled with a smile.

Paulette mimicked Meredith's actions and grinned. "Now that's another happy ending right there. Do you think she got what she came for?"

Meredith nodded. "But what do you think it is?"

"The promise of a happy ending for her. She did point out the graveyard. Perhaps…" Paulette tapped a forefinger on her chin; then her shoulders sagged. "I don't know. What do you think she wanted?"

Meredith stared at the blank black cover of the album, seeing again the photo of the three siblings, then Joe's funeral. Of all the pictures for Grace to have emphasized, why those two? She raised her gaze to meet Paulette's waiting expression and made a moue. "A happy ending?"

Silver clanked against the yellow china plate as Meredith's dad set the dining room table. He'd insisted he knew best how to lay the places for their Sunday dinner. In years gone by, Grandma invited the family to gather for a formal meal once a week. A time of sharing and connecting they often skipped during the week's activities. Shrugging at the unusual claim, Meredith nonetheless acquiesced. If he wanted to pretend to be Miss Manners, she wouldn't argue.

She made a few final tweaks to the floral arrangement she'd cobbled together from the various blooming flowers surrounding the house. Sean had performed miracles when it came to the landscaping and the abundance of fresh flowers available. The wide-mouthed, cut-glass vase held an array of spring blooms: yellow daffodils, purple bearded iris, and red and white tulips. Their combined scents softened the air.

"The salad fork goes on the outside," muttered Brock as he made his way around the table. His large fingers dwarfed the handles of the silver.

Meredith grinned to herself. Reconnecting with her parents had proven to be less painful than she'd imagined possible. They'd slipped back into her life, not judging and not annoying her. Well, other than their initial reaction to her intended future for Twin Oaks. An intention wavering with each passing hour. She'd changed as much as they had. Both had mellowed, perhaps, not expecting quite as much from each other.

She lifted the vase from the side table where she'd been working and placed it carefully in the center of the dining table. She stood back, angled her head to obtain a better view, and then turned it slowly to increase the visual impact when one walked into the room. Perfect.

Brock placed the last of the silverware on the table and stepped back, hands on hips, contemplating his efforts. "Nicely done, if I do say so myself."

"I agree, Dad. I couldn't have done better." Meredith straightened the alignment of the nearest spoon handle with the knife handle beside it.

"So there was room for improvement after all." Brock chuckled at Meredith's startled glance.

"It was only a touch off." All a matter of perspective. Paulette's chiding at the Hideaway played through her memory. She grinned. "Can't help it, apparently."

"You never could, always so precise." Brock made his way around the table, double-checking the alignment of the silverware handles.

"Leave it, Dad." Meredith gripped the back of the nearest chair. "It's about time I relaxed my tendency toward perfectionism."

"I wouldn't say that." Brock gazed at her, eyes serious. "Your talents rely upon such precision, so don't give them short shrift."

"Good point." She studied him, his strong neck and steady hand, despite approaching his seventies. "Do you remember helping me with the Twin Oaks miniature?"

A smile lit his eyes and spread across his entire face. "You did a fine job. Your first piece too. I knew then creating lovely buildings was your future."

Creating. Buildings. Two words strung together into one sentence summed her life's ambition. Or had been until Willy's senseless death, along with their little boy. At the thought, she waited for the feeling of emptiness, or desolation, to follow. But instead she longed for something else. Something *more*.

Since returning to Twin Oaks, she'd become aware of the family she'd distanced herself from. The family that, in some ways, she'd banished from her life in order to be with Willy. They'd moved away, putting a physical and psychological barrier between them and her family. Now she sat circumscribed by her heritage as well as her living family. Heck, her dead ancestors surrounded her as well. From the building itself, to the memories it contained, the furnishings used by her grandmother, parents, and sister, right down to the books, journals, and even handwritten letters handled by ancestors she'd never met. Her family, like her heritage, enveloped her.

She tried to summon up the desperate need to demolish everything in order to move forward, to push the past behind her where it couldn't hurt her any longer. She tried to recall again her husband's limp body, blood everywhere. She tried to feel the sharp pain of the bullet lodged into her womb. Nothing. Instead of pain, an undefined yearning crept through her.

"Dinner is almost ready." Paulette sashayed into the dining room. She scanned the table with its shining china and silver, sparkling crystal, and colorful arrangements of flowers. "Lovely job, you two. I'll tell Mom the table is set." With that she hurried from the room.

"Seems like old times, doesn't it?" Meredith was struck by the combination of new and familiar. Old and groundbreaking.

"Sure does." Brock snagged a side chair and settled into place at the table. "I'm glad we came to visit for a while, though we can't stay too much longer. I've got a job to do later this week."

"Yeah, I know the feeling." Her job still waited for her attention, but she'd been distracted by all the happenings here in Roseville. She'd never imagined she could be so diverted by small town happenings, either.

Meg carried in a platter of sliced roast beef and placed it on the sideboard next to the polished silver tea service. Hard to believe the teapot, coffeepot, sugar bowl, and creamer had been squirreled away for more than a hundred years and still could be refurbished and cleaned up to such a shine.

Dina walked into the room carrying a tray with steaming bowls. She added the tray to the sideboard, and Meredith caught the scent of boiled potatoes and pole beans. Paulette placed a silver basket, lined with a cloth napkin, alongside the vegetables. From the bacon and corn aroma, she'd bet a month's salary it contained some of Meg's famous buttermilk cornbread.

"That should do it. You all enjoy your meal." Meg wiped her hands on her apron. "I'll be back to clean up after I have my dinner with Sean."

"Thanks, Meg, for helping with dinner today." Dina hugged the elderly woman. "You make me look good."

Blushing, Meg headed for the door. "You're more than welcome. Ta-ta!"

Meredith watched Meg hurry away, wondering about her future after Meredith moved on. One way or the other, things must change.

"Grab a plate, dear," Dina said to Brock. "You start us off and get your hulk out of the way so we have room too."

A knock on the kitchen door had Meredith pushing back her chair. "I'll see who it is. You go ahead."

Max waited in the kitchen by the time she arrived. A tremor of something nameless, or that she'd rather not name, slipped under her skin, warming her. Her earlier realization of wanting something she couldn't define floated into her memory when he smiled at her. She grinned back, folding her arms across her chest. "You really need to replace my screen door so I can lock it."

Walking up to her, he stopped out of reach. "Yes, I do. I'll take care of replacing it this week."

His eyes, so vibrant and captivating, did their job and held her attention. Others must notice different details about a person, but for her the eyes spoke the truth of the soul.

"What brings you here?" She gripped her arms to avoid the familiar compulsion to touch him. All it would take would be to move one hand a few inches and her fingers could feel his bicep.

"The coroner's office released the skeletal remains to my custody to return to your family." He nodded toward the door and his pickup parked beyond.

"Oh. We're about to sit down to dinner." Her pulse pounded in her ears, distracting her. Muddling her thoughts. Otherwise she wouldn't have blurted out, "Care to join us?"

His eyes crinkled at the corners. "Does that mean you forgive me for the fireman's carry the other night?"

Heat crept into her cheeks as she recalled the image of hanging over his shoulder and then being plopped onto the truck seat, her skirt around her waist. "Not necessarily, but my mother would tan my hide if I didn't offer you the proper Southern hospitality."

"I'll accept, then, before you change your mind." His grin widened as he patted his stomach. "I'm starved."

"Aren't you always? Come on, then."

Before long, everyone sat with steaming plates of food before them. The aromas of the meal made Meredith even hungrier. She scooped potatoes into her mouth, enjoying being with her family. Max's presence added a pleasing tension to the atmosphere. The conversation verged on banter, laughter punctuating the meal.

Meredith contemplated Paulette's situation. Her sister's expression had softened with the passing of time at Twin Oaks. Yet she still faced an uncertain future. She had several decisions to make, not the least of which remained whether to keep her child or give it up for adoption. And if she chose to keep the baby, then how to provide the necessities. She also needed a roof over their heads. So many decisions and choices to make; perhaps the best thing for her to do was to face facts.

Meredith cleared her throat. "Paulette, don't you have some news to share with Mom and Dad?"

Paulette gawped at Meredith. She swallowed and glanced at their parents. "News?" She squeaked out the word.

"Yes. You know." Meredith paused, seeing understanding dawn in Paulette's expression. "Johnny's parting gift?"

"Mer, this isn't the time to share such breaking news." Paulette glanced at Max, and then back to Meredith.

"Did you want me to leave?" Max folded his napkin, preparing to rise.

"No, it's fine." Paulette waved him back into his seat. "There's nothing to share anyway."

"Yes, there is. You can't deny the truth forever. It will come out eventually." Meredith sipped her wine and waited for Paulette to begin.

"Must I?" Paulette's voice pleaded for commutation of her sentence.

"Yes." Meredith waited, taking several deep breaths, seeing the curiosity on her parents' faces. "Or I will."

Paulette gripped her napkin with both hands, twisting it. "If you insist." She twisted the cloth the other direction, observing her parents with wary eyes. She sighed, a long exhale releasing her reluctant admission. "I'm pregnant."

Stunned silence ended with Dina clapping her hands. "I'm going to be a grandmother? Congratulations, Paulette! I'm so happy for you."

"Pregnant?" Brock asked. "It's Johnny's?"

Paulette nodded.

"He took off for Alaska," Meredith supplied. "He said he's not ready to be a father."

Brock frowned. "Who the hell is?"

Max laughed and folded his arms. "Congrats, Paulette. That's wonderful."

"Don't rush the congratulations, folks." Paulette twisted her napkin tighter. "I'm not sure I'm keeping it. Yet."

Another moment of stunned silence followed.

"I've been thinking about that," Meredith said. "You're planning to stay here for a while, right? You have time to make that decision."

"You're not going to go through with your plan?" Paulette turned hopeful eyes toward Meredith and laid the napkin back on her lap. "If that's the case, then I'd like to stay."

Meredith hoped she wouldn't regret her offer or her decision to renege on her plan to build the park rather than a garden. "Great. I'm glad that's settled."

"If I'm going to live here," Paulette said, picking up her fork once more, "I have one request."

Meredith's protective shell erected at her sister's words. "What might that be?"

"It may seem petty, but it feels odd eating with the tea set in here." Paulette chewed slowly, her eyes darting to the sideboard.

Reflected in the shining silver were five faces turned to contemplate it. If the set had been a fly on the wall, what might it have told them about Grandpa Joe and his sisters?

Why had Grace and Edith chosen to hide the silver and nothing else? Was no other item worth hiding?

"I like having it there as a reminder of our ancestors," Meredith said.

"The obvious irony being the squabble between sisters over a man ended up with them trying to protect something valuable that led to Grace's death." Paulette popped a bite of potato into her mouth.

"A family heirloom led to a family secret, a real skeleton in the closet, so to speak." Meredith picked up her wineglass. The merlot danced in the crystal stemware, its cranberry color contrasting with the white tablecloth. She took a fortifying sip, still a touch dismayed at Max's presence and his effect on her equilibrium.

"Did you tell Mom and Dad about what happened in the attic?" Paulette plopped a piece of beef in her mouth and blinked.

"No. Should I?" Meredith didn't want to say anything, but then again why not?

"What happened?" Max asked.

"Are you sure you want to know?" Meredith asked. "It might make you uncomfortable."

"I'm a big boy." He motioned with his fork for her to continue. "Go on."

"Yes, please, tell us." Dina laid her fork on her plate and peered at Meredith.

Paulette nodded, still chewing, a smirk on her face as she winked at Meredith. *Chicken.* Meredith sighed and relayed the previous incident. "We think Grace wants a happy ending."

Brock's fork clattered onto his plate. "And how do you propose to give a dead woman a happy ending?" Brock appeared utterly perplexed by such a notion.

"That's the question." Meredith buttered a wedge of cornbread. "Ideas?"

"That's easy." Dina glanced at each of them.

"Do tell." Meredith bit into the dense yellow bread, the pieces of corn and bacon creating mini explosions of joy in her mouth.

"What, you haven't figured it out?" Dina sat back, a grin on her face. "I'm enjoying being ahead of the curve on this one, so don't mind me if I bask in this moment."

"Mom…" Meredith said, leaning forward, elbows on the table. "Spill it."

Dina's Mona Lisa smile made her audience smile in return. "She's been haunting this old place for more than one hundred fifty years because she died a horrible death at the hands of her sister. Whether accidental or not, that's a fact. So naturally, she wants to be laid to rest. And of course, the only place she'd want to be buried is beside her dearly departed brother."

"Of course." Paulette clapped her hands. "Brilliant, Mom."

"Can we do that?" Brock asked. "Aren't there rules or laws governing even family cemeteries?"

"The ME determined the remains are not Native American," Max offered. "As far as the state is concerned, you're free to bury Grace anytime you'd like."

Meredith caught the eye of each of her family members, sharing a happy grin with each. "Max has her remains in his truck." Meredith sank back, her hands falling into her lap. "I guess the next step is to plan a funeral."

Chapter Seventeen

og greeted the dawn. Whiskers tickled Meredith's chin as Grizabella sniffed her lips. She sat up, forcing the insistent cat off her. Shoving the covers away, she swung her legs out of bed and padded to the bathroom. Today they'd lay Grace in the grave waiting for her and hope she'd finally be able to rest in peace. The humidity frizzed Meredith's hair, making it near impossible to force it to lay as she wanted. She glared at herself in the mirror as she wet a comb and swiped through it, only to have it flip back up. Lovely.

A rumble of thunder rolled across the sky outside, sounding like a distant truck lumbering past on the road. So the storm wasn't too close-by. The forecast called for possible severe weather in the afternoon, but the funeral would be over by then. The family worked out the details the day before. The guests had been invited to arrive by eleven, and they'd have a brief service led by the local pastor. The pall bearers would lower the coffin into the hole Sean and Max had dug yesterday in the reserved plot beside Grandpa Joe. Knowing it would likely rain, they'd finalized as much of the preparations as they could, even though they had to do so on a Sunday afternoon. After the coffin was covered in its hole and the final benediction said by the pastor, they'd adjourn to the house for a buffet lunch.

Meredith selected a pair of navy-blue slacks, a crisp white blouse, and saddle-leather sandals. She laid the clothes on the bed, dropped the sandals on the floor beside it, and then went to her jewelry chest. Sliding open the bottom drawer, she peered inside. She fingered the strand of pearls Willy presented to her on their wedding night, remembering the love they represented. Her gaze fell on the cameo her sister gave to her the day she graduated from high school beside the gold band. A flash of light drew her attention to the triple dresser's mirror. Her breath hitched, one hand reaching for her throat. Behind her in the mirror's reflection, Grace stood in her blue hoop-skirted dress, watching her with kind eyes. The young woman must have stolen many young men's hearts with her beauty and poise. Meredith grieved for the life Grace never had chance to live. Grace pointed to the gift box lying on top of the dresser, beside the jewelry chest. Meredith locked eyes with her in the reflection, and she nodded slowly. Meredith inclined her head and opened the gift box. If Grace desired it, then she'd wear the jewelry recovered with her body in order to pay her homage. Meredith lifted Grace's ruby-and-diamond earbobs and matching teardrop necklace and clipped them on in her great-great-great-aunt's honor. She looked behind her in the mirror's reflection to receive Grace's approval, only she no longer lingered in the room.

As Meredith finished dressing, another round of thunder echoed in the distance, chasing her downstairs. Outside, the first drops of rain flashed past the window. Pushing open the door separating the hallway from the kitchen, she paused. Max sat at the dinette table, making her insides quiver at the blue-eyed assessment he aimed in her direction. So be it. She squared her shoulders, strode to the coffeepot, and then snatched a mug.

"You're here early." Meredith inhaled the aroma of the dark liquid, gaining strength from its scent alone.

"Much as I hoped I wouldn't have to do this, I can't take the chance you'd change your mind yet again." He tapped his briefcase sitting on the floor. "I've moved up the council vote to this afternoon. I won't give you the option of desecrating your grandmother's memory and her trust in you."

"You don't trust me?"

"I want to, Meredith. With all my heart." He shook his head, his luxurious brown hair flowing across the top edge of his collar. "There's no grandfather clause in the legislation. It takes effect immediately upon the vote."

She caught the challenge in his expression, and her hackles rose. She detested being told what she could and could not do. Could he do that? Or was he bluffing? She didn't know, but either way, if she burned the place down, nobody could do anything about it. She elected to change the subject rather than argue with him. Not that she meant to destroy it any longer, but he didn't know that for certain. Let him stew for a little awhile.

"Is Sue coming?" Meredith sipped her coffee, gripping the mug with both hands. The heat warmed her cold fingers.

"Yes, and bringing Jeremy."

"Nice of you to give her the time off so she could attend."

"She would have taken the morning either way, so why not."

Paulette strode in, followed by Grizabella. The cat made a beeline to her bowl. Paulette grabbed a mug and poured coffee in it, adding cream and sugar until Meredith felt ill thinking about drinking the concoction. A breeze flowed through the open window, billowing the light curtains out like the hallmark photo of Marilyn Monroe's white dress.

"I think the weatherman was wrong." Paulette claimed a seat at the table. "That cold wind is announcing the severe stuff is coming faster than they said."

"It'll be fine." Meredith heard a timer ticking. "What's Meg got in the oven?"

"Pecan coffee cake." Max rubbed his stomach and licked his lips with exaggerated smacking. "Can't wait until I hear the timer ding."

Despite herself, Meredith chuckled at his antics. "You always think of food, don't you?"

"Smells good." Paulette inhaled deeply. "Now that I'm eating for two, I guess we can grant you one meager piece, Max."

"We'll see." Max grinned at her.

Meredith sucked in a breath and almost choked when she smelled honeysuckle instead of the cinnamon and nutmeg she expected. One hand went to the pendant, rubbing it between her fingers. She coughed to clear her lungs, and then tentatively sniffed. Cinnamon, brown sugar, pecans. Hmmm. Much better. The timer dinged, and she rose to remove the pan from the oven.

"Where is Meg?" Meredith asked, setting the round pan on top of the stove.

"She said she had a pork roast to start in a slow oven at her place." Max stood and walked over to retrieve a stack of plates from the cupboard and then waited beside Meredith as she sliced the cake. His actions smacked of familiarity with the house. With her. Her hand shook as she inserted the knife tip into the crunch topping and pushed down. She shouldn't be reacting to his mere presence. He was her lawyer, not her lover. Which only made her think of their last kiss, the one she'd ended before she wanted to further their foreplay. Before he became more than her lawyer and risked her own heart.

"Here, now go sit down." She scooped a slice of cake

onto a plate and waved the knife at him to urge him to return to his seat. Away from her so she could think clearly.

"Yes'm."

"What about me?" Paulette asked. "Do I have to come there or can you bring me a piece?"

"Lazy." Meredith grinned at her as she placed a slice on a plate and then carried it to her. She set it on the table. "Just because you're with child doesn't mean you get special treatment. At least not all the time."

"I can try, can't I?" Paulette took a bite and then licked the tines of her fork to snare every crumb of the treat.

"Is everything ready for the service?" Max asked between bites.

Meredith joined them at the table. "Yes. The coroner said he wrapped her remains in the blue gown ready for burial. And I"—she fingered the pendant again and glanced at Max, then Paulette—"I chose to wear her jewelry. Do you think that's weird?"

"Not at all." Paulette gazed at her a long moment, tears glistening in the corners of her eyes. "I think she'd like that."

Meredith laid a hand on Paulette's arm and briefly squeezed. "Me too."

A couple of hours later, the first cars pulled into the driveway. Sean took it upon himself to direct traffic, assuring everyone had a place to park that didn't block the driveway. The rain had abated, the grass sparkling with traces of the latest shower. But dark clouds built in the distance, threatening charcoal mounds soaring high into the heavens. Typical rainy weather for a funeral. Some cultures believed rain on your wedding equaled good fortune. What did it mean when rain fell on a funeral? Peace?

Sean had erected a tent over the burial site the day before, anticipating the potential need to shelter the mourners now gathering at the grave. No tombstone sat at the head of the grave and wouldn't until one could be made.

Meanwhile, Sean's creativity shown through the placement of a wooden cross painted white with Grace's full name—Grace Abigail O'Connell—stenciled in black on the horizontal beam. Max assisted in herding everyone through the open gate and under the dark-green canvas. The pastor waited beside the cross, Bible open in his hands, until the small crowd stilled and fell silent.

As he intoned the opening prayer, Meredith stood with her hands folded. She hoped Grace would be pleased with the gathering. In addition to herself, the mourners included her family—Paulette, Dina, Brock—and friends—Max, Meg, Sean, Sue, Jeremy—as well as two renowned local historians and a contingent from the sheriff's office. Even the bartender, Sam, had made an appearance, bringing a carload of presumed relatives. In fact, most of the folks gathered were connected to Max, not to her except by extension through him. Yet comfort surged through her as a result of those who cared enough to take time from their busy schedules to attend the burial of her very distant relative. She hoped Grandpa Joe appreciated the resulting send-off his sister received.

Sunlight dappled the ground under the surrounding magnolia tree branches, tiny spotlights layered on the waxy leaves, spent white blossoms littering the wet grass. Thunder rumbled in the distance, accompanied by a burst of cool wind that flipped the Bible's pages.

The sound of the paper in the breeze reminded Meredith of the photo album and the idea that Grace had turned those pages to ensure her message came through loud and clear. Which reminded Meredith of Grace's image in the mirror mere hours before, linking with her silently though effectively through the medium of the reflection. Disappearing without a trace when Meredith blinked before turning to try to look at her directly.

"Amen." The pastor nodded, and several men moved to

lower the coffin into its final resting spot. With each slip of the ropes between their capable hands, contentment spread through Meredith, as though joy found purchase within. Or perhaps Grace had returned home to where her own heart beckoned. Home to be with her favorite sibling. Once the casket settled on the floor of the grave, the men hefted spades and began covering the coffin with dirt. The sound of the clods striking the wooden lid sent shivers through Meredith, but they were not cold or scary. The shivers seemed to be echoes of laughter and love from somewhere inside. Tremors like she'd never experienced before.

The pastor intoned a final benediction while the men continued to shovel dirt into the hole. When the prayer ended, the gathering paused for the space of a breath and then began making their way to the house for lunch and socializing. Meredith hung back, watching the hole fill and experiencing Grace's satisfaction spread through her. Max sauntered over to where she lingered under the trees.

"May she rest in peace." He studied her, appearing to search for something in her expression.

She nodded. "Hungry?"

"You bet. Shoveling is hard work." He patted his stomach. "After all, I only had a piece of cake for breakfast."

She cast a last glance at the fresh mound of dirt blanketing Grace's grave site. The white cross seemed to glow among the deep shade beneath the tall trees. The rain clouds roiled above like smoke in a jar. A clap of thunder made her jump. Lightning forked across the sky. "We should go in anyway."

"Right, if you can hear thunder, you can be struck by lightning. Given that we can see the lightning, the risk is very real." He took her arm and escorted her back through the metal gate, and then across the gravel driveway.

As she passed through the kitchen door he held open, she paused and gazed up at him. "I hope the worst of it waits until after everyone has safely arrived home. Our shelter would be mighty crowded if all these folks had to cram inside it."

"Not to worry. The radar isn't showing any purple yet, so we're okay. Let's have some sandwiches, shall we?"

She nodded and hurried into the kitchen, where Paulette immediately accosted her carrying a potted geranium.

"Where shall we put this?" She lifted the ceramic pot with geometric designs decorating the sides. "It's in memory of Grace from Sue. She wanted you to have something living to remind you of your aunt's life. Isn't it a pretty shade of red?" Paulette twirled the plant, examining it from all sides.

"Put it wherever you want. I'm getting something to eat." Meredith moved away from Paulette, catching up to Max at the makeshift buffet table set up in the foyer.

The double front doors stood open, creating a picturesque backdrop to the array of delicious foods. Grizabella had been relegated to Meredith's room until the luncheon ended so Meredith wouldn't worry about her venturing outside, checking out the food, or tripping someone. Before very long, the crowd thinned. The dark storm clouds continued to gather overhead, lightning fracturing the sky. Finally, the last of the mourners paid their condolences, ate their last mouthful, and drove away. The thunder and lightning drew nearer, carried by the increasing wind whipping through the trees and blowing the tall grass so it danced under the onslaught.

"Quite a view from here." Max had sneaked up on her so quietly she hadn't heard even a floorboard creak.

"I've always loved being on the porch, drawn to it for reasons I only now understand." She gazed out over the vista, the rolling hills boasting copses of trees, the lake churning in the wind, the road winding its way across the valley and disappearing to the left. The sky turned from dark gray to silver with a green cast, as though growing ill from its own increasing ferocity. She turned away from the storm to contemplate Max, drawn to him, too, for very different reasons. Reasons she must deny herself in order to protect them both. *He's my lawyer, not my lover.* "I guess it's time for you to head to town for the vote, right?"

His expression turned grim. "Why are you pushing me away?"

Before she could formulate a response, the tornado siren blared at the same time the weather radio sounded. Together, they gaped out over the valley in time to see the funnel cloud come into view and take aim on Twin Oaks.

"Oh no!" Meredith cried. "Where's everybody? We need to take cover."

"Get down to the basement," Max said. "I'll get the cat. Go!"

"I'll find everyone." She closed the double doors and then raced down the hall, searching for her family.

They found her, emerging into the hallway from side rooms as she ran toward the kitchen. Brock's stalwart expression calmed Meredith's rising panic. Her mother and sister exhibited concern but not fear.

"The tornado is coming this way. Go to the cellar. Now!" She shooed them before her, aware of Max's heavy footsteps above as he hurried to retrieve her cat.

His offer to find Grizabella and keep her safe warmed Meredith's heart. His longer stride made it faster for him to retrieve the cat than for Meredith. As long as he hurried, they'd all make it to the safety of the storm shelter.

Moments later Meredith sat with the rest of her family huddled in the basement, the radio blaring the weatherman's blow-by-blow coverage of the tornado's track. Max slammed the door at the top of the steps before pounding down to join them where they perched on the benches lining the walls. When he reached the bottom of the steps, he let Griz jump out of his arms while he took a seat next to Meredith.

Outside, the wind battered the antebellum building, rattling the windows. Rain beat against the sides. Inside, Meredith glanced from tense face to worried expression. Predicting the actions of a tornado seemed difficult at best. Even professional storm chasers died in their efforts when the tornado shifted direction so fast they couldn't escape its path.

How long would they be stuck here? Trapped in a tiny wine cellar with four other adults and one grumpy cat stalking about the room. Brock paced, nearly stepping on Meredith's feet as he maneuvered his bulk between the two benches and their occupants. Dina perched on the edge of the bench facing Meredith and Max, staring at the door, their escape route once the all clear sounded. Paulette plopped cross-legged on an oversize pillow on the floor, one she dragged downstairs with her.

Two weeks ago Meredith would have never thought to be in the same room with any of them, and now they'd been forced to squeeze among the wine bottles and emergency supplies and wait. In the very place she'd hoped they'd never need to use. She stared at the array of wine bottles, pondering whether to suggest opening one to calm her nerves.

"Do you hear that?" Max stood and walked to the base of the steps, staring toward the door.

"What?" Meredith rested her hands on her knees, prepared to join him should the need arise.

"It sounds like a train coming." Paulette wrapped her arms around her knees and rocked. "Oh God."

Max sat back down beside Meredith and put an arm around her shoulders. "The tornado is here."

The door bumped against the jamb as the winds surged and roared around the house. Max tightened his hold on Meredith, unwilling to chance her safety. When he'd finally located the cat hunkered under the bed, he'd dragged it protesting from its hidey-hole and hurried to the basement. On the way past the front windows he'd seen the tornado, debris aloft within the whirling winds, heading straight for Twin Oaks. Over the last several years, the strength and frequency of tornadoes in the area had both increased. This old property had seen its fair share of them passing over, but now it faced certain destruction. The question was how much would be damaged?

He glanced at Meredith. She'd wanted to bring the place down, and he'd fought her. Was Mother Nature taking her turn? Was it Twin Oaks' destiny to be flattened and left as only a memory for those who loved it? He swallowed his fear. He must remain stoic and supportive despite the impending violence outside the stone-and-wood structure.

"What do we do if the tornado hits the house?" Dina clenched her hands together in her lap, knuckles pale.

"That depends on what the winds do," Max said. "I've seen houses shifted off their foundations or blown away with the storm."

Meredith trembled in his embrace. She hadn't said anything in several minutes. Her fear created a vibration within her so violent it reminded him of a violinist's tremolo.

"What if the house collapses on top of us?" Paulette hugged her knees tighter.

"The sheriff's office has a list of the tornado shelters," Max said. "They'll know to hunt for us in here."

Meredith searched his face. "I'm glad you're here."

His heart swelled at her words. This woman touched his soul with those eyes. "Me too."

Brock stopped his pacing and settled on the bench beside Dina. He covered her hands with one of his. Some of the tension in his wife's posture eased.

Max hoped the twister avoided the house, but nobody could predict its exact path. Some studies suggested they followed the terrain to an extent, but how much? They didn't always stay in flat or shallow areas. Even Sand Mountain in northern Alabama had been struck, trees toppled, leaving jagged shards of trunk jutting against the sky.

Meredith tensed beneath his arm.

"Hey, where's Meg?" Meredith sat upright, breaking his contact with her shoulders. "And Sean? Oh no, they must be out there." She stared up the steps and then looked at him as if he had the answer.

If only he did. Sean, a country boy born and bred, knew how to prepare for threats such as tornadoes and would ensure they sought shelter. Why hadn't they done so already?

"What will they do?" Paulette shifted to sit cross-legged again, leaning forward with elbows on her knees. "We should help them."

"We're not going out there," Brock said. "That would be suicide."

The tension in Meredith increased beside him. Her muscles pulled tight, seemingly to the point of snapping, like his piano string. He gazed at her, drew her chin around with a light hand to fix her attention on what he needed to say. "They'll seek shelter. They've been through this before."

"Unless they've been hurt." Her eyes glistened with tears. "Or worse."

"Don't say that." Paulette's expression revealed her concern. "They have to be okay."

Dina laid a hand on Paulette's shoulder. "Sean is resourceful. They've both been through these storms all their lives. I'm sure they'll be fine."

Paulette overlaid her hand on her mother's, grasping her fingers. "I hope so."

"I can't imagine losing Meg or Sean," Meredith whispered. "What would we do without their caring assistance?"

"Or cinnamon buns." Paulette grinned, but worry weighted the corners of her mouth. She huffed a laugh. "Not funny, eh?"

"Let's not give up on them," Brock said. "Keep the faith."

The door at the top of the stairs yanked open, blasting air into the stuffy room. Sean and Meg bolted through the opening, Sean turning and wrestling the door closed behind them. They hesitated for a second on the steps, long enough for Max to realize they were soaked through. He went to the far shelf and grabbed blankets, offering one to Meg and then to Sean. Meg nodded her thanks, but Sean shook off the offer. Max tossed the unwanted blanket back on the shelf.

"Thank goodness you made it here." Dina rose to hug Meg. "We were worried sick about you both."

"It's awful." Meg sank to the bench Dina had vacated, wrapping the blanket around her shoulders. She shook her head, tears threatening. "The gazebo is gone, shattered into pieces and flung into the cemetery like kindling on a fire."

"Not the gazebo." Paulette gripped her knees with both hands. "Grandma used to hold tea parties there for me and Meredith when we were little. Remember, Mer?"

Max glanced at Meredith. She nodded, as though in a trance, her thoughts far away. He went back to slide his arm around her shoulders. The storm and her fear both provided the perfect excuse for him to indulge his desire to touch her. From the first time he'd been near this beautiful and intelligent woman, he'd been drawn to her, needing to experience her.

"Hopefully that's all that is damaged," Brock said. "From the sound of the wind, it's not over yet."

"The eye of the twister hasn't arrived yet." Meredith trembled, and he snuggled his arm around her. The roar of the wind increased until the sound hurt his ears.

"The radar shows it's moving fast." Sean leaned against the wall. "We should be clear soon. Then we can go inspect the extent of the damage."

Meredith cleared her throat and pushed to an upright position. Max let his arm drop off her shoulders but maintained contact with her, encircling her waist instead.

"I'd like to say something." Meredith paused, looking at each person in the room. "We never know when our time may come, and in case we're about to find out when our times are, I want you all to know that—" Glass breaking upstairs made them all gasp and fall silent for a moment. "Despite what you may think of me, I love you all. Coming here has changed me in ways I'd never expected. And, as this tornado threatens to do what I had foolishly considered, I've realized I was wrong."

Max waited for the other shoe to fall. What did she plan to do? He involuntarily tightened his arm around her until she shot him a questioning look. Forcing his embrace to relax, he winked at her.

"So you're definitely, positively not going to demolish it?" Paulette asked.

More glass crashed overhead. Everyone stared at the ceiling for a long moment, and then back at each other.

"No, I'll do what Grandma O'Connell wanted and renovate Twin Oaks."

Max squeezed her waist. He was overjoyed she'd finally come to her senses and recognized the value of restoring the place and living here. "You won't regret your decision."

"As for you, Max..." Meredith turned to peer at him, angling her body within his embrace. "You've been a thorn in my side the entire time I've been here."

He stiffened. What? He tightened his lips, resisting jumping to conclusions.

"You broke my door, which you still owe me a repair on. But of course, who knows what else will need fixing?" She smiled. "But we're even, at least as far as owing each other, since I owe you a dinner, I believe."

Max brushed a stray lock of hair out of her face, his index finger sliding down to brush her cheekbone. She watched him with a new openness in her startling eyes, as though she'd awakened from a nightmare. Perhaps in one sense she had, having realized the value of her inheritance, her heritage, and most of all her family. Max couldn't help himself. He kissed her.

The touch of her lips to his ignited the ever-present simmer of longing in his heart and soul when near her. "Assuming we all manage to survive, you're on."

Meredith smiled at him. "I'd like that."

"Knock it off, you two." Brock resumed his pacing. "The wind is letting up."

Max kissed her again, deeper this time, despite the groans from their audience. "Sounds like a plan."

The wind continued to roar above their heads. Meredith snuggled against Max's side, a newly discovered sense of well-being and peace filling her. The people around her were her family, both by blood and by choice. With each crash of glass she'd realized demolition of Twin Oaks would never happen at her hands. This place, so replete with traces of her ancestors, her heritage, even her childhood, provided the continuum between then and now. Her marriage to Willy had been idyllic, and she'd never forget her first true love. Yet he would not want her to stop living, to stop dreaming, and most important, he'd never want her to stop creating.

Renovating the house spoke to her in a way she hadn't heard in a long time. Too long, in fact. A whisper of possibilities for what she could create, the finishes to apply, the furniture to locate to reflect the beauty and opulence of days gone by.

More glass breaking interrupted her thoughts. She glared at the closed door, willing the storm to abate so she could assess the damage and begin to make her dreams into actions.

"I hope there's something left when all this is over," Paulette said.

"There will be." Meredith stood and stretched. "What's the radar showing?"

Brock checked his phone display. "Storm track is showing we should be clear in another minute."

"Must we wait?" Sean tugged at his open collar. "Such a small room for all of us."

Meg pulled him closer and kissed his cheek. "Not much longer, dear. You'll survive, I promise."

Meredith grinned at the elderly couple. "How long have you two been married?"

"Thirty-two years this summer." Meg took Sean's hand and covered it with both of hers.

How satisfying to have that much time together. Meredith glanced at Max. What would their future hold? Did they even have one? More important, was she ready to find out?

Griz dashed up the steps. Her meow sounded loud in the small, crowded space.

The wind quieted, and Meredith moved to the bottom of the steps. "I'm going up."

"Is it safe?" Paulette asked.

Meredith smiled in reply to the concern in Paulette's eyes. "Safe enough."

"Right behind you." Max followed her up the stairs, and together they opened the door.

"Careful, there's glass everywhere." Rain blew through the window over the kitchen sink as Meredith picked her way into the room. Glass crunched under her shoes. Max emerged into the room from behind her, and they both paused to take in the amount of destruction.

Max pushed past Meredith and lifted a six-foot limb from the floor. He dragged it to the open doorway, the broken door now lying half-in and half-out of the kitchen. Sean led the others out of the cellar to stand and gape at the damage. The rain had soaked everything, and the wind had hurled tree limbs and debris from outside through the shattered window and door. The little tiled table had been reduced to so much kindling and porcelain pieces scattered across the floor.

"Wow." Paulette hugged her waist. "What a mess."

"At least we're all safe. I want to see what else happened." Meredith picked her way across the floor and through the swinging door to the hallway. At the far end, the front doors stood wide open, the rain and wind wreaking havoc on the hardwood floors. More limbs and leaves lay blasted across the space, scratches glaring in the floorboards. One front window lay in shards on the floor, the apparent victim of an eight-foot tree limb.

"The sewing room is intact." Max shook his head. "It's bad in here but not irreparable."

"It's pretty minor, thankfully." She closed the front doors, relieved the ancient wood panels remained unharmed when they blew open. Finding solid wood doors to replace them would have been difficult. She turned to Max. "I spotted some plastic in the cellar we can use to cover the kitchen window."

"That'll work, at least temporarily."

When they returned to the kitchen, Sean already had the door propped back in place. Meg had started sweeping up the glass. Brock hefted the last of the large limbs outside, while Dina and Paulette gathered the smaller pieces and added them to the growing pile. Before long, the broken windows in the kitchen and the foyer both sported an expanse of blue tarp held in place with gray duct tape. The swirling leaves settled onto the floor as the wind inside stopped.

Meredith finished sweeping up the glass from the front hall, dumping the shards into the trash can. The gouges on the floor would be harder to clear away. She knelt down to inspect the damage. Rocking back onto her heels, she considered leaving the scarred floor as it was; a reminder to her that not all scars need to be obliterated in order for the past to not impede the future. *Sometimes our scars help show the strength we've developed through the adversity in our lives.*

"The rain's stopped." Max sank to a squatting position beside her, bringing to mind the other time, in the sewing parlor, when they'd shared their first kiss. "Did you want to check out the exterior damage now?"

She knelt in front of him, placed her hands on his shoulders and kissed him. "Yes, since the interior is secured against further damage."

They walked together through the door and surveyed the front of the property. Several large trees stood snapped midway up their trunks, leaving jagged fragments pointed to the heavens. The path of the tornado scored a barren swath of land leading up to the side of the house, though thankfully skirting the building. Following the trail of desolation, Meredith and Max strolled around the house.

The beautiful white gazebo peppered the backyard and family cemetery with pieces of wood and metal. Tears smarted Meredith's eyes. The gazebo had held as many memories as any other part of the plantation. Most recently of sisters sharing secrets among the fairy lights. But those memories, both old and new, were all the more cherished because of their uniqueness.

"I'm sorry, Meredith."

She glanced at his sad eyes. "It's okay. I'll rebuild it." Meredith tread onto the stone foundation. "Complete with fairy lights."

Max stepped up behind her and wrapped his arms around her waist. She leaned her head against his chest and sighed. She never thought she'd feel contentment with another man, yet here she stood among the debris of the gazebo with Max holding her, comforting her. Amid devastation she found comfort. A tear trickled down her cheek as she surveyed the snapped and flung trees, the battered wrought-iron fence, and the gazebo's white boards strewn across the yard like so many matchsticks. Leaves rustled behind her, but she didn't move when Max shifted his weight. His solid support meant more to her than she had ever hoped to experience again.

"It could've been worse." Paulette strolled up to stand with them. "At least no one was hurt."

Meredith exhaled, knowing she spoke the truth. The others trailed outside to witness the damage. She pushed away from Max's embrace, the rush of cool air on her back making her shiver. Dragging in a deep breath, she detected wet earth mixed with the aroma of early spring flowers but no whiff of honeysuckle. She smiled, knowing Grace finally did rest in peace.

"Well, I'm so glad we had this chance to spend time with you, a ghost, and a tornado." Brock quirked an eyebrow. "So worthwhile making this trip to be with my girls."

Meredith chuckled, a lopsided grin forming. "Glad we could entertain, Dad."

Dina smacked Brock's arm. "Be serious, will ya?"

"What?" Brock assumed an offended look, though his grin belied his attempt.

Sean laughed, clasping Meg's hand. "I'll grab the wheelbarrow and start cleaning this mess up while we still have daylight."

"I'll grab my gloves and start on the boards." Meg hurried away with him, hand in hand, toward the shed.

"So, Paulette, do you still want to live here?" Meredith smiled at her sister.

"Of course." Paulette crossed her arms and gazed at Meredith. "Why?

"We've got our work cut out for us."

Paulette hugged Meredith. "I'm in, don't worry."

Meredith turned to Max and angled her head, assessing his serious expression. She squeezed his hand. "What about you, lawyer dude? Are you in too?"

The sun lowered behind the plantation house, casting long shadows across the yard. Meredith cradled a glass of wine, its fruity tones intoxicating after the hard work everyone had put in clearing debris all afternoon. Her folks had already taken off for home, worried about any possible damage at their place from the rampant storms. Paulette had pleaded a headache and taken a cup of tomato soup and crackers to her room to recuperate. Meg and Sean had retreated to their home for the evening as well. That left Meredith and Max on the porch, alone.

Max insisted she relax and reconnoiter her thoughts, her plans. He settled onto the two-person swing at the corner of the wraparound porch, sipping some of her dad's whiskey on the rocks. His gaze weighed upon her, though she pretended not to notice he watched her actions. She scanned the yard succumbing to the deepening shadows. Stars twinkled in the distance, innumerable and mysterious.

He was right. She did need to determine her next steps. What should she do with the family plantation? Ten bedrooms seemed an awful lot of wasted space if they always sat empty. Of course, Paulette and Meredith would each occupy one, and Paulette's baby would occupy another. What about the other seven? She rubbed her forehead with her thumb and index finger, massaging the tightness lodged above her eyes.

"Are you okay?" Max's deep chocolate voice reached her, his concern apparent.

"I've been worse." She glanced at him, and then back to where the gazebo once stood. "Thanks for all you've done for me, Max."

The swing creaked, followed by Max's footsteps approaching. His hands gripped her arms, and he turned her to face him. His eyes glowed in the soft lighting. She smelled his spicy aftershave overlaid by the scent of his honest labor on her behalf. Crickets sang as background to the last strains of the birds crooning themselves to sleep.

"When I look at you, I see the most beautiful woman in the world." Max slipped his hands down her arms to grasp hers. "But more even, your courage and your deep love for your family shines from your soul."

"Max, I—"

"Shhh. Let me finish." He kissed her, a soft pressure that thrummed through her. "You attract me like bears to honey, or steel to a magnet. I must touch you, feel you beneath my hands. You've become my obsession."

"Is that a good thing?" She laughed, sounding nervous to her own ears.

"I believe so." He pulled her closer and kissed her. "I know you've been through a very rough time, losing both your husband and your child. I can't imagine the enormity of the challenge you faced, working through the grief."

She closed her eyes, a flash of the old pain searing her

gut. She opened her eyes and worked her lower lip between her teeth, drawing his attention to her mouth. "It's been the most difficult time of my life."

He speared her with his gaze. "Grief is a tunnel, Meredith, not a destination. We pass through it, no matter how long or dark it may be. We find a way through it, a way to light the path so we come out the other end ready to face the rest of our lives without the ones we've lost. Whether the way is through religion or family or yelling and screaming. But we always find a way to traverse the grief tunnel. Always."

She'd never thought of grieving the way he described. She searched his eyes, where caring and concern shone. And something else. She leaned closer, delving deep into his expression. His lips pressed together and then relaxed at her nearness. Captivated, she reached to kiss him, pressing her mouth to his as a thank-you for his understanding, and as a giving of herself to this man who attracted her like—now, what did he say?—bears to honey and steel to magnets. She, too, couldn't help being drawn to him despite all her protests.

His arms slipped around her, crushing her against his hard chest. His mouth opened to her tongue, seeking entrance. He tasted delicious, the whiskey he drank heightening his natural essence and combining with the wine she'd consumed. The notes of sweet and smoky harmonized, building to a crescendo of sensation flowing through her. She rode the wave, amazed she could once more experience the pleasure of kissing. Max ignited a passion in her unlike any other she'd known. He deepened the kiss, one hand clasping her breast, and all analytical thoughts disintegrated into the sheer bliss of being with a virile man. Of being with Max.

When they mutually ended the kiss, they contemplated each other for a minute, a soft smile on their lips.

"I do believe you've helped me find the light at the end of the tunnel." Meredith rested her hands on Max's chest, his heart thudding against her palms. "Thank you."

He inclined his head and winked. "The pleasure is definitely all mine, my lady."

"What do we do now?" She traced a finger across his polo shirt, circling one button with her pinky. He'd broken through her defenses, awakened her to feelings and sensations she'd attempted to bury after all she'd been through. Now her body sang with need, want, desire. She could fly she felt so free and happy.

"Whatever feels right." He kissed her forehead, the tip of her nose, and then pressed a long kiss to her mouth.

She returned his kiss, savoring the physical connection almost as much as the sense he meant what he said. Knowing she needed him as much as he needed her. She ended the lip lock, took his hand with a wink, and led him, unprotesting, upstairs.

Chapter Eighteen

eredith raised the window two inches, allowing the early morning breeze to flow through the sewing room. She returned to the rocking chair, sipped from her coffee mug, and stared at the stack of Grandpa Joe's journals and letters. Beside them, Grandma O'Connell's research binder was open, white pages filled with notes from her efforts.

Since Meredith intended to restore Twin Oaks, the contents of those pages and pages of information became source material for matching the present to the past appearance of the house. Grandpa Joe's journals reflected his view of the layout and contents. The many letters included references to who visited, what they did while there, and also the ambiance the visitors sensed about the house. Plus, the genealogical research showed the number and categories of residents as well as their occupations. A virtual treasure trove for the renovation expert to delve into for specific nuances to the completed restoration.

She set her mug back on the table and lifted a leather-bound journal. Laying it on her lap, she ran a hand over the embossed cover. Would she ever tire of pausing for a moment to ruminate upon holding the same book as her ancestor? Ever since Paulette pointed out she was about to dispose of her Grandma's books—ones Grandma held near and dear—Meredith had developed a sense of connection through the paper and leather and ink. If only there were a way to establish that same sense of connection for all her descendants so no one else would ever propose to do what she'd briefly considered.

"Hey," Paulette said, sauntering into the parlor. She carried a sketch pad, several pages flipped open, a pencil in hand. "What are you doing in here?"

"Thinking." Meredith laid the journal back on the stack. She raised an eyebrow at the sketch pad. "What's up?"

"I thought I'd try my hand at designing again. Have I lost my touch?" She turned the pad to face Meredith.

The dress featured a flouncy skirt and fitted bodice with tulle overlay and cap sleeves. The heart-shaped outline to the bodice featured a plunging neckline, which would highlight a woman's décolletage, though the overlay softened the effect to a more feminine allure.

"That's beautiful." Meredith rose to move closer for a better view. "If the skirt were floor-length, you could also use it for a prom gown."

Paulette examined the drawing and then smiled. "Yes, a few tweaks here and there and I could also make this a formal, or even convert it into a hoop-skirt design. Brilliant."

Meredith stilled, her thoughts racing.

"What?" Paulette asked. "You look like you're far away all of a sudden."

She blinked and then smiled. "I have an idea."

Paulette raised an eyebrow. "Yes?"

"We could make Twin Oaks into a partial B&B with a small museum dedicated to Twin Oaks history. Maybe even host reenactments of the Civil War encampment and balls." She waited for Paulette to follow her reasoning. "You know, with the ladies dressed in their finest and the gentlemen in uniforms and suits?"

"You want me to design the dresses?" Paulette's smile illuminated her entire face.

Meredith bobbed her head. "We could make this place our home as well as our business. What do you think?"

She squinted at Meredith. "Are you asking me to stay? Permanently?"

"Yes, if you want to." Meredith grinned. "And your baby, of course. I can help you raise him or her. We'd have Meg and Sean to help, as well."

"And Max? What about him?"

"I don't know, but will you stay? Please?"

"But why, Mer? You told me you'd strangle me if we ever lived under the same roof again. And we nearly did. So why now?"

Meredith hugged her and then stepped back. "Because even though we may not always see eye to eye, we are sisters. We're family, and family sticks together. I hope we can be friends once more."

A long moment of silence followed, with the two women eyeing each other. Meredith hoped Paulette would agree, because her plan solved all their problems for a change, rather than creating more of them. She waited, wanting her to weigh the pros and cons and make a choice like she had when deciding to raise her child. Meredith appreciated the difficulties her decision would bring, but with all of them working together, the hardships would be minimized.

Paulette nodded with a smile. "Yes, and thank you, Mer."

Meredith hugged her, holding on longer than she'd hugged anyone in years. After several minutes, she ended the embrace and stepped back. "Come on, we have work to do."

The next day the house was almost returned to normal.

New glass panes had been installed and only the scarred floorboards recalled to mind the terror of the tornado. Meredith closed the journal she'd been reading, rocking back in her grandmother's favorite chair. The sun streamed through the sewing-room windows, beckoning to her. She pushed to her feet and down the hall to the kitchen.

Walking outside, she drank in the sense of solitude and serenity gracing the property. She'd heard on the news the night before that the tornado that rampaged through her part of the county classified as an EF1. Not such a big event in the grand scheme of things, but certainly big enough to shake them up. The stone foundation that once supported the graceful gazebo appeared stark in the afternoon light as she walked by. Locating the artisan to recreate the elaborate ironwork to decorate the roof would take time. But she had all the time in the world. She grinned at the thought.

Sean had cleaned up the yard and cemetery faster than she'd ever believed possible. He'd even managed to straighten the fence, though some of the iron showed stress marks from the twisting and untwisting. More reminders of how Twin Oaks had suffered and grown stronger as a result. She pushed open the back gate and emerged into the expanse of the meadow. The waving grasses had dried out since the severe weather passed through. If not for the barren gazebo foundation in the middle of the yard, no one would ever know anything bad had occurred. She spotted her objective, standing sentinel in the center of the field, and strode toward it.

The fairy tree's gnarled trunk and branching limbs welcomed her. She laid a hand against the bark, the rough textures familiar beneath her roaming fingertips. As she gazed up through the mass of green leaves, two puffy white clouds floated across the bright sky. This small tree represented both the passing of time and the sense of time standing still. As it grew a little each year, it marked the passage of the days and weeks. Likewise, the longer it graced the meadow, it represented the constant presence of the O'Connell family. Must be the fairy's magic that enabled one living thing to encompass both concepts.

"Dear fairies, wherever you may be," Meredith said, grasping a branch with both hands, "I've come out here today to thank you. You've watched over us, me and my ancestors, for many generations. You've protected Twin Oaks and all it stands for, and I'm deeply grateful."

The late spring sun held more heat than previously, making her forehead bead with sweat. No, that wasn't right. Her Grandma had always said Southern women do not sweat, they *glisten*. She smiled. Okay, so she was glistening. A lot.

A cool breeze lifted the hair from her warm neck, sending a delightful shiver through her. The meadow stretched in all directions from this point where she stood. Much like her view of her future. Her options had increased tenfold since making the decision to move to Twin Oaks permanently. Her boss hadn't been too happy. She mentally shrugged. He'd get over it. After all, she could design multimillion-dollar homes for the firm from wherever she lived. More to the point, though, relying on her creativity brought her much more satisfaction than she'd thought possible. And, of course, her commitment to Paulette's and the baby's future played a significant part in her decision.

She wondered again whether the child would be a girl or a boy. She'd welcome her or him no matter. In addition to reconnecting with her parents, she'd rediscovered her sister, and in six and a half months she'd become an aunt. She'd also discovered all the people who, though not related by blood, figured into her larger family. Meg, Sean, Sue, Jeremy.

A blues riff drifted on the afternoon breeze. She scanned the meadow, letting her gaze pick out details she'd skimmed over in the past. Daffodils and jonquils littered one corner of the meadow, their cheery yellow and white blossoms vivid against the green grasses. Many other wildflowers dotted the expanse, their tiny spots of color dancing in the gentle wind. The breeze turned cool. Her gaze darted across the field, finally landing on what she equated to the cooler temperature.

In the shade of the old magnolias, Grace paused regally, a smile on her lips. Her sequined gown glittered in the shadows of the tree. She nodded at Meredith and then turned as though she'd heard someone call her name. Following her glance, Meredith gasped. Standing deeper in the shade of the magnolia, Joe waited. He was striking in his Confederate uniform, saber at his side and a wide red sash around his waist. He saluted Meredith, a crisp movement of his right hand. Then he lowered his hand and extended it toward Grace, palm up. Grace smiled at Meredith once more, hiked her skirt and walked to Joe. Taking his hand, she let him tuck her hand around his elbow. He gave Meredith one last nod and a smile before they turned and strolled into the cemetery. Slowly their image dissolved.

Meredith's smile remained intact long after they had disappeared. She marveled at how she'd helped them to find lasting peace at Twin Oaks, something she'd dreamed of happening for her as well. And she could finally admit she found happiness despite her best efforts to destroy the very thing instilling peace within her.

The crunch of tires on gravel drew her attention to the pickup truck coming up the drive. Max's green vehicle bounced slowly closer. Not wanting to return to the house quite yet, Meredith figured Paulette would let him know where she'd gone. The day proved too lovely, the tree too inviting for her to stay inside.

She grabbed a low-hanging branch and swung from it, feeling joy return to reside in her soul. The action reminded her of her tomboy days, days she and Paulette spent together climbing trees, riding bikes, and playing baseball. She pendulum swung a few more times and then dropped to the ground. Lying on her back, she explored the bright blue sky with its scattering of cotton-ball clouds. A pair of turkey buzzards spiraled above her, slowly lowering their flight to determine how tasty she'd be. As children, the two girls used to lure the buzzards in and then jump up to scare them away. Such a morbid game they'd played, but it brought a wry smile to her lips.

Max strode up to where she lay, his footsteps sending small shocks through the ground. "Hey, beautiful."

She sat up and smiled at him. "Hey, yourself. Care to join me?" She patted the grass beside her, and Max folded his legs to sit down.

"I have some good news." He leaned over and kissed her lightly on the lips, his eyes glowing.

"What's up?" Meredith put a blade of grass between her thumbs and blew on it, producing a whistling type of sound.

"You're pretty good." Max clapped, then sobered. He took her hands, the grass blade fluttering to the ground. "I've been made senior partner."

"Wonderful. Congratulations." She helped him celebrate with a quick peck on the mouth. "What does that mean?"

"It means the county council passed my ordinance to protect historic homes like Twin Oaks." He squeezed her hands, pulling her closer to him. "It means I have everything I've worked for all my life, except for one very important element."

"What?" Her heart skipped a beat at the smile illuminating his eyes.

"A wife."

"Oh." Her heart fluttered, and she couldn't prevent a silly grin from emerging on her face.

"So what do you say?"

"About what?"

"You know…"

She shook her head, not wanting to admit she did. But was she ready for such a serious commitment? "You want to move in with me?"

"What? No. That's not it."

"Oh. Then what?"

"Will you marry me?"

"Why?"

"What do you mean, why?"

"This is rather sudden, you have to admit." She couldn't let him think she was too eager, right? "Why do you want me to marry you?"

"Because we're good together."

"Oh, we make a good team?" Really? There must be more to it. She loved him. But he'd never said how he felt. Marriage didn't require the couple to love each other. Take all the arranged marriages that had occurred through history for political reasons or merely for convenience. She could only marry for love. Her heart sank. What if he *didn't* love her?

"No." Max scrubbed a hand over his smooth jaw.

"We don't?"

"Well, yeah, we do, but that's not why." He dragged a hand through his hair. "This isn't coming out the way I'd planned at all."

"So how did you plan it?"

"I was much more debonair in the truck on the way over here. Let's start over." He stood up and then pulled her up beside him. His eyes sobered as he peered at her, taking deep breaths. He squeezed her hands. "Over the last few weeks I've discovered something missing in my life. Or more explicitly, *someone* missing. A woman who challenges me to be more than I could be on my own. A woman to love me and to care for me, and whom I can love and care for. In short,

Meredith O'Connell Reed, I love you. I want to spend the rest of my life caring for you, laughing with you, loving you. Will you give me the honor of becoming my wife?"

"You're sure about this? I don't want you to rush into something you may regret later." She fought to keep her expression serious as she gazed at his gorgeous blue eyes, the ones that first caught her notice despite her resolve to never be with another man. She watched his tempting mouth tighten as he considered her question.

"Meredith…"

She bit her lip and then smiled as she punched him on the arm. "Of course, I'll marry you, you dolt."

Max let out a whoop, then scooped her into his arms, and swung her around three times. He set her down and drew her into his embrace, kissing her in the shade of the fairy tree.

Meredith's heart filled to bursting. "I love you, James Maximillian Chandler."

"I love you, Meredith, and I will until the day I die."

She kissed him again. "I'll love you forever. An undying love."

The End

Thanks so much for reading *Undying Love*! I hope you enjoyed Meredith and Max's story. Paulette meets Zak in the next story in the Secrets of Roseville series. Turn the page for a sneak peek at *Haunted Melody*!

To find out about new releases and upcoming appearances, please sign up for my newsletter via my website at www.bettybolte.com. I send out a monthly newsletter with book news to share with my readers, upcoming events and signings, and even a few favorite recipes, puzzles, and other doings!

I'd love to hear from you! Feel free to send me an email at betty@bettybolte.com, find me on Facebook at AuthorBettyBolte, follow me on BookBub, or connect with me on Twitter @BettyBolte.

You can always find an updated list of the titles in this series, as well as all of my other books on my website, at www.bettybolte.com/books/.

Thanks again for reading!

Sneak Peek of

Haunted Melody

Secrets of Roseville • Book 2

Betty Bolté

*P*aulette eased behind the steering wheel of her little white car. If her belly grew any bigger, she'd have to trade in her favorite vehicle because she wouldn't fit. Or be stuck at home, waiting for Meredith to take her places. She shifted into drive and jammed down on the accelerator until the tires spun on gravel. Easing off the gas, she drove down the driveway and out onto the highway, heading for Roseville. The tune to Bob Dylan's "On the Road Again" echoed in her mind. First, she must explore ways to reverse a conjuring spell. If Grandpa wouldn't cooperate, then she'd have to take matters into her own hands. Poor Meg refused to enter the parlor without either Meredith or Paulette to escort her, which of course meant a disruption to their day. At least their guests had no clue the ghost of her grandfather Patrick had arrived, and she planned to keep it that way.

The Golden Owl Books and Brews boasted an impressive collection of tomes on witchcraft and wizardry. She'd noticed the section when searching for the local history books earlier in the year. Surely the three sisters who ran the place could help her find answers. Although, the last time she'd shopped there with Meredith, they'd hesitated to wait on them. It had been odd, really. The three women had looked askance at them, wary and watchful.

She parked the car and pried herself out of it. Locking the door, she crossed the sidewalk. The baby elbowed her, and she briefly rested a hand on her belly. Less than two months until her child would be in her arms and the seeming volleyball she wore under her maternity top began deflating. Then, serious weight training could be incorporated into her routine again. Maybe she'd try Zumba or kickboxing. Sounded like a good plan. After she had her baby and cleared the house of ghosts.

The little bell jangled above the door to announce her arrival. She spotted the sisters working in different parts of the store. While not quite triplets, they bore a strong resemblance to one another. Slender with two sporting varying shades of brunette hair and the other a tawny blonde, no one would accuse them of being strangers. Three pairs of eyes noted her entrance and then turned away. Why? What made them so reticent toward her? Still, she needed answers.

She strode through the store, mindful of her balance, and slowly climbed the spiral staircase to the second floor where the books on mysticism and magic waited. It was bad enough she could see ghosts, now she sought a way to use magic to rid the plantation of her grandfather's presence. Life sure had taken some strange twists.

The nape of her neck tingled. She shrugged the sensation away and kept moving. Glancing over her shoulder, she noticed the tallest of the sisters watching her. She gave her a smile and was heartened by its return. Maybe with some time the suspicion between them would dissolve.

She moved on through the stacks, scanning the titles on

the spines of hundreds of books. *Ghost Busting for Beginners*. *A Historiography of Spirits and Ghosts*. *Spectral Contacts and Solutions Through the Ages*. She'd never realized how many volumes existed on ghosts and spirits. Such a variety of approaches, ways to analyze or apply techniques and the belief systems behind all of it.

Slipping a candidate from a shelf, she perused its table of contents, and then put it back. She chose another, then another. Lots of information had been written about the history of hauntings and ghosts. Very little apparently on how to help them find peace. Or more specifically, how to reverse a spell's results.

"Need some help?"

Paulette looked up from the book in her hands to see the tall brunette sister; the one who had smiled at her earlier. The younger woman regarded her with curious hazel eyes beneath pencil brows. Up close, Paulette detected blonde strands mixed with the luxurious milk chocolate hair pulled up in a banana clip. Her black polo sported the store's owl emblem embroidered over the left breast. She wore creamy slacks and comfortable shoes. Very practical attire for working in a bookstore. Paulette considered her own decadent flowery maternity blouse over stretchy black corduroys and matching pumps. By comparison, she was overdressed. Her fun, dangly earrings seemed like overkill. "I can't seem to find what I need."

"Maybe I can help. I'm Roxie." The woman stuck out a hand, and they shook.

"Paulette. Glad to finally meet you." She motioned to the rows of colorfully bound books, a rainbow of covers. Faced with having to state her mission, she cringed. What would Roxie think of her desire to learn magic? If the townspeople learned of her need, she'd be ostracized, shunned. Nothing more than the spinster sister. Johnny had once meant the world to her, but he left her with nothing but a broken heart. A kick reminded her of the other thing Johnny had given her. She laid a hand on her belly. She'd always have her child. But apparently it fell to her to rid Twin Oaks of ghosts for everyone's peace of mind. "I'm not sure how to explain what I'm even searching for."

"Start with the general topic and we'll take it from there." Roxie shrugged. "You know that much, right?"

"Sort of." Paulette read the signs posted on top of the many rows of books. History. Self-help. Mysticism. None suggested instruction on how to use spells effectively. She peered at Roxie. "I need to know everything about magic. And spells and stuff. For…a, um, a party we're throwing at Twin Oaks."

Roxie grinned and pointed at the Mysticism section. "You're in the right place. See?"

Paulette moved closer to the shelf Roxie indicated. "Well, my problem is these all discuss the history and beliefs. I need—or rather my *friend* needs to figure out how to reverse a spell—"

"A friend?" Roxie folded her arms across her chest and lifted one brow. "Does your *friend* realize how dangerous incantations can be?"

Indeed, Paulette understood firsthand the dangers of tinkering with magic. She had a ghostly grandfather hanging around to prove it too.

"Yes. It's necessary though." She glanced around the large room, relieved no one lingered in the vicinity who could eavesdrop on their conversation. "Can you help?"

Roxie studied her for the span of two deep breaths. "Can I trust you?"

That wasn't what she expected to hear. Surprised, she chuckled then sobered. "I need a book. Or a witch, if you know one."

Roxie raised both brows, her gaze intensifying. "I do."

Again, not what she expected to hear. Paulette blinked

twice and smiled, a chill inching through her. She swallowed and drew a long breath. "In Roseville?"

"Of course. Where did you think?" Roxie laughed, her smile wide and teeth reflecting the overhead lights.

She hadn't known a witch lived in such a quiet town. How could she? She'd been too busy with the ghosts. But she supposed they kinda went together. Given she had summoned her grandfather using a spell, after all. And why she came looking for guidance on how to clear the house of the specter. He needed to rest in peace, or at least go away. She'd rather he be content, given he was her grandpa. Maybe he'd go back and be with her grandma, happy and peaceful for all eternity. A good thought.

Paulette glanced around the room, spotted an elderly woman wending her way through the stacks and rows of books. She peered at Roxie and whispered, "Can you tell me who the witch is?"

Roxie shook her head and marched to a different aisle of books, one closer to the balcony railing. "Let me show you something that might give you the answers you seek."

Paulette trailed after the woman, aware customers below could see but not hear them. Why bring up the subject, then refuse to answer the question? Didn't Roxie trust her? Small wonder, since they'd known each other for all of three minutes. Roxie stopped in front of books on witchcraft. She glided a finger over the spines, landing on a small, black book with script lettering. She slipped the tiny volume from its home and handed it to Paulette with a little flourish.

Basic Witchcraft by Peggy Golden. On the cover, the familiar owl, featured on the sign hanging outside, perched on an open book with a single lit candle next to it. She opened the cover and looked up at Roxie. "What's this?"

"A beginner's manual, of sorts."

She opened it to the table of contents, several intriguing chapters beckoning her. She definitely qualified as a newbie when it came to spells and spirits. She spotted a chapter titled "Spellcrafting" and flipped to it. Pleased to find sections for writing, preparing, and casting spells. Yes, the book would help. "Thanks. You knew right where to find what I need. Do you have the inventory memorized?"

Roxie chuckled. "No. But that book is special to me and my sisters since our mother wrote it."

Paulette looked at the author's name again. "So that's why the store's called the Golden Owl? Your last name?"

Nodding, Roxie started toward the staircase. "I have to get back to work. Feel free to look around."

"Right." Several other titles had piqued her curiosity. "I'll linger here a bit and see what I find."

"Great." Roxie turned back and smiled at Paulette. "You're not as prickly as we thought. I hope you'll come back again."

"I'm sure I will. Thanks." Wonderful. Paulette looked over the railing, half expecting the other two sisters to have gathered below as an audience. She'd developed a reputation as the prickly sister. Figured. All her life she'd been misunderstood, left to her own devices to struggle through as best she could. Somehow her personality made others uncomfortable. She'd have to work on being nicer.

The little bell jangled, drawing her attention to the entrance. *Oh. My. Goodness.* She heard in her mind The Weather Girls singing "It's Raining Men" as she stared from her place at the railing. A tall, dark-haired, gorgeous man in black jeans and a tan pullover sweater that accentuated his skin coloring strode into the store, paused to allow another strikingly handsome man to pass through, and closed the door. Her pulse tattooed a rhythm in her ears as she sharply inhaled. What a hunk. Both of them, for that matter. Hunk number one scanned the first floor in one blazing pass, and then lifted his gaze to spear Paulette's appreciative stare. She'd never seen a man with such an arresting appearance, despite the bruise on his forehead. Gunmetal gray eyes met hers, high strong cheekbones and a jaw framed by black hair. Wide muscular shoulders tapered to an abdomen she'd bet good money boasted a washer board of muscles. His heavy brows raised as he did the guy once-over and then turned to his buddy.

Her earlier buoyancy deflated a smidge, but she smiled at Roxie. "Looks like you have customers."

"Cool." Roxie glanced at the men, curiosity infusing her expression, and started toward the first floor. "Very handsome customers too. I'll talk to you later."

"Right. I see you have your priorities." Paulette's chuckle died away as she tracked Roxie's progress down the steps.

She kept one hand resting on the rail, leaning over so she could follow the woman until Roxie reached the two strangers. After a brief exchange, she led the men toward the back of the store. The dreamy one who'd so blatantly assessed her earlier appeared to be about her own age. If she weren't about to have a baby, she'd try to make his acquaintance. As things stood, however, she wouldn't burden any man with another man's child. Doing so seemed too desperate to contemplate. Because she couldn't allow herself to be involved with anyone. At least, not under the current circumstances.

When the threesome passed the base of the spiral staircase, dreamy glanced up and winked at her. Startled, she jerked back and spun away, heart racing. *Damn.*

www.ingramcontent.com/pod-product-compliance
Lightning Source LLC
Chambersburg PA
CBHW021002120726
47905CB00009B/2822